The Bunyip Wakes!

Keith Garvey

Cover design by Allan Cornwell and Rosie van der Elst

Titles in the series:

Tall Tales from the Bush Volume 1 ISBN 1 875 169 31 8
Tall Tales from the Bush Volume 2 ISBN 1 875 169 32 6
Tall Tales from the Bush Volume 3 ISBN 1 875 169 33 4
ISBN 1 875 169 34 2 (Set)

Printed in Australia by McPherson's Printing Group

Produced for the National Direct Marketing Group by:
Allan Cornwell
25 Churchill Road
Mt. Martha Vic 3934

National Direct Marketing Group:
Books Plus (VIC/SA)
Books First (NSW/QLD)
Premier Books (WA)
Meander Books (TAS)

To the courage and fortitude
of my friends in Kerry,
who have the will
to keep on keepin on.

Also by Keith Garvey

The Funny Bugger.
Shout for the Adder.
Slowly Sweats the Gun.
Where the Blacksoil Ends.
Night of the Dingo.
My Uncle Harry.
Uncle Harry Rides Again.
Uncle Harry Returns.
More Tales of Uncle Harry.

Rhymes of a Ratbag.
Ditties of a Deadbeat.
Blacksoil Ballads.
Absolutely Australian Verses.
Songs of a Shearer.
Digger Ditties.
Cattle-Camp Collection.

Dinkum Little Aussies.
Vanishing Australians.

Contents

Contents

The Bunyip Wakes

Night was close. There was still light in the west, a wan glow marking the sun's reluctant retreat, fading away behind the grey drift of rain that curtained the river timber. Like a sad shroud it fell slow and silent, a winding sheet spread by Nature to farewell the dying day. In the twisted limbs of a dead gum, stark and skeletal, a mopoke emmited a melancholy croak mournful and depressing to the last extreme, like a dirge of complete sadness and unbelievable woe. It was a time when the black men stayed close to their fires, for they believed that on rainy nights the terrible bunyip arose from the gloomy waters, and sought its prey as the bush lay in the grip of darkness. It was a myth unproven, but aside from myth and legend, the dark bed of the bush holds many secrets, some of them terrifying beyond belief until disclosed.

The hooves of the buggy ponies made a sodden staccato thudding on the wet ground as Sir Edward Penterham drew the steaming pair to a halt at the home yard. The big Englishman climbed stiffly down, oilskin coat crackling, to be immediately met by Towser Watson, handyman on the property called New Suffolk, where Sir Edward bred blood horses of high quality, as well as walers, the half throughbred, half stock-horse type so popular with the British Army as remounts.

"Got somethin' bleedin' funny to report, Sir Edward". Towser raised a claw-like hand in a half salute. "Tem sheep yer bought for the larder. When I wuz gettin' the milkers up to-day, I finds one of 'em dead".

Sir Edward regarded his employee without emotion. In his worn jodphurs, greasy woollen jumper and Balaclava cap, the ex-steeplechase jockey resembled a rather shop-soiled gnome. The big Englishman smiled tolerantly. "I wouldn't worry greatly, Towser. All creatures die, some without obvious reason".

Towser rubbed a nose that carried a permanent bend, one of several physical disfigurments collected in

7

the pursuit of his hazardous profession of earlier days. His hoarse Cockney voice was skeptical. "Hit's oney got one mark on it. Where hit's 'ind leg was".

"Pray be more explicit", Sir Edward ordered, and Towser cast a mystified and uncomprehending look at his employer.

"Explain more fully".

"Summat's cut its 'ind leg orf an' swiped it".

Sir Edward stood pondering for a moment, then smiled as the evident solution occured to him. "Some wretched swagman has killed it and taken only a leg. A habit the scoundrels have".

"Just two 'undred yards from the 'ouse? Not on yer life, Sir Edward. No swaggie 'ud be that game. And there ain't hany marks on it, oney where the leg wuz lopped. A swaggie would have cut it's throat".

Sir Edward pondered again, wiped water from his ginger moustache, and came to a decision. "Take charge of the ponies, Towser. But first point out to me the position of the sheep, and I will inspect. Hello, here comes Joe. He can accompany me".

Joe Walsh drew the prancing grey colt to a halt, and dismounted with the grace of a swallow. He was hatless, his flaming red hair disarrayed by the rising night-wind, his perpetual smile revealing even teeth white in a florid face. Joe was a crack rider of the district, and until his wedding to Tilly Hobbs, Sir Edward's hired help, he had been notorious as the leading Lothario. Bushmen claimed that anything Joe could catch he could ride. And the reference was not made about four-legged animals alone. But the flash young ringer's days of philandering were over now. Three children over a space of three years, plus a devoted wife, kept Joe chained to his job as horse-breaker at New Suffolk.

The ringer swung down at Sir Edward's call, and listened while Towser, prompted at time by his boss, told of his recent discovery. Then Sir Edward hitched up his belt, over which the beginnings of a paunch was starting to hang, and set off to the spot pointed out by the old groom. Joe followed at a discreet distance, leading his mount as he made leisurely work of rolling a cigarette.

At the foot of a stunted gum lay the sheep's carcase. Eyes and tongue had been removed by the crows, and strings of bloodied intestine protruded through holes made by the ravening beaks of the predators. But there was no way in which to account for the completely missing hind leg. Joe blew a long streamer of smoke, then addressed his employer. "Somethin's took a whole leg. Clean as a whistle. Now what the hell would do that?"

"A dingo?, queried Sir Edward.

Joe shook his head. "Dingo don't chew hind legs off and carry 'em away. And as far as it bein' chewed off, it could just as easy have been cut off. It's crow-picked so much yer can't tell. A lot of swaggies who hate the landholders think it a joke to kill a sheep and only take the hind leg. But they always cut its throat. And they wouldn't be game to do it this close to the homestead. I would say, that be the state of the carcase, it was killed last night, before the rain fell. If it was killed after the rain started, there would be tracks".

"Can you see any form of track, Joe?"

Joe shook his head. "That's a thing that's out of my style, Sir Edward. You'd have to send to town for Bert Murrika. I'm a ringer, not a tracker. And now it's rained, I doubt if Bert would find anything."

"It's something of a mystery, but the loss of a sheep is of jolly little importance. And by Jove, it looks as if the weather is clearing". He gestured to the east, where the lifting clouds revealed a patch of sky, tinted saffron by the last light of the departed sun. "Our next big job is the marking of the colts on Saturday. I have arranged with Tom Andrews to lend me Andy Bronson and Darkie Edwards for the day, so we won't be short of assistance. Are you feeling fit, young man?"

"Fit as a cat in a cream factory, boss". Joe grinned as he ground out his cigarette, then his florid face assumed a serious expression. "Y'know, I can't help

9

thinkin' there's somethin' funny goin' on when I look at that sheep".

★ ★ ★ ★ ★ ★

Joe Walsh unchained the gate of the stockyard and flung it wide. The fifteen newly branded and doctored colts left in a trot, heading for the nearby river, chastened by their recent ordeal. Herb Hilliard, Sir Edward's veterinary expert, placed the bloodied castrating instruments in the bucket of disinfectant dosed water, then washed his hands. Nearby the two Karragatta stockmen waited their turn at the bucket. Darkie Edwards was long and lean, his strain of aboriginal blood evident in sad dark face and black curly hair. Andy Bronson was big, broad and burly, a man to be reckoned with in a rough-and-tumble battle. All eyes welcomed the sight of Mary Hilliard approaching with a large tray of sandwiches and brownie, and an urn of tea. Herb was first to partake of the refreshments his wife delivered, and with raising of hats and an announcement of "thank yer, missus", Andy and Darkie followed. At the stockyard gate, Sir Edward Penterham and Joe Walsh stood remarking on the qualities of the colts. The discussion was interrupted by Andy, brandishing a large sandwich.

"This mutton reminded me of somethin' I forgot to tell yer, Sir Edward. Up on the ridge near the boundary gate, when I come through this mornin', I seen one of yer ration sheep dead. Somethin' had took one of its hind legs".

Joe gazed open-mouthed at Sir Edward, and the Englishman returned the gaping stare. Joe was the first to find speech.

"That's twice".

"Yer mean it happened before?, Andy queried.

"Second time", Joe replied. "Hind leg pinched, no other mark only crow pecks".

"The sheep you found this morning, Bronson", Sir Edward cut in. "Any bad mutilations other than the leg?"

10

"Looked as if it was only done last night. Crows were there, but they hadn't done much damage. Looked to me as if the leg was haggled off be somethin' with big sharp teeth. No other wounds or marks".

"Sounds like a bunyip of some kind". Darkie Edward's quiet voice was tinged with humour.

"D'yer believe in the bunyip, Darkie?", Joe asked.

"Well no, I don't". The coloured man showed even teeth in a dark smile. "But there's a lot of people do, even some of the whites. My mother was a half-blood. She believed in it, and the old murries used to tell me about it when I was a little feller. It's a spirit that comes out of the river at night and takes different shapes. A lot of blokes claim to have seen it, but none of 'em ever come up with the goods. Just a tale some of the Old People cooked up a long time ago and it grew as it travelled".

"I dunno so much". Andy reached for another sandwich. "This is a bloody big country we live in. A new country. And wild. There could be things hidin' in the bush and the rivers that nobody's ever set eyes on. Soopernatcheral things".

Joe Walsh grinned at the big ringer. "Holy Smoke, Andy. You ain't superstitious are yer?"

"Me old man was a Danish seaman", Andy replied. "He reckoned there's all sorts of unknown monsters in the sea. Could be the same here in the rivers. Krakens and things".

Sir Edward produced a large linen handkerchief, wiped his terrifying moustache, and placed his empty pint-pot on the tray. "Enough", he announced. "It does not become a man of your physical strength and courage, Bronson, to believe in demons. Let us go and examine this unfortunate sheep, and hope the kraken sleeps".

The sheep lay on a scalded patch of ground some half a mile from the homestead, and crows rose up in a black cloud as the four horsemen approached and dismounted. The mutilated carcase was a repetition of the one Joe and Sir Edward had viewed three days previously. The Englishman addressed Darkie.

11

"Do you have any tracking experience, Edwards?"

"Not that yer could count on". The swarthy ringer ignited a thin cigarette. "I used to go out at times when I was a boy, with old Joe Binghi. He was the police tracker at Roma. I'll look, but I reckon it's a job for Bert Murrika".

Darkie cast a narrow circle around the sheep, then pointed a long finger. "There's marks all around, but they're shapeless. See, a line of 'em goin' towards the river, just blotches".

"By Jove, I can see them myself". Even to Sir Edward's inexperienced eye the indentations were plain on the bare patch of red earth, but they were shapeless, no more than a scuffling on the gritty surface.

Andy Bronson grinned. "Bunyip always covers his tracks. An old murri told me".

"Might be one of them kraken things yer mentioned, Andy", Joe Walsh remarked.

"This old murri", Andy continued, "reckoned the bunyip is like a man, and it's covered with long red hair. Got four big claws on each paw, and one big tusk in it's upper jaw. When it grabs a victim, it drives the tusk into the victim's skull. And it never leaves tracks, only smudges on the ground. And it smells like fish".

"Enough!" Sir Edward turned to his mount. "Though I do not believe in unsubstantiated legends, this is quite mysterious. Joe, we must be on the alert. There is an answer somewhere. Here is payment for your services, lads. You may now return to Karragatta, and I advise you not to be misled by myths".

He handed the two ringers a square of folded paper each. Each man pocketed his cheque carelessly and without a glance. Then after mumbling a brief thanks, they turned their mounts towards Karragatta. Andy slewed in the saddle, waved his hat and shouted, "look out the bunyip don't get yer, Joe".

"Look out he don't get YOUR hind leg, yer big bludger", Joe shouted back, "there's more beef on yer than me".

12

Once out of sight of the station, Andy inspected his cheque and smiled. "Three quid for only half a day. The old Pom always pays well if yer do a good job".

"He ain't mean", Darkie agreed. "But never stir him up. He's like a mad bull if he does his block. I think yer had him in a bit, Andy, when yer started talkin' about sea-monsters and things".

Andy's smile grew wider. "No harm in havin' these immy-grants on a bit. I bet he's thinkin' about it now, my oath he is".

Back at the yard, Sir Edward was addressing Joe in serious tones. Though he had poo-poohed Andy's suggestion of Bunyips, a lingering doubt remained in his mind. Could it be possible that some predatory monster unknown to man lurked in the vast acres of the Australian outback?

"What is your opinion of bunyips, Joe. Do you think such a thing exists?"

Joe handsome face broke into a grin, and it was the reckless grin of confident youth. "If bunyip was around, Sir Edward, I think somebody would have captured him before this".

"True", the Englishman agreed. "But the strange deaths of the sheep remain unexplained, Joe".

"Yer dead right, boss". Joed assumed a thoughtful expression as he pushed back his hat and wiped his sweating forehead. "There's more rain on the way, I reckon. Hope we don't get it".

"Why, dash it all, we could do with a follow up".

"I know, Joe said grimly. "But the old murries reckon that on rainy nights the bunyip wakes".

Sir Edward turned away, the earlier lingering doubt growing tormentingly larger. Was Joe serious?

★   ★   ★   ★   ★   ★

Sunday was still, sunny and peaceful, and Monday followed the same pattern, but with an increasing temperature that brought heavy clouds in mid-afternoon. Darkness came, and with it a steady drizzle of rain de-

13

scribed by Joe Walsh as being "fine as a frog's whiskers and cold as a Laplander's nose". Sir Edward, though a member of the British Peerage, never hesitated to assist his employees with their many duties, and to-day he pitched in with a will, his gaze shuttling ever so often to the dark line of gums that marked the river, and soon the big man's uneasiness became apparent to Joe.

"Yer ain't worryin' about the bunyip, are yer Sir Edward?", Joe queried. "Old Andy was pullin' our legs a bit, yer know, about them sea-serpents and things. He's a bit of a card, and likes takin' a fall out of blokes. What ever haggled the sheep, it was no bunyip. There ain't any such thing".

Sir Edward's face was serious as he addressed Joe in the increasing gloom. "But who knows, Joe, if some prehistoric creature is not roaming the night. Think of the stories about the Loch Ness Monster, and the Nandi Bear of Africa".

"Tripe, boss". Joe's breezy laugh was a trumpet-call of disdain. "Good night, and sleep well. Nothin' to fear".

"Never the less, I will have the old Service revolver close at hand", Sir Edward replied. "A good night to you, Joe".

He strode off in the direction of the house, and Joe turned to Towser Watson. "What d'yer reckon, yer Pommy bastard. Bunyip or not?"

"So sich bleedin' thing, yer colonial bastard". Towser displayed a scattered collection of jagged and multicoloured fangs in a gargoyle grin. "But just in case, I'm barrin' the door of me soddin' 'ut ternight".

* * * * * * *

Tom Andrews, longtime manager of Karragatta, Old Well Dressed to the ringers because of his always neat appearance, addressed Andy Bronson as the big rider released his tired horse.

"The grey mare by Danshiel is looking for a bit of affection, Andy. Tomorrow morning you can lead her over to the stallion at New Suffolk".

14

"Goin' to be an awful wet ride". Andy was without enthusiam.

"I don't want her to miss out", Andrews replied. "You can have the rest of the day easy, mending harness".

"Orright, I'll start early. Might hear more about the bunyip", Andy grinned.

*　*　*　*　*　*

Mrs Joseph Walsh, formerly Miss Matilda Hobbs of Spitalfields London, surveyed her husband across the tea-table, as he wolfed corned beef and slurped cabbage and onion sauce. Though plain of face and fat of figure, Tilly was a cook far above the ordinary, and had long ago found the way to Joe's heart via his stomach. Now her Cockney voice, loud and ungrammatical, was charged with contempt and disbelief.

"It's oney another of big Bronson's tall tales. The wind gets in 'is ear and blows 'is tongue about. Soddin' bunyips! Ain't hany such thing". She pushed a plate of rice pudding at Joe, who flashed a tantalising grin.

"He's there all right, ole girl. He's got long red hair all over him, and four long claws on each hand, and...."

"A bleedin' great tooth 'e sticks in people's brains", Tilly cut in. "If 'e 'appens to stick in your 'ead, or Andy's, it'll break orf in the wood".

Joe's widening grin showed he was not offended. "I'll have some more corn bull before the puddin' ", he announced.

"Must 'ave a worm in yer as big as a tiger snake". Tilly reached for the carving knife. "Bigger glutton than the bunyip yer tellin' lies about".

"No lies". Joe's voice was sincere, but his eyes twinkled. "He's most likely watchin' right now, waitin' for the night to get a bit darker. Then look out!"

*　*　*　*　*　*

The wind moaned eerily, driving the fine droplets of rain in continuous gusts against the windows of the

15

homestead, sighing sadly in the branches of the box-trees. Sir Edward sat at his office desk, trying to study accounts for the past month. His wife and the twin children were far away at her brother's sheep-station in the Dalby area, and loneliness hung heavily on his broad shoulders. Herb and Mary had retired to their quarters at the rear of the homestead and Towser would now be snoring in his hut by the stockyard. The big man was finding concentration hard, and the night was growing late. With a stifled yawn he arose and sought his bedroom, placing his old Army revolver on the dressing table within easy reach.

* * * * * *

Old Jack was the only dog on New Suffolk. He had arrived uninvited one cold day, and nobody worried when he made the place his home, for he was harmless, content to scrounge a ration of scraps and keep out of mischief. Never suspicious or aggressive, he camped at night undisturbed under the warm stove recess that joined the kitchen. But to-night he awakened suddenly, the old infallable canine instinct telling his something was not quite as it should be. Out there in the rain-swept yard danger skulked in an unknown and terrifying form, and Jack rose and rushed from his retreat, emitting a string of thunderous barks that would have awakened the long dead occupants of an Egyptian tomb. And it brought Joe Walsh out of the heavy slumber that claims all men who spend long hours in the saddle, while in the homestead Sir Edward sat up fully awake, for Old Jack was a dog friendly to everyone, and he seldom barked at all.

* * * * * *

Andy Bronson smoked quietly by the kitchen stove as his wife packed his saddle bag with lunch for the morrow. She was a slim wiry blonde woman, a complete contrast in colouring and physique to Andy, whose dark hirsute bulk and bone would have been noticeable in any company. A wail arose from the ajoining room where the

16

two small children slept. "Dad, there's somethin' walkin' on the roof. I can hear it".

"There's nothin' there", Andy called. "Go to sleep or the bunyip'll get yer".

There was immediate silence, and Rita Bronson smiled at her placidly grinning husband. "One thing about this bunyip scare it keeps the kids in order. I'm glad it's only a tale".

Andy immediately feigned to be incensed. "It's no tale mum'. He comes out on rainy nights, he's all covered with red hair, and he's got four long claws on each hand. He's got one big tooth in the middle of his top jaw, and he sneaks up behind yer and springs on yer, and drives the tusk inter yer brain".

"Well you're pretty safe, old boy", the woman replied. "Let's burrow up. You've got an early start in the morning".

   ★ ★ ★ ★ ★ ★

In the darkness Tilly gripped Joe's arm, and there was fear in her whispered tones. "Wot's wrong. Wot's Jack barkin' at?"

"Some thievin' cow, most likely. I'm goin' to look". Joe was dragging on his boots. "Swagman, most likely".

"Luvaduck, don't go!. Tilly's voice shook with fear. "It might be the bunyip".

"Thought yer didn't believe in the bunyip, ole girl. Keep quiet while I take a look". Supremely contemptuous of bunyips, Joe stepped into the outer darkness, clad only in long underwear and boots, at the exact moment that Jack's frienzied barking ceased as though cut off with a knife.

The night was a shroud of impenetrable blackness, but knowledge of the territory guided Joe to the big house. The rain was a fine mist, but as he reached the homestead yard thunder growled overhead. Noiselessly he entered the gate and stepped onto the wide verandah near the store room. It was then that the smell hit his

17

nostrils, a foul decaying odour like the stink of a dingo den, tinged with the sickening effluvia of river mud long floodbound. Too late he heard the sinister pad of feet behind him, then the darkness exploded in a blaze of stars. Sir Edward emerged from his room even as Joe's body thudded to the floor, candle held high and revolver levelled, and in the weak, guttering light his eyes caught the movement of a weird leaping something that sprang from the verandah into the rain-washed night. Sir Edward fired in wild haste, and there followed a terrifying screech, then silence except for the beat of the suddenly increasing rain. In a shocked second the big man was beside Joe's sprawled form, then footsteps sounded as Herb and Mary, awakened by the shot, arrived at the scene of violence. A bull's eye lantern bobbed in the outer night as Towser Watson made approach.

"By Jove he's hurt bad. What a dashed bad show! What to do!" Sir Edward was on the verge of panic, looking anything but an English peer with his hair and moustache all awry, and his powerful legs and bare feet protruding from beneath his short nightshirt.

"Be calm. Sir Edward". Mary Hilliard had taken the time to fling a robe over her night attire, and she was cool and collected. "Herb, a mattress and pillows, then go and get dressed. You too, Sir Edward. And please be quick".

Five minutes later Joe lay on a spread mattress, his head propped high as Mary clipped away the bloodstained hair that surrounded a nasty looking wound in his scalp. "He's had a heavy blow from something sharp". The Englishwoman had gathered some nursing experience in her youth "back 'ome in the Old Dart", and she swabbed the gash expertly. "All we can do is keep him quiet and wait for him to regain consciousness".

"By Jove, shouldn't somebody go to town for the doctor?" Sir Edward's voice was anxious.

"A doctor will only tell you to let him rest", Mary replied. "I don't think it's a terribly bad concussion. There's no blood from his nose or mouth. Some brandy later on may help".

"In the meantime, let us get him into a bed", Sir Edward ordered, then suddenly he remembered Tilly. "Good Heavens, Matilda and her children are alone, and the monster at large! They must be brought to the homstead at once". With revolver at the ready he headed in the direction of Joe's cottage. Stumbling through the gloom he reached the dwelling and pounded on the door. Tilly knew if it had been Joe he would have entered without sound, and she emitted a squeal of fear.

"Op it, ooever yer are. I ain't goin' out to get eat be the soddin' bunyip".

"It is your employer", Sir Edward shouted. "Get dressed and bring the children. Joe has been attacked by some unknown creature".

Tilly gave another wail of terror. "Knew there 'ad to be some truth in Bronson's tale. I'm 'urryin' as fast as I can, Sir Edward".

Shortly Sir Edward's entire retinue was gathered on the verandah, where several hastily hung lanterns flung light through the drifting drizzle of rain. Herb Hilliard spoke sharply.

"There's something you should see, Sir Edward.

Sir Edward's hair stood as Herb pointed to a mark on the floor near the door of the store-room. It was the print of a giant paw with four long mandibles plain to see, etched in wet mud. Towser's harsh voice was suddenly loud.

"I bin waitin' to tell yer, boss. Old Jack's dead. Somethin' drove a big 'ole in 'is 'ead, clean through the brain".

"By the Lord Harry!!" Sir Edward's voice was a shocked whisper. "Could Bronson have been telling the truth after all?"

*　*　*　*　*　*

Day broke grey and depressing, gloomy cloud banks hanging low and smothering as funeral shrouds. The wind whistled in the dark tops of the belars like the painful and irregular breathing of a dying consumptive.

19

Towser Watson, mounted on a powerful black waler, listened attentively to Sir Edward's final orders.

"Give my letter to Senior-Constable Murdock, and answer all questions carefully and truthfully regarding the matter. It is a matter of jolly big necessity that he or Trooper Claffey return with Bert Murrika. Whatever this monster, this bugaboo may be, it must be laid by the heels. You should make good time on Officer, he's a dependable mount. Thank the jolly Lord the river has not risen. But nevertheless be careful at the crossing".

"Won't be as 'ard as steerin' a baulky one over Beecher's Brook. I'll do the job, boss. Never 'ave no fear". Towser headed for the river at a canter, and Sir Edward turned to the homestead, his mind a turmoil of fear and foreboding that he was unable to shake off. He remembered vividly the charge of the Dervishes at Khartoom, when he was but seventeen years. He had stood and fired cooly and without fear or panic at the shrieking hordes of desert men, neither giving or asking quarter. But dread of the unknown, the supernatural, was finding it's insiduous path into his redoubtable character.

He was brought back to earth by the thud of hooves, and the trumpeting squeal from Duke of Suffolk. The blood stallion patrolled the rails of his yard emitting a staccate of whinnies, for he had smelled the mare led by Andy Bronson. The big ringer was hatless, and rain dripped from his oilskin as he swung down and greeted the Englishman with a water-melon smile.

"Awful day, ain't it, Sir Edward. Mare here for the Dook. Old Well Dressed didn't want her to miss out". Big and burly and confident, Andy was always a man to lean on in time of trouble.

"You arrive at an opportune time, Bronson", Sir Edward said. "Joe was attacked by some strange creature last night. A creature exactly like the bunyip you described. There is a frightening paw-print, just as you told us. It killed our dog by driving a hole in the skull, and it also struck Joe a violent blow on the head. He is unconscious".

20

Andy stood thunderstruck, his mouth open wide enough to swallow an emu egg. "You ain't havin' me on are yer, Sir Edward?"

"I'm not spoofing, if that is what you mean. It is my belief that a dangerous creature lurks nearby. I have sent to town for the police and the tracker".

Squelching footsteps announced the arrival of Herb Hilliard. The squeals of the stallion and the whinnying of the mare were producing a Bedlam of sound, and Herb almost had to shout to make himself heard.

"Joe's regained consciousness, Sir Edward".

"Come with me, Bronson", the big Englishman ordered. "You are a friend of Joe, and may understand him better than I. Herb, take charge of the horses".

Herb took the reins of Andy's bedraggled mount, and the halter-shank that held the amorous mare. Andy followed Sir Edward to the room where Joe lay under the watchful eyes of his disturbed wife and Mary Hilliard. The horse-breaker's face was wan and colourless, but his breathing was deep and strong, and recognition showed in his dull gaze as he saw Bronson.

"Andy, ol' mate". The voice was slurred but legible. "It...stonkered me. Smelt like...like...a bag of dead fish. Come up behind me".

"Did yer see it, mate?". Andy leaned close to Joe, his massive shoulders obscuring the pale face from Sir Edward's gaze.

"Too dark. Stunk, it...did. Thought yer was kiddin'...Andy".

Joe's voice died away as his eyes closed, and Mary Hilliard spoke sharply. "That's enough, Andy. Let him rest now, and he will recover soon".

Silently the two big men tip-toed from the room, and in the rain-swept yard Sir Edward turned and addressed Andy in mystified tones.

"Dash it all Bronson, but everything that old black told you seems to be coming true. Can it be possible there really it a bunyip?"

Andy's dark eyes failed to meet Sir Edward's fiery

blue ones. The big ringer's broad face bore a hangdog expression, like a school-boy caught stealing apples. His voice was slow and uncertain.

"Whatever this thing is, Sir Edward we gotter find it. I'll stay and give yer all the help I can".

"Capital, Bronson. The police and tracker should arrive during the afternoon. In the meantime, there is work to be done. Herb and I are behind schedule with our daily duties. I thank the Lord that Joe is recovering".

Andy grinned. "Blokes like Joe take a lot of killin'. I'll give yer a hand with the work. With a bit o' luck the trap might get here earlier than we reckon".

Andy's hope was fulfilled. Towser Watson had covered less than half the sixteen mile journey to town when he ran into the police patrol. Trooper Mick Claffey read Sir Edward's letter, and it's contents brought a wide grin to his duck-billed Irish face. He turned to Bert Murrika, the squat half-blood whose ability at bushcraft and tracking was a legend in the district.

"Bunyip out at New Suffolk, Bert. Think you can find him?"

"No chance. No bunyip any more".

Claffey grinned. "Thought the blacks believed in bunyips".

Mostly a lugubrious type, the dark man showed a flash of humour. "No bunyip any more. Go away when Captain Cook come".

"We best be lookin' into it, anyway". Claffey reined up his mount as he spoke. "Old King Ned's a big wheel in these parts. I don't want a reprimand for neglectin' him".

* * * * * *

The council of war was held under an overcast sky that threatened more rain. Sir Edward had given Claffey an elaborate description of the strange and violent happenings on New Suffolk, but the trooper seemed unconvinced whenever the bunyip theory was mentioned. The group comprised Sir Edward, the trooper, Towser, Herb

22

and Andy, while a few feet away Bert Murrika squatted smoking, knowing the show was his, awaiting his cue to commence the performance. Claffey, beefy red face drawn with concentration, turned now to his tracker.

"What you feller reckon, Bert?"

"What I reckon?". Murrika's voice was soft, the fluid tones of the aboriginal. "This feller you want, he's not far away".

"How d'yer make that out?", Claffey queried.

"Come". Murrika led the group to the awning of corrugated iron covering the concrete path that led from verandah to garden gate. A few faded pink blossoms remained on the rose bushes on either side, sheltered from the rain. With a large black forefinger, the tracker indicated a bloom on which reposed a dark ragged stain. Sir Edward's scalp crawled.

"By Jove, blood!!"

Murrika's finger travelled to Sir Edward, and his ungrammatical English was slow but confident.

"Boss man hit him when he shoot".

Again the dark finger pointed, this time to the garden fence, for the first time Sir Edward noticed the sagging top rail, broken almost in half. Murrika slouched forward, and pulled from the cracked timber a large tuft of red hair.

"By Jove, red hair!" Sir Edward's voice was hoarse. "More proof of the bunyip! Your story is true, Bronson, without doubt".

Andy was silent, eyes on the ground, but the tracker's thick lips stretched in a wide grin.

"No bunyip, this feller. Bunyip spirit feller, him don't bleed. This feller hurt. Him not far away".

"What feller is he, Bert", Claffey asked, but the black man ignored the question, and spoke volubly.

"What any wild feller do when he's hurt? Kangaroo, dingo, pig, any feller. Look for safe plant. Where safe plant? Down there in ti-trees".

All eyes followed the pointing finger. It travelled, wavered and became steady. The ti-tree clump it indi-

23

cated was a good quarter-mile away, so thick and impenetrable it appeared as one huge single growth.

"You reckon it's in there, Bert?", Claffey's voice was doubtful.

Murrika nodded, and began to fill his pipe.

"How the devil does he know?", Sir Edward burst out.

"This feller know". The tracker's voice was curt, indicating that he would say no more on the matter.

Sir Edward turned to Claffey, and his voice was uncertain. "Well, now what is the procedure from here. Has anybody a suggestion?"

"My oath. Go and capture the bludger, whatever it is". The remark came from Andy Bronson.

Sir Edward gazed at Andy as if he had not heard correctly.

"You mean go into the forest and try to overpower this...this monster...bunyip? You cannot be serious, Bronson".

"Why not?" Andy grinned. "I'm game to mix it with him. And I'm dead sure of good support from you and the trooper. Yer both got pistols. Just show him to me, Bert, and I'll see how good he is".

Confidence flowed suddenly over Sir Edward like a tidal wave as he gazed at Andy. With muscle-loaded arms protuding from the rolled sleeves of his flannel shirt and pillar-like legs bulging the fabric of his moleskins, the big ringer looked capable of handling any form of monster, real or imagined. Sir Edward became in a second the competent military strategist.

"Bronson, you will lead the advance. The trooper and I will flank you with pistols at the ready. The tracker will bring up the rear. Herb and Towser will remain here. The women must not be left without protection. Any questions?"

"Just one thing". Bronson removed his spurs and hung them on the fence. "If yer get cause to open fire, be careful where yer pointin' them bloody things. Let's go".

The rain was a thickening mist now, the clouds a

24

low-hung smothering gloom wrapping the river flats in a pall of dismal woe. The ti-tree clump seemed ominous, charged with an unknown menace beyond human comprehension, a dark labyrinth holding morbid secrets awakening from a cloister erected by Nature in the long dead past. The quartet halted at its dank and sinister edge, and a muffled grunt from Murrika caught the attention of the three whites. The tracker indicated several long red hairs that hung from a broken bough, and a shiver bounced and capered up Sir Edward's spine.

"Bunyip feller in there", the black man whispered. "You bet".

Under the thick green canopy of foliage no grass grew, and again Murrika pointed, this time to the deep, shapeless indentations on the wet earth. The tracker's hoarse whisper sounded frighteningly loud in the funeral stillness, and his finger touched a dark blood smear on the bark of a low-hanging bough, a clue invisible to any eyes but those of the tracker. Andy moved forward into the feral catacomb of verdure, and with doubt and trepidation Sir Edward and Claffey followed, revolvers gripped. Murrika brought up the rear, to all appearances calm and undisturbed.

As the group advanced the light in the depth of the clump grew less, until it was little brighter than late twilight. Our safety lies in numbers, Sir Edward thought. It won't attack four of us. Suddenly up ahead a stick cracked loud in the silence, and Bronson broke into a run, dodging between the tree-trunks and ducking the low boughs. Sir Edward sought to follow and fell full length over a trailing root, bringing Claffey and the tracker down in a struggling entangled heap on top of him. The Englishman was first on his feet and he blundered forward as a piercing screech sounded close by. Crashing through the impeding foliage he burst into a small clearing, and the scene that caught his eye was to be remembered until the end of his days.

Andy Bronson was locked in furious combat with a huge hairy creature, that stood fully a head taller than the

25

stocky ringer. Andy's left hand gripped the right wrist of the monster, forcing back the clawlike hand that held a murderous-looking pick-axe like instrument. Sir Edward went into action even as he heard the thud of Claffey's boots behind him. Leaping forward, the Englishman brought the barrel of the revolver down with stunning force, just as Andy drove a tremendous right-hand punch home. Claffey clicked the handcuff's shut on the hairy wrists. Sir Edward stood back shaken and amazed. "Good Lord", he gasped. "It's a man!!"

It was undoubtedly a man that lay groaning on the dank earth, a huge hirstute brute with tangled red hair and beard as long as the tail of a brumby mare. The creature was clad in a weird garment composed of animal skins, and its feet were wrapped in soiled canvas bound on with twine. Andy pointed to the pick-axe that lay on the ground and announced what each man was aware of now.

"That's the gadget he used to kill the dog and clobber Joe. And to hack orf the sheeps' legs. The canvas and twine he must of pinched somewhere. God knows where he got the skin suit".

"But where the devil did he come from in the first place", Sir Edward ejaculated.

"Out of a woman, same as the rest of us", Andy grinned. "There ain't any doubt he's a human bein, and stinks like a country dunny".

Sir Edward's eyes flew to Bert Murrika. The black man was lighting his pipe, a cunning expression on his dark face. He spoke softly. "Him white-feller bunyip. Catch him easy. Never catch black-feller bunyip. Him spirit feller. Not leave tracks".

"You black wretch!" Sir Edward's voice was wrathful. "I think you were aware all the time that it was a man".

A babble of disjointed words caused all eyes to focus on the captured prize. The 'bunyip' was sitting up, speaking rapidly in what was without doubt a foreign tongue.

"By Gad, he's speaking French". Sir Edward, a

linguist of note, sounded more surprised than ever. "He says he surrenders, and will give no more trouble".

Claffey pouched his revolved. "Let's get him to town, Sir Edward, and see what we can find out about him".

Andy Bronson inhaled and blew a long streamer of smoke. "Now I've heard the bloody lot. A French bunyip. Next we'll turn up a German kangaroo. Hey, look, will yer. He ain't got any thumbs".

The big ringer's amazed statement was indeed true. Each of the 'bunyip's' long hairy hands lacked the thumb.

"That accounts for the print on the verandah", Claffey said. "Come on, let's get the boyo to a place of safe keepin'."

The 'bunyip' was hoisted to his feet, and for the first time Andy notices the blood encrusted furrow along the upper left arm, where Sir Edward's wildly-fired bullet has scored a hit.

"Christ, he's lucky he's here", Andy said. "So is Joe, for that bloody matter".

" 'Tis nice and quiet he is now", Claffey said, "but 'tis happier I'd be if you rode to town with us, Andy".

"I'll be in that, my oath". The ringer's voice bubbled with eagerness. "The bit of excitement's made me feel horrible bloody dry, even it if has been rainin'".

"I will also accompany you", Sir Edward announced. "It will be necessary for somebody who speaks his language to be present".

*　　*　　*　　*　　*　　*

"It's a fair dinkum bunyip all right". Andy Bronson, his third pint half empty, addressed the open-mouthed crowd in the bar of "Boney" Morton's Royal Hotel. "It's got four long claws on each hand, it's all covered in red hair, and it's got a great big fang in its top jaw, and it sneaks up behind yer and drives the fang inter yer head. That's how it got Joe Walsh".

"How did yer catch it, Andy?", enquired a mesmerised onlooker.

"We sneaked up on it and grabbed it. Took three of us to subdoo it".

"Did it kick up a noise at all?"

"It done a lot of jabberin', but I couldn't understand what it was sayin'," Andy replied quite truthfully.

"What will happen to it now". This from Elsie, the barmaid.

"Dunno, me love". Andy grinned. "That's up to the traps. Fill me up another pint".

"On the house, Andy", "Boney" Morton announced, realising Andy's presence was responsible for the brisk increase in the evening's usually mediocre trade.

The crowd grew larger and more amazed as Andy's tale became more lurid with every drink.

* * * * * *

At the jail, the bunyip had undergone an amazing transformation. Bathed and with wound dressed, hair and beard clipped short he looked what he was, a normal male human. Still handcuffed, and clad in an old khaki shirt, too-small moleskins and canvas shoes, he sat across the office desk from Sir Edward and Senior Constable Murdock.

"He's a bally Frenchie, no doubt", Sir Edward told the trooper. "But he refuses to tell anything, and demands to see the French Consul. What is the procedure now, Constable?"

"Looks like a trip to the city for Claffey", Murdock said. "It's lucky you can speak his lingo, Sir Edward. I'll pack him off under escort tomorrow. I wonder how the devil the bugger got here, and where he started from".

"That we should know in a few days time", Sir Edward said.

* * * * * *

A peaceful week passed, and Sir Edward journeyed

29

to town. His first port of call was the police barracks, where Murdock presented a full explanation on the bunyip and its behaviour.

"Believe it or not, Sir Edward, the man is an escapee from one of the French penal colonies in Guiana. His name is Pierre Ledoux, known among the criminal element as Le Poilu, the Hairy One, and he was a pretty bad gang member in Paris. He betrayed a fellow gangster, whose friends cut off Ledoux's thumbs as punishment. Soon afterwards he was convicted of murdering his mistress, who was a prostitute. He was then packed off to a penal colony for life. I have no details of how he escaped or got across to the mainland of Australia. Possibly he stowed away on a ship. Any way he got here, and his fear of capture made him like a wild beast. It's a save bet he will be deported, and the French can have the joy of him".

"To think", Sir Edward said, "that Bronson and Joe really had me believing there is such a creature as the bunyip, and at the end they really believed it themselves. In fact the only one who did not believe was your tracker. And he, being a native, should have been the believer".

Murdock smiled knowingly. "Old Bert's a lot smarter than many of the white people. By the way, how is young Walsh?"

"Quite recovered", Sir Edward replied, "And he adamantly states that he is going to seek a safe hiding place next time the bunyip wakes".

Riding South Again

The rider came in from the south, the hooves of his horse lifting small puffs of red dust from the dry, arid surface of the track. Ruby halted in her work of polishing the bar-counter, watching him dismount. A group of magpies scattered from their perch on the tie-rail, and scolded noisily as he hitched up. The big bay horse assumed a hipshot posture, and stood with head hanging. Fresh sweat gleamed wetly on its shoulders and flanks, announcing the fact that it had been ridden at a fast gait for several miles.

The rider stood gazing at the open doorway, seemingly unsure of what his next move would be, then with what appeared a certain reluctance mounted the verandah. He brushed dust from his worn clothes, eyes studying the nameplate over the doorway, then stepped up to the bar. Ruby took note of the sun-darkened, handsome face under the wide brim of a dirty felt hat with a broken crown. His endearing smile radiated confidence and revealed a set of startlingly white teeth, perfect except for a gap in the top row. He's handsome, Ruby thought, and young too, but I'll bet he knows his way around. A capable stockman, I'll wager. Capable at anything else, too.

"I'll have a beer please, missus. Hot day, ain't it?" The voice was soft and courteous but ungramatical. "Seems like the pub's changed hands since last time I come through. Bloke named Tim Wallace was the publican then".

"My husband and I bought Mr Wallace out nearly a year ago", Ruby replied. "He has gone to Blackall to-day, drove our barmaid in. She is getting married this evening. Lucy girl, Bonnie".

"Bonnie?" There was a flash of interest in the young ringer's eyes. "There was a Bonnie here when I come through last, couple of years ago. Awful nice lookin' girl. Tall with reel fair hair".

31

"That's the same one, Bonnie Milton. She was a Blackall girl. Took her a long time to recover from a tragic love affair. But she's on the right track this time, with a grazier that is well to do, and completely devoted to her".

It was evident that the women was prepared to gossip. The ringer smiled fleetingly.

"There's a broken heart for every stone in Queensland. And like the stones, they're easy cast aside. I suppose this girl fell for some cove who wasn't serious".

"Exactly", the woman said. "Bonnie took me into her confidence, told me the full story. He was a drover named Clarrie Commerford. Came from Boulia. You wouldn't know him, I suppose?"

"I come from Boulia". The ringer took another pull at this beer. "Know Clarrie and his three brothers well. Had a pretty hard upbringin', those boys. Their father died when they was little, and the mother worked like a nigger to rear 'em.

"There are some remarkable women in these frontier outposts". Ruby's voice carried a firm note of conviction. "I lived all my life in Sydney before I came out here. The courage and fortitude of these outback women never ceases to amaze me".

"Yer dead right", the ringer agreed. "And let me tell yer, the greatest one I ever knew was Clarrie Commerford's mother. But to get back to this girl Bonnie. What was the strength of her affair with Clarrie?"

"I don't suppose there's any harm in telling you about it". Like most women who are often alone, Ruby welcomed a chance to gossip. "When John and I took over the hotel, Bonnie was very depressed, and she wasn't long telling me her troubles. It seems that a drover named Harry Hickey passed through on his way back to Boulia after finishing a job. This young many Commerford was tailing the horses, and he stayed on at the hotel for a few days. Of course Bonnie was the attraction, and she fell for him in a big way. He took a job breaking horses on a nearby property, and stayed for more than two months. The romance went like a bushfire, until one

32

night Commerford made it clear that he wasn't the marrying kind, and that he was riding on, as soon as his job cut out. A few days later Bonnie told him that she was pregnant, and expected him to stand by her. He agreed to do so, but the following week-end found him missing. He never came back''.

"That sort of thing happens pretty often'', the ringer said. "And tell me, what happened when the baby came along?''

Ruby smiled shrewdly as she refilled his glass. "There wasn't any baby''.

"Holy smoke!'' The young man's features showed shocked disbelief. "How did that come about?''

"It was a desperate lie that Bonnie told to try and keep him'', Ruby said. "She wasn't **pregnant**, but she told him she was, in hopes of trapping him into matrimony. I suppose where ever he is, he has a bit of guilt on his conscience, and he wasn't as guilty as she made him believe. For a long time she lived in hopes of his return. Then a man came into her life who was respectable and financially secure, and she accepted him''.

The ringer produced tobacco and began to roll a cigarette, a thoughtful expression on his rugged countenance. After a brief silence he spoke. "She was a real nice girl. It's good to know she found a way out of her troubles. D'yer reckon she thinks as much of her new bloke as she did of Commerford?''

"I'm quite sure she doesn't'', Ruby said emphatically. "But it was evident as time went by that Commerford wasn't going to return. Had he really loved her he wouldn't have left in the first place''.

"Perhaps she should have waited a bit longer'', the ringer replied. "He might have repented and come back''.

"Not from what I hear of him'', Ruby said. "Rumour has it that he is a very faithless type. Out for any girl that comes along. Even black ones''.

"That sounds like Clarrie, alright'', the ringer said ruefully. "It's an interestin' story, missus''.

34

"When you go back to Boulia you will be able to pass it on to him", Ruby said.

"I don't reckon Clarrie will need to be told anything", the ringer replied. "I had it in me head to ride north lookin' for work, so I mightn't see Boulia for a while. Be sure I'll tell me mates what good service and attention yer give, and that the beer's extra bonzer. It's quiet to-day, I reckon".

"Always is in the early part", Ruby said. "The drinkers will be arriving any time now".

"Well I'll say good-bye and push on. Best of luck and thank yer".

He made what seemed to Ruby a rather hurried departure, mounting quickly and putting his horse to a canter until he reached the main track that ran north and south, where he pulled in to a walk. Ruby's eyebrows shot up in surprise. Her late customer had turned his mount's head to the right, and was riding south again.

* * * * * *

Day was falling into dusk, and lights were springing up in the houses at Barcaldine. In the common horsebells clanked. At the drovers' camp flickering firelight shone on Harry Hickey's red moustache, ragged and uncombed as the tail of a brumby colt.

The boss-drover looked up as Charlie Commerford stood up and pointed to the south, where a rider on a swift walking bay horse was approaching the camp.

"He's back", Charlie said in a surprised tone. "Jesus, he must've pushed the bay along. Wonder what the story was".

Hickey knocked the ash from his pipe, smiling as he spoke.

"We'll never know what the story was, Charlie. Whether it's a good girl, or a harlot, he never skites about his conquests".

Monsieur Le Frog

Maggie stood in the kitchen doorway, holding the letter in a chapped red hand while Ned unloaded the firewood from the dray, then removed the harness from the sweating old horse. Freed of its bondage, it made off immediately towards the creek, where the spring grass grew green and tender. Ned smiled at his mother, wiped sweat from his red forelock and reached for the water-bag that hung beneath the sagging roof of the lean-to. His voice was dry.

"That oughter keep the home fires burnin' until I get back from Ginna Gudgeree, mum".

Paying no heed to the remark, Maggie Lynch held out the letter to her tall son. "Ye told me to scan any mail for ye, Ned. This is all the way from Scotland. From an old friend of yours. Often ye have told me of the baby ye rescued in Flanders. That's who this letter is from".

"Monsieur le Frog! Jesus, how did the little bugger find me". Ned's red face registered complete surprise. "It's more than twenty years ago. He'd be grown up now. Funny thing that the Scotch nurse never wrote".

"And of course ye got ye facts roight at the toime". Maggie was smiling secretly now, emotion broadening the Dublin brogue she had never quite lost.

"My oath I did". There was a quiet pride in the gun-shearer's rough demeanour. "Somethin' I always been proud of, grabbin' that little boy out of the mud and cartin' him to safety. I often wonder what become of him. It's just as clear in me mind as it was the time it happened".

* * * * * *

Night was falling, and behind the retreating men shell-fire rumbled, punctuated by the red flashes of the guns. British troops had been flung back by the sheer fury of the German advance, mounted on a five mile front, forcing a deep salient into Allied territory. Fighting almost

36

to the last man, an Australian division had inflicted casualities on the enemy that almost equalled their own losses, until the order to retire came down the embattled front line.

The misty rain that came so often in the wake of battle was falling steadily, soft and clinging as a winding-sheet for the fallen. Long lines of soldiers and civilians walked listlessly, weary and exhausted, their one thought to escape from the scene of carnage. Ambulances both horse-drawn and motorised churned through the tenacious mud of Flanders, overloaded with casualities still living, passing the slower travelling field-guns that had been rescued by determined gunners while their mates had made a last-ditch stand.

Ned Lynch plodded doggedly, the shard of shrapnel in his thigh burning like a hot brand, his mind dulled by the horror he had been through. Beside him Casey walked steadily, his freckled face a pale patch in the increasing gloom. The right sleeve of his tunic was gone, hastily hacked away by Ned with a bayonet, and the tightly drawn field-dressing on the upper arm was dark with blood that still oozed in a slow seep.

Both men were weaponless, their rifles abandoned when the retreat was ordered, for wounded men have a better chance of survival if unburdened on the march. Ned was limping badly, but his wound had ceased to bleed. Though worn, weary, wounded and hungry, still he thanked his lucky stars for delivery, and for that of his brother Sid, who was behind somewhere, substituting as a stretcher-bearer. Ned mustered a weak grin as he addressed Casey.

"Stay with it, mate. We're awful lucky to still be in the land of the livin'".

"Jesus, I feel awful bloody groggy, Ned. Christ knows how far to a dressin' station. And no sign of a bloody medic anywhere".

"Don't chuck it in, Len". Ned's voice grew sharp as he realised his mate was weakening. "We're here, and that's more than a lot of our mates back there can say.

37

We'll live to fight another day".

"Christ, I hope we'll never have to. I'd give the bloody world to see **Kikkajikalong** again".

"We're goin' to see home again". Ned's voice carried a confidence he was far from feeling. "If there's only two men left in the world when the war ends, it's goin' to be you and me, Len".

"Jesus, I wish I could be as cocksure as you". Casey managed a weak grin, then halted suddenly, pointing with his uninjured arm. "Hey, look at that!"

A few feet from the roadside lay what was evidently a dead woman, the bloated corpse straining against the clothes that constricted it. A shell-splinter had torn half the head away, and blow-flies had already been busy. Hardened soldier though he was, Ned almost gagged at the sight. It was not the body that caught his attention, but the small child that sat beside it. No more than a year old, it was howling lustily.

"Jesus!" Casey's voice was a pitying croak. "Poor little coot. I'll bet it's his mother".

The child ceased to cry as Ned moved closer, then it raised two small arms in a gesture of supplication. The short black curls were mud smeared, as were the patched garments, and the dark eyes gazed hopefully at the two soldiers. Casey spoke again.

"Bloody hell! Wonder why someone hasn't picked him up".

"Someone has now". Ned swung the baby up on one long arm, and immediately the child clasped him around the neck, it's dirty face breaking into a woebegone smile.

"What yer goin' to do with him?" Casey enquired. "We gotter keep movin'. Nearly too dark to see".

"Cart him along", Ned said. "Some woman's sure to take him. Christ, but he stinks awful! Enough shit in his napkin to fertilise a Chinese garden. I'll bet he's bloody hungry. Looks as if he's been here a couple of days. A little Frenchy. Monseiur Le Frog, I'll call him".

38

"How the hell will yer keep goin'", Casey asked doubtfully. "Yer lame as a duck now".

"Me old man walked beside a bullock team for thirty years", Ned said. "On a lamer leg than mine. We can't leave the little bugger, Len. He's a little beaut. Look how he's cuddlin' up to me".

"I didn't think of leavin' him". Len sounded suddenly ashamed. "But why hasn't some of the Frenchies picked him up?"

"Because it's every bastard for himself", Ned said grimly. "All thinkin' about keepin' in front of the German advance. We should be passin' reinforcements headed for the front at any time. That's if old Lord Haig hasn't got all hands wiped out. Come on, mate, and look after that arm. Let me do the worryin' and the carryin'."

They trudged on, borne by the escaping crowd that seemed endless. Soldiers of many nations mingled with French civilians who were homeless now. Old men and women carrying bundles or pushing carts and barrows that held hastily gathered belongings, countless children, mothers pushing infants in prams. Human flotsam, drifting listless on the mounting tide of war. An ambulance roared past carrying a load of wounded, their cries of pain clearly audible to the marching men. Ned's voice was grim.

"That could easy be us singin' out in there, Len. Let's make the most of our luck and step it out. If some of the drivers see we're wounded they might pick us up".

They never knew how long or how far they stepped it out before a troop-laden lorry drew up beside them. Willing hands lifted them up amid a mixed bag of Allied soldiers. Ned found himself sandwiched between Casey and an English private who offered a thin packet of cigarettes and scratched a match. Like starved dragons Ned and his mate inhaled and belched smoke, while the baby howled and slobbered.

"Wye the byby, myte? Brought him along to reload for yer, I s'pose". The chime of Bow Bells was evident in the Tommy's rude speech.

"Found him along the road back". Ned exhaled a blue cloud. "Mother got skitted. Well, I think it was his mother. He hasn't stopped cryin' since I got him".

The Cockney leaned forward, stabbing a grimy finger at Ned. "Know wye, myte. 'E's empty as a drum. Hungry, the little tyke is. I know. Got two er me own back in Lunnon. 'Ere, cop this".

Rummaging in his pack, the Tommy produced a dented can. "Tin er milk I scrounged", he announced. "Now 'ow ter get the soddin' thing open".

A match flared, outlining the bearded profile of a French soldier, a dark and sinister-looking poilu who would have been a typical "old sweat" in any man's army. A bloodied bandage was wrapped around his head, and his hands gripped a Lebel rifle with the long wicked bayonet still attached.

"Bli'me, 'ere's one cove 'oo stuck to 'is guns", the Tommy announced. "Let's 'ave a bit more light on the subject".

He bunched several matches and struck them simultaniously, as the poilu detached his bayonet. Even in the weak light, dark flakes were easily discernible on the blade.

"Cor, this bloke's reely bin in it over 'is boots", the Tommy remarked. "Wish I could savvy 'is bloomin' lingo.

The French soldier swiftly punched two holes in the can with the bayonet's point, then handed the former to Ned with a voluble remark in his native tongue.

Tipping the baby's head back, Ned trickled the milk into the small open mouth. Monseiur Le Frog gagged and gasped, then became silent except for bubbling swallows.

The lorry chugged on, the occupants speaking little, minds still numbed from the holocast they had been through. Casey seemed in a stupor, his breath coming in painful gasps, and Ned knew that exhaustion and the wound were bringin his lifelong mate to the point of callapse. The Cockney soldier produced another packet of cigarettes.

41

"Where did yer score all the smokes, Tommy?",
Ned asked as he lit up.

"Tell yer the truth, I took 'em orf a dead bloody officer".

"Jesus! Ned's voice was a shocked whisper.

"No sweat, Cornstalk. 'E didn't need 'em. Good
and bloody dead 'e was, like a lot more poor blighters.
Told us the war wouldn't last a year. Like bloody 'ell".
The Tommy's face in the cigarette glow was drawn, his
speech bitter and disillusioned.

Ned's attention was taken by a cluster of lights
ahead. The dressing station was close at hand, and he
roused Casey. "Nearly there mate". Ned tried to sound
cheerful. "Don't chuck it in".

The lorry wheezed to a stop, its radiator throwing out
a plume of steam. Ned scrambled off, his wounded leg
almost collapsing, the baby clinging to him with all the
strength of its tiny arms, while the French soldier helped
Casey down. The Cockney, wiry and unwounded, sprang
off and melted into the crowd without a word of farewell.

They made staggering steps to the verandah, Len
leaning heavily on the shoulder of the burly poilu, who
had abandoned his bayonetted rifle. An orderly stepped
forward.

"How bad is it, soldier?"

"Not too bad", Ned said. "Me mate's worse. See to
him first".

"This way". The orderly led them along the dimly
lighted verandah to where several wounded men lay leaning against the wall and smoking. Soldiers silent and dull-
eyed, apparently stunned by the knowledge that they
were still alive. Ned sank down gratefully, still holding the
now sleeping baby. The Frenchman helped Casey to a sitting position, then turned to Ned, a smile on his bearded
face.

"Bon jour, mon copain".

" 'Ooray mate, and good luck". Ned gripped the
outhrust hand, then the poilu turned and disappeared

into the darkness, leaving Ned's life as abruptly as he had entered it.

"Jesus, there goes a mate", Casey whispered. "The Pommy bloke was orright too. Wonder when it's all goin' to end".

"Whatever happens, Len, we've done our share. Though it ain't very much to skite about".

"That's right", Casey said. "And we both left a brother on Gallipoli".

Ned carefully laid the sleeping baby down beside him, and his voice was hard. "We gotter be thankful that our people back home are safe, Len. The war won't ever reach 'em".

The minutes dragged by. More wounded arrived, sitting down thankfully on the right, while the line to Ned's left grew fewer.

"Soon be our turn", Casey said. "What the hell are yer goin' to do with the kid? Yer can't take him to Blighty".

"I'll think of somethin'". Ned was stubborn, determined. "I ain't goin' to desert him, whatever happens. I've took a fancy to the little bugger".

Footsteps sounded, brass buttons gleamed, and two English officers made their way along the verandah. Their pressed and polished attire gave mute evidence that they had not arrived from the battle-field. They halted at sight of the sleeping baby. The younger one, a lieutenant, pointed his cane at Ned.

"That child, soldier. Where did it come from?"

Ned saluted without attempting to rise. "It was abandoned, sir. I carried it along with me".

"Are you aware of the order that no time is to be wasted assisting civilians?"

"Didn't receive it, sir."

"What's your name and regiment?"

"Private Lynch, sir B Company, First Australian Battalion".

"Colonials". The contempt that went into the word

43

made Ned wince. "Why did you retreat?"

"Orders, sir".

"By Colonial Officers, of course". The remark was a sneer.

"By an English Major, sir". Casey spoke for the first time. "He was a brave man and a humane one. And he won't be giving any more orders".

The remark seemed to enrage the lieutenant, for he stepped forward and held the cane an inch from Casey's nose.

"Speak when you're spoken to, soldier, or I'll have you on a charge".

"Enough". The major's voice carried a Dublin accent, and for a fleeting moment Ned thought of his mother. "If ye wish to impart discipline, Lieutenant, let it be to men who are not wounded and exhausted. There are no better fightin' men than the Orstralians. Soon ye will have the chance to find out".

The officers moved on, the Lieutenant throwing a sullen glare at Casey. Len's voice was bitter as they drew out of earshot.

"Pommy bastard. They're all the bloody same".

"No they ain't. Remember the bloke give us the milk. They ain't all the same. Up yer get, Lennie boy. It's your turn".

A nurse was beckoning from a lighted doorway. Len struggled to his feet and made unsteady entry. Ned waited for what seemed an eternity, then the nurse appeared again, her gaze inquisitive as she viewed Monseiur Le Frog. When she spoke it was with a Scottish accent.

"Who's next?"

Ned struggles to rise, and his game leg gave way. He floundered like a landed fish, then the girl was beside him, lifting with her strong hands thrust under this armpits. He came erect, and leaning far forward, snatched up the sleeping baby. The nurse spoke sharply.

"Here noo, ye canna bring the child. Put it doon".

"He comes with me". Breaking free from the girl's grasp, Ned lurched through the door, his wounded leg

44

giving agonising pain. The room was ringed with kerosene lamps, and in the centre reposed a table draped with a bloodstained sheet. The medic who stood beside it was young and slight, steel-rimmed spectacles gleaming, apron blood blotched, a tray of bloodied instruments beside him. His haggard face broke into weary smile at sight of Monsieur Le Frog, who has awakened and was howling lustily.

"A mascot I suppose, Digger". The voice was undoubtedly Australian. "Put it down somewhere and hurry. Others are waiting."

Ned deposited the baby near the wall, and at that moment an Army sister entered from a door at the rear. She addressed the medic.

"Can you come for a moment, doctor? There's a bad case outside".

Wordlessly the surgeon followed the woman, and Ned turned to the Scottish girl, who was eyeing the baby doubtfully.

"Ye shouldna hae brought it, soldier. Against orders".

"Blast the bloody orders! There he was, sittin' up beside his dead mother, yellin' his little heart out. God knows how far I carried him. Can yer help me save him? I've sorter got to love the little bugger". Ned's voice was pleading.

The girl's uniform was smeared with blood. Dark hair shone bronze in the lamplight where it straggled from beneath her cap. She stank of sweat and antiseptic, and her face was drawn and pallid with fatigue. But the dark eyes that appraised the lanky Digger were wet with tears of admiration.

" 'Tis a roight guid mon yer are, soldier. To think of another's loife when ye own was at stake. And wounded, too".

"Look after him, will yer. Please say yer will. I'm done in, and I'll be in the ambulance soon, and there won't be room for him", Ned was becoming incoherent, almost at the end of his tether now.

45

The girl turned swiftly to a stand near the door, and snatched a notebook and pencil. "Tis against regs., but I'll look after him somehow. If ye can make sacrifices at a toime loike this, I can too. Tell me yer noime and address back home".

"Ned Lynch, K-i-k-k-a-j-i-k-a-l-o-n-g". Ned spelled the name of the little bush town carefully, then added New South Wales, Australia. "And yours?"

"Morag. Morag MacAvoy. Get on the table, quick! I can hear the doctor coming!"

Footfalls sounded, and the doctor came through the door. Paying no heed to the crying baby, he spoke to the nurse in a harsh disciplinary tone.

"Why isn't this case ready, nurse. Smarten up, our night's far from over. Leg wound, is it? All right, down on your back, Digger".

Thankfully Ned sank down, then rose on one elbow. "Me mate Casey. Yer last patient. How is he?"

"In the ambulance. You'll be with him soon. Get ready for dreamland. Breathe it deep".

The chloroform hissed in the makeshift mask, and a peace that he had not known for days came to Ned Lynch, a painless, comforting peace that ended in unconsciousness.

* * * * * *

Maggie held out the letter, a cunning smile on her face.

"Read it, Ned boy. 'Tis a shock ye are in for".

Wordlessly Ned accepted the missive, and began slowly to read, ignoring the date and the Glasgow address.

Dear Mr. Lynch,

I write in hopes that you are still "on deck". This letter may never find you, but I sincerely hope that it does, and that you will reply.

I am the baby you rescued in Flanders so long ago, grown up now. I will be as brief as

46

possible and if this finds you, and you reply, I will write again and give a more detailed account of what happened after Nurse McAvoy took charge of me. I was destined never to remember her.

She got me across to Scotland, (not without some difficulty), and her mum took charge of me. Soon after her overdue leave, she returned to France, and was killed when the ambulance she was riding in received a direct hit from a German shell.

Morag was an only child, and after her death Mr. and Mrs McAvoy would not part with me. They adopted me legally, (again not without difficulty), and I have lived with them ever since. I became a school-teacher, and knew nothing of my adoption until I was perhaps twenty-three years old, and had decided to marry. Mum and Dad told me then that I was a French war-orphan, and how I was rescued. I was upset at first, but soon realised how lucky I was to be alive, and to have such wonderful parents.

Mum then showed me an old note-book of Morag's and in it was the address of my deliverer.

I want to thank you with all my heart, Mr. Lynch, for your brave deed, and hope you are hale and hearty, and that life is good to you now. Please write if you receive this letter.

Living in hopes,
Margaret Morag McAvoy.

★　★　★　★　★　★

Ned stood thunderstruck, unable to tear his eyes from the clear and neatly written signature. Then he found voice.

"Strike me silly! Monsieur Le Frog was a girl!! And me thinkin' all these years it was a boy!"

Maggie smiled, a smile of adoration at her lanky son.

"What matter, Ned boy. It's what ye did that counts".

"I s'pose yer right, mum", Ned replied. "But I just can't picture a girl. Madamoselle le Frog just don't sound right. She'll always be Monsieur Le Frog to me".

Sort of Complicated
(Joe Walsh)

Smart alecks tell yer it's a wise man who knows his own father. Be that as it may. There's somethin' I do know for sure, after spendin' all me life on the stations and stock-camps. It's a wise cattleman who knows his own beef on the hoof. Things can get sort of complicated.

Out on them big Queensland runs, cattle wander a lot in a dry time, sometimes a long way too. When a general muster's held after a drought, all the strange brands in the world turn up, and unless yer an expert, it's hard to say who belongs to which. And too often a brand's put on with a half-cold iron, and it heals in all the scaley designs in the world. An earmark means nuthin'. A smart duffer can alter it with one stroke of a sharp pocket knife. Makes things sort of complicated.

It was in 1905 that I was ringin' for a bloke we called Rusty Ned Cook. He was a real bloody scoundrel, had done time for cattle and horse duffin', and topped up his record with a degree at Boggo Road College for half-killin a copper. He was just about unbeatable in a rough and tumble fight under Kelly's rules, and blokes who knew him trod softly.

I was only about sixteen then, but I could ride a lot better than most blokes, and Cookie hung on to me because he needed a man who could take the ginger out of the rough ones. Like all drovers of the time, he was all the time tradin' and swappin' in horses, and quite a lot used to appear in the camp overnight. I didn't ever ask Ned how he came by 'em. Could have made things sort of complicated.

It was durin' that stint with Cookie that I found out just how thick-headed some blokes in the cattle-game are. Not the ringers, but the coves that command authority. A lot of 'em wouldn't wake up if yer fired a cannon in their ear, they'd reckon it was a spring breeze blowin'.

49

Things started with a bloke named Shelby. He was a dealer from down in New South, and he came up round the brigalow country buyin' cattle here, there and everywhere, big lots and small. Cookie had the job of takin' 'em south over the border for grass. He started at Taroom, where we picked up five hundred head, every brand and colour and type in the world. I was tailin' the horses, while Cook, Crocodile Jones, Vince Burnside, and a blackboy we called Target handled the cattle. Jones was a tough old ringer, past sixty and he knew more about cattle than a parson knows about the Bible. Burnside was a loud young cove, all skite but a good stockman just the same. Target could hardly talk Engish at all.

By the time we got to the border we had over eight hundred head, as we were pickin' up small mobs that Shelby bought as he went on ahead of us. We crossed over at Goondiwindi, and the feed was something yer don't often see. The job was real holiday. It was at Boggabilla we struck trouble.

Cookie and Vince and Crocodile got on the grog at the pub, and they had three days of a bender. The cattle went everywhere, because two men couldn't hold 'em. Me and Target were ridin' day and night until the other boys got sobered up and came to their senses. All hands were in the saddle then, but when we finally counted we were fourteen head short. There were some pretty sharp boys around the place, and some of 'em took advantage of Cookie's lapse to aquire a few head.

Rusty Ned didn't try to shift the blame on to anyone. He knew he'd done the wrong thing by gettin' on the booze with his men. He had a plan for makin' the numbers right, but he didn't know I was awake up to it. I always went to bed early, unless I had to sleep away from the camp with the horse when feed was patchy, or when I had to do the dog watch. One night they reckoned I was asleep, and they're talkin' at the fire. Didn't reckon I was listenin'.

"We won't have any trouble gettin' fourteen head",

Cook says. "We got such a mixed mob that yer wouldn't notice any particular beast that walked into it. We swipe one here and one there 'til we get fourteen head. The further south we go the more likely we are to strike cattle in paddocks that have come down earlier, and are waitin' to cross over at Wodonga. We better keep young Joe in the dark. If the traps got on the scent he might get the wind up".

"What he don't know can't hurt him", Vince says.

So that was the great plan. Don't let me know what's on, and of course no worries about the blackfeller, because he couldn't talk the lingo much. Also he used to sleep well away from the camp and make his own little fire at night. The blacks were pretty downtrodden in those times.

On we go, the stock gettin' fatter and quieter all the time. It was late spring, and the weather was grand. Old Crocodile was the cook and packer, and he had all the spare time in the world to put on slap-up feeds. Round the fire at night we used to yarn, or Vince would sing the popular songs of the day. Swagman often camped with us and told of any major happenin' that might be news, and we were always meetin' other drovers with somethin' to talk about. Camp-fire tales and songs were a lot more interestin' than all this potted entertainment we get on the radio and screen to-day. We had no set destination, just follerin' the grass, but we reckoned the mob would be sold when we got to the Victorian border. And as far as I knew the three bold duffers hadn't as yet grabbed any cattle to make the numbers right.

We were gettin' close to Coonamble when Shelby lands unexpectedly with an agent named Baxendale. They looked the cattle over, and fairly danced with joy.

"You've done a great job, Ned", Shelby says. "No losses, of course?"

"None at all", Cookie says, but I can see a few worry lines spring up on his forehead. He's thinkin' of the fourteen head that went missin' at Boggabilla. Then Shelby drops the bombshell. Him and Baxendale have conveined a sale at Coonamble on the forthcomin' Friday. We've got four days to get to the yards and draft up..

Away goes authority, and Cookie and Vince and Crocodile are sittin' in their saddles lookin' pretty discouraged, each thinkin' the same thing. How to present the right number of cattle. Things were gettin' sort of complicated.

We camped that night on one of the Goobreganna boundaries. It was a big station that ran Hereford cattle, in a district that was mostly all sheep. I knew somethin' was on when the big three caught fresh horses and tied 'em up, but I didn't ask any questions, as they didn't know I listened in when I was supposed to be asleep.

About twelve o'clock they ride off. The moon was big and bright as Alladin's lamp. A great night for skullduggery. I went to sleep and didn't wake 'til daylight, when I had to go after the horses. Crocodile was buildin' up the fire, and Ned and Vince were still in their swags. I heads the night-horse for the sound of the bells.

It was full light when I got the cuddies together, and just as I expected, three of 'em's got dry sweat all over 'em, a sure sign they'd been hard-ridden. When I got to camp the blackboy had gone to the lead of the cattle, and Crocodile was packin' up. Ned and Vince were pushin' the tail-enders ahead. I grabbed some breakfast and got the horses movin'.

I didn't go far when I hears a whip goin' and cattle bellerin'. Then I spots Vince dealin' to a small bunch that's tryin' to get back. I canters up and gives him a hand to get 'em movin' ahead. Fourteen of the bludgers, neat little Hereford steers all alike. They hadn't been well branded, all the brands were smudged and scaley, but I had no doubt where they came from, and that they were tryin' to get back to home ground.

"Jesus, what's got into 'em?", I says real innocent like. "They never put on an act like this before, in all the weeks they been on the road".

"Cattle can do funny things", Vince says. "Yer can get back to the horses, I can handle 'em now".

52

I had first watch that night, and Ned took the second one. I was coiled up listenin' for a while, and sure enough Crocka and Vince start talkin' in low tones about the fourteen Herefords, as they're drinkin' tea by the fire.

"It's a hell of a bloody risk", Vince says in low tones. "Some bludger's goin' to spot 'em, this close to their own dunghill".

"We got a hell of a mixed mob", Old Crocodile says. "And the brand on them little fellers is pretty badly put on. Hard to tell what it is, seein' they ain't shed their winter coats yet, and they got no earmark. We put one here and one there in different pens, and no bugger will notice 'em. As the agents always says, "The mob will be drafted into lines to suit buyers". There's going' to be a hell of a lot of lines in a mob like this one. The main thing is to split the hot ones well up. No two of 'em in one pen. This bloke Baxendale is new to Coonamble, so he won't spot anything, and Shelby wouldn't remember what half the cattle he bought looks like".

I went to sleep then. It's hard to keep awake after a long day in the saddle. First light saw me out and around the horses, and as I was headin' 'em for camp I sees fourteen little Herefords makin' back down the fence at a trot, lookin' real homesick. They'd got past Target, who was doin' the dogwatch.

I cantered over and turns 'em back, and as I got back to the horses I sees Vince run over on foot with his whip and fires a few volleys behind 'em. Not a word was said as ₐne boys caught their horses for the day. I wondered if Rusty Ned knew I was awake up.

We still had 'em when we gets to Coonamble saleyards. Next mornin' Baxendale took charge of the draftin', and he knew his job, believe me. In fact he knew it too well to suit Rusty Ned's ambitions. Two of the little Herefords come chargin' up the race and Bax sings out, "put them in a new pen. They're a cut above what's been coming through".

"I don't reckon they match. You orter split 'em", Ned says.

53

"What's wrong with your eyes this morning, Ned", the agent replies. "Put them together in a new pen".

That was how it went. When we finished the draftin', Baxendale's got the lines drafted up beautiful. Shelby comes along and compliments him, but he didn't get any compliments from Cookie. The fourteen Hereford were on their own in one pen.

We boils up and has a feed, and by that time the buyers are turnin' up. I hears Bax say to Shelby as he points a finger. "There's Mr Markson, the manager of Goobreganna. He must be looking for restockers".

Cookie and Vince heard it too, and I could fairly hear 'em sweatin'. Poor old Crocodile looked too scared to even sweat, and I hears Ned say to Vince; "It's a case of hope and bloody pray now".

The sale gets off on a high note. Baxendale was just as good at sprukin' as he was at draftin'. Be the time the first line of pens were sold Shelby was grinnin' like a goanna that's broke into a fowl-yard. But Cookie and his two guilty mates wasn't. Nearer and nearer they comes to the dangerous pen of fourteen Herefords. At last they gets there.

"Here's a quality lot", Bax sings out. "Fourteen top Hereford steers. What about three pounds to start them?"

"Done", says a loud voice right beside me, and I nearly faints. The bidder is Mr. Markson of Goobreganna, where the fourteen steers belong.

They went up in five bob bids until they reached five pounds five, then were knocked down to Goobreganna Station. The sale went on and from that point Markson let his head go and bought over three hundred, all Hereford steers.

The sale finishes, and Baxendale orders me to put all Markson's cattle in one yard. When I finished I knew any danger was past. All Hereford steers look alike when yer push 'em into a mob. The poor silly bastard had bought fourteen of his own cattle, and let Cookie off the hook as far as deliverin' the right number. But there was one more bit of a scare.

Cookie was undecided whether to pack up and head for home, or camp for the night at the yard. We were debatin' the matter when up comes Shelby, Baxendale and Markson, and with 'em is a Sergeant of Police. I could hear the three bold duffers tremblin' in their boots, but Bax gives a big smile and pulls out a bottle of whiskey.

"I always shout for men who do a good job", he says. "My three friends will join us". I woke then why the copper was there. There ain't a bigger bludger in the world than the average policeman.

We all has a whiskey, and then Markham asks Cook if he wants the job of takin' the cattle to Goobreganna. "It's on your road home", he says. "A little extra money for you, and don't have to go out of your way".

Ned agreed. The whiskey had stiffened his backbone, as well as the knowledge that Markson wouldn't wake up if yer threw him in a tub of hot water.

We only took three days to get to the delivery point, because we had fourteen good leaders. Them little Herefords was awful keen to get home again. We didn't see Markson, the alert cattleman. One of his ringers made the count and took delivery. Then it was the long road home for us.

I never worked for Rusty Ned Cook again, although I saw him from time to time over the years. I took a job on Karragatta, got married and give the drovin' best for a quiet life. And I ain't sorry. When yer work for blokes like Cookie things can get sort of complicated.

Lament of Plain Bill
(Ned Lynch recalls)

Lots of people tell yer that it's possible to hear voices from the dead. I reckon that when a bloke's dead he's very dead indeed. Just the same, in all walks of life yer strike men and women who reckon they can hear the voices. I suppose hearin' 'em couldn't do yer much harm, but takin' notice of 'em could be dangerous. Superstition has sent a lot of sane blokes over the foo-foo line. My mother was born of shanty Irish people, and they're about the most **superstitious** mob in the world. She used to tell us kids about banshees and goblins, and leprechauns roostin' on toadstools, but none of it ever rubbed off on me. There was only one time that I had cause to believe in the soopernatcheral, and until I found out the strength of it, I was scared stiff. It was a long time ago, when I was a young feller.

Me and me brother Sid had swagged it into Bourke, lookin' for shearin'. There was a hell of a drought on, and work was scarce. We had a few quid between us, so we decides to make enquiries in the nearest pub.

There was a long sandy-headed bloke at the bar, takin' his time over a pint. The slow way he was drinkin' made me think he didn't have the finance for a refill. Yer could tell be the bend in him, and the callouses on the knuckles of his lefthand, that he was a shearer. He throws us a big grin. "How are yers, boys", he says.

"Lookin' for a pen", I replies.

"Pretty hard just at present", he tells me. "The hill's gettin' steeper, but yer got to keep climbin'".

Just then a big bloke with a grey moustache comes into the bar. Wide hat, garbadine strides, Baxter boots. A man-on-the-land for sure. He didn't waste any time on preliminaries. "Are you men shearers?", he asks.

"I am, name's Lynch", I says, and points to Sid. "Me brother's a rouseabout."

"I'm a shearer", the pint-sipper says. "Bill Plain". I reckon Plain Bill would have suited him better.

"There's six hundred ration wethers at Dullmore to be shorn", the big nob says. "I'm Caisley, the manager. Only three days work, but if you men are unemployed it may suit you".

"Yer on", Plain Bill says. "A quid would be handy right now. The hill's gettin' steeper, but yer gotter keep climbin'".

Sid and me agrees, so away we goes in Caisley's waggonette, that was loaded up with plunder for the station. It was fourteen miles out, and the closer we got to Dullmore, the more dull it looked. At last we arrives, and gets off at the huts. There's an old warrior camped there with one eye, and a tea-towel tied around his head. He had no boots, and feet like a camel, only not as clean.

"Me name's Oney", he says. "I doin' the cookin. When yer dig in, come for tea. I got somethin' special on".

He saunters off, and I give Plain Bill a doubtful look, but he only grins. "The hill's gettin' steeper", he says. "But yer gotter keep climbin' ".

The special was corn meat and spuds, and the junk was that salty that is must have been soaked in the Pacific Ocean for a week. But it wasn't as bad as the big heap of scones, hard enough to tile a bathroom floor. "Thank God we're only here for three days", Plain Bill says. "The hill's gettin steeper, but yer gotter keep climbin'.

Next day we sail into the wethers. Mr Caisley worked on the wool-table with Sid, and a grubby-lookin' ringer did the musterin' and pressin'. "No need for a classer", Caisley says. "Only three grades of wool here, long, short and shitty". That just about summed up the whole operation.

They were far from fast shearin, full of grass-seed. Plenty of body wrinkles too, and the weather was as hot as hell. But we plugged away at 'em, and I got to say that Bill was a good, uncomplainin' mate, and a good shearer, even it he wasn't a gun. Every time we pulled up to light a smoke, he'd shake the sweat out of his hair and give a hard grin and the same old remark. "The hill's gettin' steeper, mate. But yer gotter keep climbin''.

We cut out at dinner-time on the third day. Caisley paid us cash, so I reckoned the wool cheque was due to hit his own personal bank account, unknown to his directors, and the owners back "Ome". We had a final go at Oney's special tucker, and took the track for Bourke.

We got to town just on dark. It didn't take Bill long to get drunk, and the cops lumbered him, along with a few more blokes who were kickin' up a noise about the wrongs of the workin' class. Sid and me camped on the bank of the Darling that night, and next mornin' Bill comes to say hooray. He had decided to head for Nyngan, on the not too kind advice of the law. We shook hands and watched him tramp off to the east. When he was about a hundred yards away he stops and turns as it he had forgot somethin'. "The hill's gettin' steeper", he sings out. "But yer gotta keep climbin'.''

I struck him again about six months later, at a shed out of Brewarrina. It was a fast team, and I was as flat as piss on the road to get me average. We were all nervy and irritable from workin' at too much pressure. All except Bill. He just plugged along behind. "No sense in bustin' yerself", he says. "Be lots of sheep when I'm dead and gone. The hill's gettin' steeper, but yer gotter keep climbin'.''

I don't know if the hill Bill was always talkin' about was any rougher than the necks of some of the old ropy wethers we were battlin' with, but I was bloody glad to cut out. When we got into Bree I find that Bill's got a wife and four kids in Sydney, because he wired money to 'em. He confided to me that the lady was livin' with another bloke, and Bill hadn't been home for three years. "She's a good mother, Ned. That's about all yer coud say in her favour. But yer can't let kids go short". Whether he was saint or mug I couldn't decide, but I had a lot of respect for him after that.

It was a good while later on we were in Coonamble,

and Bill we finds, is yardman at a pub. And let me tell yer he looked bad. Thin as a starved emu, and pale as a new-born ghost. "I ain't been too well", he says, shakin' hands. "Good to see you blokes again. The hill's gettin' steeper, but yer gotter keep climbin'."

I landed two days work, shearin' stud rams. There was nothin' goin' for Sid, so he stayed camped on the river at Coonamble. When I gets in after cuttin' out, he passes me on the sad news. Plain Bill had died in his sleep, and is to be buried that afternoon. God knows what killed him. The doctor said it was a heart attack, but yer wouldn't know for sure.

A lot of the quacks in those days couldn't tell con-sumption from a broken leg. Anyhow, whatever it was, the hill had got too steep for him to keep on climbin'.

We fronts for the funeral. His Mum and Dad were there, a pretty old couple, and a few other relatives. I didn't know any of 'em, the crowd was mostly pastoral workers. The local Union Rep. was givin' a lot of help, and he asked Sid and me to act as pall-bearers, along with two other shearer blokes.

It was a hell of a bloody ordeal for me in the church, listenin' to the long-winded sermon the sky-pilot dished out. I been a dead-set atheist all me life, to the sorrer of me devout Catholic mother. I only hoped the Golden Stairs would be easier for Bill to climb than the hill he was always talkin' about. Anyhow, at last it was over. We gets the box loaded and starts for the cemetery.

We follered the hearse on foot. It was a horse-drawn vehicle in those days. The grave was up on a bit of a rise, and we had about twenty yards to carry Bill, on an uphill climb. There'd been a shower of rain in the night, and we had to tread careful on the slippery ground. We were nearly to the grave when I heard the voice, and so help me God I nearly dropped the coffin!

It came over real soft and clear, like it was comin' from a long way away, but yer couldn't mistake the words. "The Hill's gettin' steeper, boys. But yer gotter keep climbin'."

We puts the box down, and the parson starts givin' Bill another helpin' hand into Heaven. I was shakin' like a poor wether that's just been shorn, wonderin' if Bill has come back to life again. Then Sid comes up beside me.

"It's alright", he whispers. "I heard it too. It was the bloke on my side of the coffin'."

Talk about bloody relief! I tell yer, it swamped me like a flood. When we got back to town, I didn't feel right until I knocked over a big double rum, and I never was much on for the hard liquors. I'm chasin' it down with a beer when Sid comes over with the bloke who parroted Plain Bill's stock remark. He was a shearer from the south named Bob Hannon.

"Sorry I scared yer", he says. "I thought we was goin' to slip arse over head and drop the coffin'."

"No harm done", I says. "But yer could have thought of somethin' different to say. I was dead sure Bill was still on deck. Or speakin' from the bloody hereafter".

"It was Bill's great sayin' when things were hard", Hannon says. "It must have been in me mind. He was a real good bloke to have on yer side when the goin' got rough".

That was the only time I thought that dead men could still contact the livin'. I've heard blokes argue on it all day and night. But just for now I've talked enough anyway. There's a lot of little jobs to be done round the place, so I better make a start on 'em. They won't do themselves, so here goes. The hill's gettin' steeper, but yer gotter keep climbin'.

The Lifticoola

The weather was cool, for it was late autumn and the days were growing shorter as winter approached. The land was dry, sadly in need of rain to ensure a growth of verdure before cold weather set in. Rainfalls in the outback are always inconsistent, and the bright yellow automobile was coated with a film of red dust as it chugged to a stop in front of the Pride of Erin Hotel. Painted a garish shade of green, it was the only building of style in the small settlement of **Kikkajikalong**.

The occupants of the car, a young man and woman, alighted and removed their dust coats, then hand in hand entered the parlour of the hotel. It was evident to any onlooker of keen perception that the couple were newlyweds. The woman was at once impressed by the clean little room with its simple furnishings, where green was again the predominant colour.

"Oh, Harold! What a dee-lightful little place! We simply must have lunch here. Don't you think it is quite unique."

"Absolutely, Murial my dear". Harold was evidently deeply in love with his wife. "But so quiet. No quick service, it seems".

The inner door opened to admit mine host, Patrick Gilhooley, late of Athlone, Ireland. The ex-pugilist's craggy face displayed a gargoyle grin. Muriel surveyed the battered countenance with a mixture of distate and fear. Gilhooley's voice was a hoarse whisper.

"Welcome to me humble hostelerly, young people. 'Tis from the city ye come, I would wager. Now what would ye pleasure be?"

"My wife is keen to have lunch here in the parlour", Harold replied". She is very impressed with the place. I hope my request is permissible".

"Shure, 'twill be no trouble at all", Gilhooley wheezed. "Sit ye down and rest while I make arrange-

61

ments. 'Tis roast mutton and spuds we have, with a spotted dog to foller''.

"A spotted dog, what's that?'', Harold enquired doubtfully.

Gilhooley grinned. "Faith, 'tis a name the bush laddies have for a plum puddin''. Muriel's face displayed an expression of relief as Gilhooley made silent departure, and a man entered from the sunlit street, immediately catching the eyes of the city visitors.

The newcomer was indeed a striking figure. lean and muscular, almost as dark and swarthy as an Indian, he walked with a swaggering step that denoted confidence and strength. His Blucher boots were worn and dusty, and worn moleskins were supported by a belt decorated with silver studs. A black serge waistcoat also displaying much silver, plus pearlshell ornamentation, was worn over a red flannel shirt, and a red scarf tied pirate fashion failed to hide long curling black ringlets. The man raised a hand in a half salute. Gold teeth flashed as he smiled under an inky Lord Kitchener moustache. The voice was deep and musical.

"Real bonzer day, don't yer reckin?'' Without waiting for a reply he turned to the small serving window at the end of the parlour, leaving the two visitors with somewhat amazed expressions.

"Now what and who would that chap be'', Harold whispered.

"I don't know'', Muriel said in an awed voice. "He looks like a buccaneer escaped from Treasure Island''.

Gilhooley entered bearing a tray, and with a flourish deposited it on the table. Harold addressed him sotto voce. "Who is the chap across the room? He is quite a striking type''.

"Handsome too'', Muriel added. "Like a Greek scholar''.

"Faith 'tis a strikin' spalspeen he is for shure''. Gilhooley's rasping whisper was low "That's Ted Romany, the flashest bullock-driver in this great land. The son of a gypsy mother and an unknown dad''.

Muriel's attention was distracted by the steaming lunch. There was sufficient on the loaded plates to feed four hungry people. The lady from the city was greatly impressed.

"My word, you certainly serve a substantial lunch".

Gilhooley's cauliflower ear twitched. "Bejabers, 'tis niver short of food we are in the bush, even though niceties may be lackin'. Besides, 'tis a land where men work hard, and need large amounts of food to keep goin'. Taker yonder bullocky. All that is on ye tray would only be an entree for the rascal".

He departed, and the newlyweds attacked the repast, finding that a little more than half the feast was sufficient to sate their hunger. Harold, plying a toothpick diligently, noticed that the gaudy bullocky had consumed two whole pints of beer, and was sipping a third. It was then that the small dog entered the bar and sat up before the teamster.

"Oh, look Harold. What a dear little dog. I think he's hungry". Muriel arose, and taking a scrap of meat from a plate, crossed the room and smilingly addressed the gypsy. "You surely won't mind if I give your little dog a present".

"Go ahead, missus". Gold glittered in the dark, reckless smile, "He's a cert to enjoy it".

The dog sat up, eyed the meat in a most appealing manner, and held out a small paw. Muriel was captivated as the meat was taken daintly from her fingers. The tit-bit disappeared at one quick gulp, then the dog rose to all fours and capered around his benefactor.

"Oh, Harold isn't he delightful. He is absolutely the most unique dog I have ever seen".

The dog was without doubt unique in appearance. It was white with one black ear that flopped, while the other stood up stiffly. A black ring circled one eye. The legs were so short as to nearly allow the creature's stomach to touch the floor. The lifted tail curled tightly over the back, revealing a shiny black anus the size of a shilling. And the brown eyes held a pleading and trustful expression that won Muriel's heart. She addressed the big teamster.

63

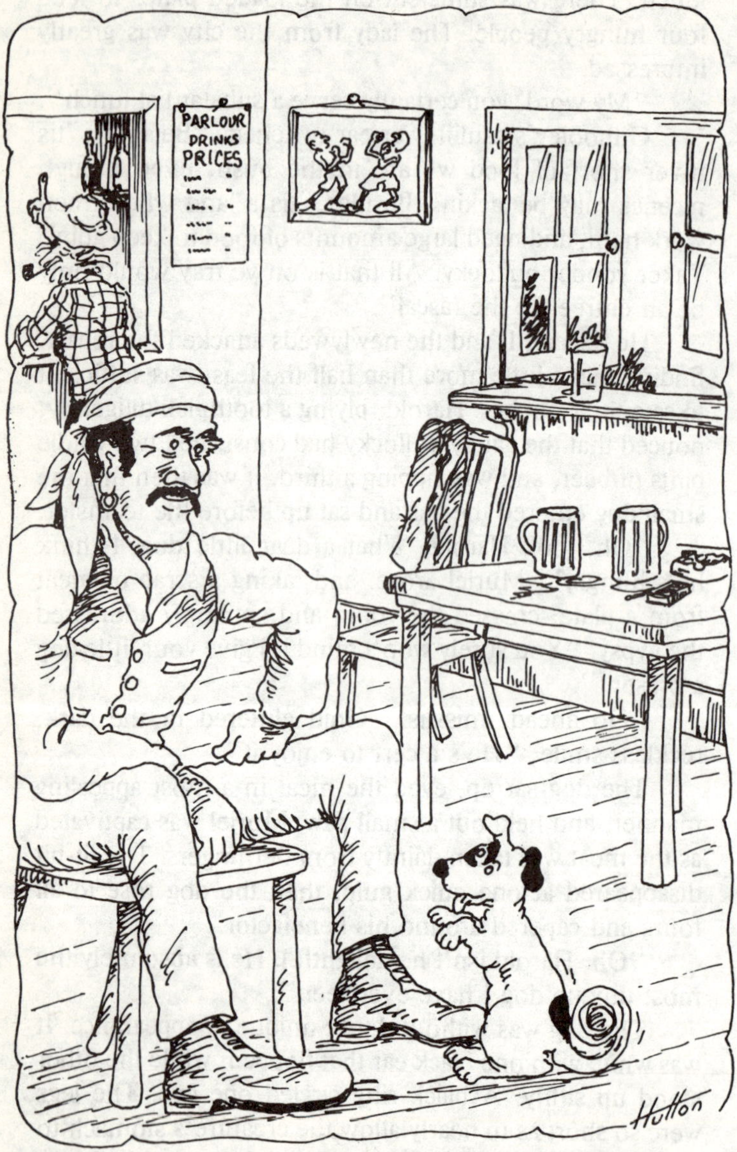
PARLOUR
DRINKS
PRICES
Hutton

"He's such a dear. What is his name?"

"His name missus, is Lifty".

"A strange name. Why do you call him that".

Romany took another sip at his beer, his smile a gold and white slash now. "Because, missus, he's a fair dinkim Lifticoola".

"A Lifticoola. Why that's a breed of dog I am not aquainted with".

The teamster placed his pint on the table and produced tobacco. "Theyre' a breed yer seldom see in Australia. Come from Roumania".

"Oh, how exciting. All the way from Roumania".

"How I happen ter have him", Romany went on, "me mother was a Roumanian gypsy. Brought a pair of Lifticoolas out with her. We kept breedin' 'em over the years, but they got crossed up with other types, and the true breed has just about died out. That little bloke would be one of the last genuine Lifticoolas in Australia. Sit up for the lady, Lifty".

The dog obeyed, sitting up and waving its forepaws in a quaint and endearing manner. An ideas blossomed in Muriel's mind, and with a flattering smile she addressed Romany.

"Of course, a man of your kind and loving ways would never think of selling him, would you?"

"Now I'll surprise yer". The black gypsy eyes were full of guile. "If I could get a fair price, and know that he was goin' to a good home, I'd sell him".

"But surely you're joking. How could you part with him if his species is so rare".

"Well it's like this. When a man is a teamster, he's got to have cattle dogs. Savage ones, and I've got three of 'em. They deal to the little bloke, savage him and take his tucker when I ain't lookin'. And I'm afraid that he's goin' to get kicked under the waggon by one of the polers and a wheel will go over him and squash him flat. So when yer take it by the whole and look well into it, he's better in a good home. I hate partin' with him, but I got to think of his welfare".

65

"Oh, Harold we must have him. Please". Muriel could not believe what she fondly imagined was her good fortune.

"Of course, my dear". Harold was more than happy to satisfy the wishes of his young wife. "Now as regards the price, Mr. Romany".

"Well as I've told yer, his type is pretty rare. I was goin' to ask ten pounds, but seein' as yer like him so much, he's yours for a fiver".

"Done!" Harold produced a purse and handed over the required sum. "Do you require a receipt?"

"No need, me word is me bond, and I'm sure yours is the same".

Muriel lifted the dog in her arms, and was stroking its head as it tried furiously to lick her face, its grotesque tail waving like a flag.

"Look at that", Romany said. "He really likes yer. Yer luck's in to-day alright. Not often yer can guy a genuwine Lifticoola for a fiver".

Mary Gilhooley had entered silently despite her huge bulk, and was collecting plates and eating utensils. Harold settled the dinner bill, and with a voluble farewell went through the dusty sunlight to the car, his enraptured wife carrying the obviously contented little dog. A receding dust cloud marked their departure, and with a cunning grin Romany hied himself off to the dining room, where Big Mary and Judy Lynch were serving dinner to several transient shearers who were passing through.

"I'll have dinner, everything on the menu", gypsy announced.

"Is there naught in ye tucker-box, ye dago rascal?", Big Mary asked with a smile.

"Plenty", Flash Ted replied. "But I just made a successful deal, and a bloke has to think of his welfare'.

Half an hour later, fully replenished, the gypsy crossed the road to where his team lay dozing in the yokes. He took a battered felt hat from where it reposed on a wheel hub, pulled it over his red turban, and was unscrewing the brake, when he heard a soft footfall. He turned to find Judy beside him.

"Ted", she said, "I was listening in when you sold the dog to those two Sydney ducks. Where did you get it. I've never seen it around the pub, or with any of the teamsters".

Flash Ted fingered a gold ear-ring. He knew Judy Lynch could always be trusted to hold her tongue.

"Tell yer the truth Judy, he come to our camp out on the ridge at daylight this mornin', lookin hungry. I give him a feed and he follered the waggon to town. I dunno where he come from. Queer lookin' little bugger. Part kelpie and part fox terrier be the look of him, with a bit of dashchund chucked in. Useless poor little bugger, gets in the bloody road".

"Well what did you mean when you said he was a Lifticoola. I never heard of one".

"Just somethin' I thought up on the spur of the moment. Yer noticed how he lifted his tail up over his back? That was to cool his shiny little black asshole. Lifticoola. D'yer savvy?"

"You're a crooked scoundrel, Ted Romany", Judy sounded serious, but her violet eyes were smiling.

"Not a bit, The buyers were satisifed, and yer can't blame a bloke for lookin' after his welfare! Gee Split! G'wup there Polish!" There was a clank of bar-chains as the resting bullocks rose to their feet. The whip cracked, and the leaders swung into the road to a thud of linch-pins. Judy retired to the parlour where Mary met her with an enquiring gaze.

"He didn't tell me anything", Judy stated quite untruthfully, and the big woman turned away, disappointment plain on her face.

Judy was silent and thoughtful during the afternoon, and as the day waned Mary was moved to ask the reason for her employee's silence.

"Tis quiet ye are, girl. Is somethin' troublin' ye".

"Not really, Mary", Judy replied. "I keep wondering why in all the stories we read, the people from the city always outwit the yokels from the bush. It doesn't always happen that way''.

Matter of Necessity

The evening was as yet early, but there was a cold bite in the air, an announcement by the elements that winter was not far off. Ernie Lynch scouted well beyond the sickly circle of light from the lantern that hung from a gunwale of the waggon, seeking a log for the diminishing fire. Finding a long dry brigalow that was to his liking, he hoisted it on a shoulder, and with limping steps making his lameness evident, he carried the wood to the blaze and deposited the end in the flames. Two yards away Romany raked coals from the oven-lid with a pot-hook, then lifted the hot cast-iron disc. The damper showed up crusty brown and steaming.

"She's done, and she's a bloody dazzler", the gypsy stated with a smile that revealed his gold caps in the fire-light. "What say we tap her with a bit of butter and treacle before we burrer up?"

Lynch's reply was to fill the billy from the keg slung under the waggon. He was a serious and silent man most of the time, displaying little humour or cheer. Placing eating utensils, treacle, and a tin that formerly contained axle-grease, but now was used as a butter-pot by the teamsters. He deposited his armful on the square canvas where Romany was slicing enthusiastically into the damper with a murderous-looking knife.

"It's a bastard havin' no meat in the camp", the gypsy said. "I'm only half a bloody man without meat. Never mind, termorrer night we'll be camped near Marimbindi mill paddock. Once it gets dark, this old knife will be slicin' chops. Always a few wethers in that little meadow, and they're always fat".

One night you'll be caught, Ted", Ernie Lynch said heavily. "You're too bloody darin' for yer own good. A lot of traps would give a year's salary to get somethin' on yer".

"And you're too bloody honest for yer own good". Romany's gold ear-rings glittered in union with his teeth". Ned and Sid and Tug don't mind moonlightin' one if they're hungry".

"My boys are men now", Lynch said soberly. "I always tried to discourage 'em from dishonesty, but they fell into the ways of the hard-up people. They're takin' the chance of bein' caught. I only hope they never are".

"Tell me, Ernie", Romany said, "If you was reel hard-up, wouldn't yer shake somethin, if doin' so would relieve the pressure".

"Only if it was a case of reel necessity", Lynch replied.

"Well, I s'pose yer can't blame a man for playin' it safe", Romany said thoughtfully. "The billy's boilin".

He reached for the tea-tin, and at that moment Clipper, Ernie's cattle dog, rose from under the waggon with a warning growl, his bristles raised. "Somebody comin'," Lynch said, "get back under the waggon, yer old bludger".

Clipper retreated, still rumbling suspiciously in his throat, and a man stepped into the firelight, dropping a thin swag. His greeting was delivered in a weak, husky voice. "Hope I'm not makin' a nuisance of meself. I'm starved out".

"Well yer won't starve in this camp", Romany said, taking note that Ernie was already at the tucker-box unloading more victuals. Black gypsy eyes made careful appraisment of the visitor. Lean and stooped, white hair sticking out from under a faded brown bowler hat, the man gave an instant impression of frail poverty. A tattered coat covered a threadbare-fronted shirt. Old serge trousers, sans knees, dragged their frayed bottoms on laceless canvas shoes. The thin face, displaying several days of snowy whisker, was pinched with hunger.

"Yer tuckered out all right", the gypsy said. "Look as if yer been dead for a week. Bog in, mate, and fill yer tank".

"There's one tin of bully left", Ernie announced.

"Bust her", Romany ordered," before we find we got a bloody corpse on our hands".

70

The transient ate slowly, drinking mug after mug of hot strong tea. Romany's shrewd black orbs noticed the trembling in the hand that held the pint, the sunken eyes and bloodless face. Symptoms that announced some form of fever or ague, evidently the result of hunger and exposure. Ernie Lynch spoke softly and with concern.

"Yer look pretty crook, mate".

"It's the cold change, I reckon". The man moved closer to the fire, and Romany threw on more wood. "I can't stop this bloody shiverin'. But I'm bloody grateful to you blokes. Lucky I spotted yer fire. Down to me last half-quid, and been cuttin' meself short to make it last out. Yer wouldn't have any sort of medicine, I suppose".

"Got castor oil", Ernie Lynch said hopefully. Both Ernie and his Irish wife Maggie believed that castor oil was the elixer of life, and would cure any ailment known and unknown to man. The swagman shook his head, and was seized by a fit of shivering. Romany smiled slyly at Ernie.

"We got another kind of dope. But it's sort of forbidden. What d'yer reckon Ernie?"

Ernie's grey eyes were shrewd, and he flashed a rare smile. "I reckon it's a matter of reel necessity".

Romany arose, moved to the waggon-box and removed a brace, loosened the chuck and fitted a small nail-bit, while Ernie broke a twig from a low hanging myall branch. He began to pare the dark-grained wood with a pocket knife, while the gypsy raised the lashed tarpaulin that covered the waggon. A fifty gallon keg was revealed, dark wood shining from a recently applied coat of varnish. Flash Ted grinned at the ague ridden traveller, whose pinched face wore a puzzled expression.

"This", announced the gypsy, "is what yer call a cuppin' and bleedin' operation'. Yer ready, Ernie".

"Just about". Lynch had cut the sliver of wood to the required size, and procuring a hammer from the waggon-box and a pint from a hook on the gunwale, stood ready for the performance. "Tap her low down", he or-

71

dered. "So the pressure up top will drive out a good stream".

Romany cranked the brace swiftly, withdrew it and placed a thumb over the hole. "The pint", he ordered, and taking it from Ernie's hand held it under the perforation. A thin brown stream trickled into the pint, and the smell of rum rose on the air. In the matter of a minute the small receptacle was filled up. Ernie inserted the wooden plug in the hole and the trickle of rum stopped. Carefully the tall teamster tapped the plug tight, then carefully pared the end to a level with the stave that had been punctured. He looked enquiringly at Flash Ted.

"Bloody bonzer! The colour of the plug matches the keg dead bloody right". He turned to the visitor, who had watched the performance with an amazed expression. "Now mate, here's somthin' to hunt the devil-devils out of yer".

"Christ, how and where did yer learn that trick", the shivering man asked.

"Just somethin' the professional bullocky has to know, when a matter of necessity arises". Flash Ted poured a nip into a spare pint, added hot tea and sugar." Down the hatch she goes, mate".

With a shaking hand the man took the pint and tossed the contents in one quick swallow. He gasped, coughed and showed watery eyes. Romany retrieved the pint, poured a liberal dose and drank it straight. Not a nerve twitched in his dark, handsome face as he expelled a deep breath and surveyed the remaining liquor.

"There's just a nip left", he announced. "I'll mix yer another one, then inter yer swag and get warm. Me old limpy mate's getting some extra nap ready for yer". He pointed to where Ernie was unrolling a small tarpaulin and two spare blankets.

The second dose of bullockys' medication was administered, rendering the patient to the point of collapse. He lurched to the spread swag, removed his shoes and fell down. "I really 'preciate you blokes", he mumbled.

72

"Like to have had a yarn, but I can't bloody keep awake".

By the time Ernie spread the blankets and turned back the tarpaulin, the uninvited guest was dead to the world, his snores sounding loud in the silence of the bush night. Romany flung out the stale tea, filled the billy with fresh water from the keg and hung it over the blaze. It boiled quickly and fresh tea was made. The teamsters ate the treacle smeared damper and drank the hot brew gratefully, indulging in speech only when the meal was over. Slowly Ernie Lynch filled his pipe as he addressed his mate.

"I wonder what the strength of that poor bugger is and why he's on the track".

"Christ only knows", Romany scratched a vesta on his bootsole and lit up. "There's a bloody lot of things that can put a bloke on the track to-day".

"I'm glad we was able to give him a bit of help", Ernie said. "And pinchin' a bit of Gilhooley's rum ain't on me conscience. When a man's hard up, doin' the wrong thing often becomes a reel bloody necessity".

✱   ✱   ✱   ✱   ✱   ✱

The teamster's camp was astir before daylight, and the transient traveller, to all appearances recovered from his illness, ate breakfast with them by the light of the camp-fire. With profuse thanks he slung his swag and departed for town, while the bullockies yoked up the swiftly-mustered oxen, and turned their heads in the direction of the small settlement called Kikkajikalong, the home base. Sundown saw them unyoke at the mill paddock that was an outstation of Marrambindi. Supper was eaten and the utentils washed, then Romany walked quietly away in the shielding dark, followed by Pedro, his well-trained cattle dog. Ernie sat and smoked by the fire, replenishing it from time to time with wood gathered earlier. It was almost two hours before Flash Ted returned with a sheep slung across his shoulders, its legs tightly bound. He deposited his burden on the ground,

73

while Pedro, an innocent but capable assistant, lay down close by, the firelight reflecting the gleam of his yellow eyes. No word was spoken as the gypsy swiftly skinned and gutted the sheep, and hung the steaming carcase from the gunwale of the waggon. The skin, cut into thin strips for easy burning, was fed to the flames, and the hungry dogs quickly disposed of the offal. Romany washed his hands as Ernie threw tea in the steaming billy.

"Fry for breakfast", Romany grinned. "And won't I bloody well enjoy it. And pinchin' the bastard ain't on me conscience. The bloody squatters have got plenty".

"I suppose yer right", Ernie said in a rather grudging tone. "Yer reckon I'm too honest, Ted, but the truth is it's fear for the wife and kids if I had to do time that keeps me on the straight and narrer. You got nobody to think of if yer were lagged".

"I can see yer point", Romany agreed. "But when yer hard up Ernie, doin' the wrong thing often becomes a necessity".

Failure to Identify

The day was miserably hot. A mid-morning sun beat down with a concentrated intensity on the weathered houses of the small Queensland town, causing the iron roofs to contract and crackle. Mr. John Playfair, J.P., wiped his perspiring brow with a large handkerchief as he surveyed the motley collection of humanity gathered in the gloomy court-house. The magistrate's bench was simply a table and chair that fronted a cheerless room equipped with long wooden stools. In this remote frontier outpost justice was dispensed without the pomp and splendour so seemingly necessary to the courts of the cities. No bailiffs stood to attention, no bewigged barristers brandished briefs as they addressed champagne-pickled judges, no reporters scribbled, no jurors sat bored and cynically amused by the inconsistencies of the travesty called justice.

On the uncomfortable furnishings onlookers sat among the several miscreants who were due for trial on a variety of small charges. Standing by the bench was Mounted Trooper Charlie Wheelan, sweat running down his beefy red face.

Mr. Playfair cleared his throat. A man who always looked for the better qualities of his fellows, he was loth to impose heavy penalties for minor misdemeanors. He tapped the table with a heavy potato-spoon that served as a gavel.

"Court is in session. First case please, Constable".

Constable Wheelan consulted a large, dirty exercise book. The department had not supplied him with official note paper and ledgers for several months. Officialdom has little regard for small and isolated bush villages. After leafing through the dog-eared tablet for what seemed an eternity, Wheelan announced in a loud voice the name of the offender.

"Cecil Commerford. Step forward and face the bench".

A wiry young man rose and came to the table, walking with the short, springy steps of one who spent most of his time in the saddle. He was darkly handsome, with the black curly hair common to people who own shanty Irish forebears.

Constable Wheelan's hoarse voice droned the charge. " — that on Saturday last the aforesaid Cecil Commerford behaved in an unruly and offensive manner, to wit he rode a savage and dangerous horse into the bar of the Sundowner Hotel, and demanded that the beast be served a drink".

Mr. Playfair eyed the slim, dark ringer without emotion. "How do plead, defendant?"

"Not guilty, yer Worship".

No concern showed on the face of the police-officer, but the J.P.'s registered surprise. "Are you represented by counsel?"

A stocky man in moleskins and a worn Donegal coat rose from his seat on the foremost bench. His head was almost completely bald, a contrast to his lower profile, that boasted a long red walrus moustache. He spoke loudly.

"I represent the defendant, yer Worship".

"Are you a lawyer?" Mr. Playfair queried.

"No yer Worship. I'm the defendant's employer, and he has asked me to help him".

"Hmm. Quite in order. Step up beside the defendant and state your name and occupation.

"Henry James Hickey, cattle drover".

"Let the first witness for the Crown be called".

Charlie Wheelan flourished his exercise book. "I'm the first witness, yer Worship".

"Proceed", Mr. Playfair ordered.

"On Saturday last", the trooper began, "I was called to the Sundowner Hotel. There I found the defendant seated on his horse in the public bar. He was in a sad state of intoxication, but was able to lead his horse out side. The barmaid on duty asked me to charge him with riotous behaviour as well as drunkeness. She claimed the

76

horse tried to kick and bite her. I then arrested the defendant without trouble. Mr. Hickey came later and produced bail".

Wheelan put the book in the pocket of his tunic, and the J.P. bent his gaze on the boss-drover. "Any questions, Mr. Hickey?"

"Just a couple, yer worship, I'd like to ask if the trooper would be able to identify the horse defendant rode, if he saw it again".

"Yes", Wheelan responded. "It was a bay horse with four white feet and a blaze. A very noticeable animal".

"And was it a mare or a gelding?"

"I couldn't say truthfully".

"Thank yer, that's all". Hickey bowed to the bench.

"Next witness, please".

Wheelan consulted his book again. "Arlene Kitteridge, step up please".

A tall and graceful young woman in a loud purple dress festooned with black lace came forward. She sported a black hat with a waving red plume that almost touched the rafters, crowning a face with a haughty and contemptuous expression as she gazed at Hickey and Commerford. She took the oath, placing a delicate hand on a Bible that looked as if it belonged to the original publication of the Holy Book. Wheelan led off.

"You are a barmaid at the Sundowner Hotel, Miss Kitteridge?"

"As you well know, constable".

"And on Saturday afternoon you sent for me, stating there was trouble at the hotel".

"I did".

"Please tell the court the nature of the trouble".

Miss Kitteridge pointed a dramatic finger at Commerford. "That man was in the bar drinking for two hours. He then mounted his horse and rode it into the bar. He then said, "give the horse a long beer, young lady. It's dying of thirst".

There was a muted titter from the audience, and Mr.

Playfair pounded for silence with the potato spoon. "Continue, witness", he ordered.

"I refused the defendant's request, and the horse snapped at me. Then it swung round and delivered a terrible kick".

Wheelan consulted his book again. "That's all, your Worship."

Harry Hickey's voice was courteous as he addressed the barmaid. "D'yer reckon, young lady, that the horse defendant rode could have injured people in the bar, or damaged anything".

"Of course. It was a vicious and uncontrollable creature".

"If it was as yer say, how did defendant manage to ride it into the bar when he was fallin' down drunk".

The question brought Miss Kitteridge up short. She was left speechless, and the judge banged with his makeshift gavel. "Answer the question, witness".

Harry Hickey waved a hand. "No need. Tell me miss, would yer know the horse again if yer seen it?"

"Of course. It had white legs, and it was a male horse, too".

"How did yer know that?"

There was a stirring in the congregation, and smiles showed. Miss Kitteridge flushed, then regained her composure. "I could tell by the shape of its head".

Hickey's face broke into a shark grin. He was radiating confidence now. He turned his attention to the judge.

"Yer Worship, the defendant's horse is in front of the court-house right now. I would like the witnesses to identify it".

"To what purpose". The J.P. appeared mystified. "You are making a strange request, possibly a quite unnecessary one".

"I will prove to the court that the witnesses are not capable".

Mr. Playfair gave the matter thought before deciding. A city man, he had always regarded country people as

78

bumpkins, but Hickey's performance had caused him to have reservations.

"Your request is granted", Mr. Hickey. You, the defendant and I will accompany witnesses to the horse at once. Court is adjourned for half an hour. Everybody rise".

There was a general scramble to vacate the room.

There were several horses hitched in front of the Sundowner, but a bright bay with four white stockings was easily the most noticeable animal. The judge and his four attendants drew to a halt, the crowd keeping a respectful distance. Constable Wheelan identified the horse at once, pointing to it and remarking "That's the one for sure".

The J.P. turned to the gaudily-dressed girl. "What say you, Miss Kitteridge?"

"That's it. The gelding with the white legs. Don't go near it. It is dangerous, and will kick and bite. I'm sure it's the same one".

"She's right on one point", Harry Hickey said. "It's the horse that Cecil was ridin' on Saturday. I'll show yers just how dangerous it is".

He went boldly up to the horses head, dropped to his knees, and to the amazement of Mr. Playfair, crawled between the animal's front legs, then between its hind ones. Rising, he swung into the saddle, then lifted himself backwards over the cantle. With a loud yell he slid over the horse' rump and grabbing the tail pulled hard. The J.P. stood open-mouthed with amazement. Throughout the entire performance the animal had not moved from its semi-slumbering position, taking no heed in any way of Hickey's actions. Hickey bowed to the magistrate, a grin on his long face.

"I think I just proved the young lady wrong on the other two points. The horse ain't dangerous, and if yer take a good look yer Worship, you'll find it's a mare, not a gelding".

A ragged cheer arose from the onlookers, and Miss Kitteridge, utterly deflated now, was unable to find

79

speech. Mr. Playfair's face bore a smile of what seemed enlightenment. "Come", he ordered. "Let us return to the court".

* * * * * *

"Court resumes". The magistrate banged with the potato spoon. "If the prosecution have no further witnesses, the defence may proceed".

"The defendant will take the stand", Hickey announced." He wishes now to plead guilty to the charge of drunkeness, yer Worship".

"Take the stand, defendant", Mr. Playfair ordered. "You may proceed, Mr. Hickey".

With a hangdog expression of complete repentance on his handsome face, Cecil took the oath, and there was an expectent silence in the crowd as Hickey began.

"Your name is Cecil Commerford, and you are twenty-three years old?" "Yes".

"You support a wife and four chilren at Boulia, and you also help support a widowed mother?"

"Correct".

"Ever been charged with an offence before?"

"This is the first time".

"How did you come to ride the horse into the bar?"

"Well y'see, I was pretty drunk, the beer was awful strong, and when I got on the old mare, I fell on her neck, and havin' no control, she made for the nearest shade, that was the bar."

"Did yer ask the barmaid for a beer for the horse?"

"I cant' deny it very well, because I can't remember it".

"That's all, yer worship". Hickey addressed the J.P., who turned to the trooper.

"Any questions, constable?"

"Nothing more, your Worship". Charlie Wheelan's blue eyes were twinkling with surpressed laughter. The crowd awaited expectantly as Mr. Playfair debated silently. After perhaps ten minutes the judge tapped with his spoon and began to speak.

80

"I have never tried a case in the far out country, and I must say that the bush, as its citizens call it, has some rather surprising characters, not the least of them the defendant's horse. After witnessing the docility of this beast, I do not think it impossible that the horse took charge of an intoxicated rider, and walked into the bar of the hotel.

"Miss Kitteridge testifies otherwise, but after her failure to identify the animal's sex, plus the fact that she misled the court regarding its temperament, I have no option but to disregard her testimony. Therefore I find the defendant not guilty on the offensive behaviour charge".

"Regarding the charge of drunkeness, to which defendant pleads guilty, I must consider the fact that he is a first offender, a man of good character who does not shirk responsibility to his family. Although his guilt is admitted, I will not impose a fine, but if he comes before me again I will not be so lenient. The defendant will now stand".

Cecil rose quickly, as Mr. Playfair pointed a threatening potato spoon at him.

"Cecil Commerford, you understand that if you appear before me again, no consideration will be shown. If you are wise you will heed this warning, think of your wife and children, and refrain from drinking. You are discharged".

Silently Cecil bowed to the bench, then turned and departed with Harry Hickey at his side, the latter throwing his shark grin at Miss Kitteridge, who returned the gesture with a malevolent glare. Mounted and heading for their camp on the common, Hickey broke the silence.

"We'll rest up to-day, and head the plant for Boulia in the mornin'. I want to make fifty miles at least tomorrer".

"I'll be glad to move", Cecil said. "I think that copper knew more than he let on".

"You've never been there before", Hickey said. "Nobody knew yer. That long sheila took it pretty hard when the beak scrubbed her evidence".

"Yer couldn't blame her", Cecil grinned. "When yer tell the truth in court and get disbelieved, it's a bit hard to take. She wasn't a bad looker, but I'll bet if yer tumbled her, she'd chase yer after it was over, snarlin' like a dog when it don't get the right bone".

Hickey smiled, but made no comment.

*　*　*　*　*　*

Dawn broke red, and Hickey swung the billy over the blazing sticks that Cecil had placed on the fire, before going after the horses. A tinkle of bells sounded, then a thud of hooves. Hickey took up winkers and bridle as the horses came to the camp. Shepherded into the corner where the van was parked, they moved restlessly as the boss-drover caught the two harness horses, then called to Cecil.

"What are yer goin' to ride?"

"Catch Earthquake". Cecil pointed to a stocky bay gelding with a wide blaze and four white stockings. Not without some difficulty Hickey bridled the evidently temperamental beast, and tied it to a fence-post. Commerford stepped down and stripped his gear from the night-horse.

After tea was made and breakfast eaten the drovers harnessed the patient van horses. Then Cecil picked up his saddle and grinned at his employer.

"Yer better grab a cheek-strap, and hang onto his head 'til I get the gear on him. Fifty miles orter take the stingo outer him, but I don't reckon he'll ever be quiet".

Hickey took hold of a bridle-strap and pulled the bay's head hard towards him, while Commerford saddled up. The horse lashed out as a crupper was adjusted, but Cecil was standing in close to the beast's flank, and the spirited kick was wasted on the wind. Girth and surcingle were drawn tight, and the rider rose to the saddle with a graceful skill born of long practice. Hickey sprang back, and Earthquake exploded in a series of twisty bucks, squealing like a stabbed hog. Cecil rode high and easy, evidently in complete control of his mount. Earthquake

broke into a canter, tried with another abortive effort to dislodge his rider, then gave up altogether.

"Jesus, I don't know how yer rode him in and out the bar without wreckin' the place", Hickey said. "yer had a lotter luck".

"He ain't a bad one", Cecil replied. "Just a lot of piss and wind. Hey look what's comin'. The bloody John Hop!

Charlie Wheelan drew his fat police-horse to a halt and dismounted. The sun was barely up, but the beefy trooper was sweating already. His smile was wide as he walked to the fire, took a pint from the tuckerbox and helped himself to tea.

"Hope you don't mind", he remarked. "I came out early to give you a bit of advice, young Commerford. You and your boss did a good job of pulling wool over the magistrate's eyes yesterday, but everybody wasn't fooled. I knew all about you before the case came on. You're not married, you haven't got four kids, and you've been up before the beak three times before this for riding horses into pub bars. But along with your three brothers, you do support a widowed mother, and you never shirk the hard part when it comes to getting a living. Boulia is a long way from here, but I have ways and means of finding things out. The Commerford boys are well known for the devilment they get up to when they drink. They are also well known and highly respected for their hard work and honesty of purpose. So for the latter reason I kept mum yesterday".

The trooper drained his pint and replaced it, then stared long at Cecil, his expression hardening noticeably.

"But let me tell you something else. If you come back here and get up to any antics again, I'll see you get fined to the extent that a year's wages won't square it. Now I'll wish you luck, and go off to attend to some duties. Think well on the advice I've given you".

He mounted and pointed a fat finger at Cecil's mount. His voice was hard, but humour lurked in the blue eyes.

"That's a horse I've seen somewhere before. A bay gelding with a blaze and four white legs. He seems bloody familiar".

Cecil and his employer were silent until the trooper was well on his way, then the young ringer spoke in an awed voice.

"Jesus, he knew all about us".

"There ain't much the buggers don't know", Hickey replied. "The beak was a mug, but there was no failure to identify about Wheelan. Let's get on our way. It's a long step to Boulia".

From the Mouths of Babes

The long day of toil was over for the teamsters, and the camp-fire grew brighter as dusk deepened. The three waggons, loaded with freshly cut logs, were ready for the trip to the sawmill, and the bullocks would be yoked at dawn. Ted Romany threw tea in the billy, then set the steaming receptical on the portable table. Ernie Lynch filled his pint, while Long Joe Tanner spooned a second helping of corn meat and spuds from the camp oven. Romany shot a gold-toothed grin at his lanky mate as Joe straightened to his full six feet six.

"Jesus, yer can eat, yer long bastard", Romany said. "That's why yer never put on weight. Yer gorge so much that yer get poor carryin' the load about".

"M-m-man's g-g-otter eat", Long Joe stuttered. "D-d-don't see y-you goin' hungry when there's m-m-mutton in the c-c-c-camp".

Romany poured tea, took a full shank of mutton from the pot and tore at it like a starved dog. Between mouthfuls he announced, "We might be eatin' Darkie termorrer. He's awful sick".

"Jesus, don't remind a man about it", Ernie Lynch said savagely. "Any other bullock than Darkie could have got crook and things wouldn't have been too bad. But it had to be Darkie".

Darkie held the responsible position of near-side leader in Ernie's sixteen bullocks. In any team the near-side leader is the most important beast, controlling his mates like a capable sergeant major, swinging the squad to left or right as ordered. Darkie was a polished exponent of his art, but now he was stricken with some strange muscular malady, and was unable to take up his usual job. Ernie could not make up his mind regarding a substitute, for in his entire team, including four spares, none measured up as a mate for Snowy, the off-side leader. It was Joe Tanner's stuttered suggestion that decided Ernie.

"P-p-put L-i-izard up leadin, and I'll use one of me s-p-p-ares".

86

The remark was applauded by Romany. "Reel good idea. Joe's had Lizard near-side leadin' a few times. He should be able to handle it."

We can try it," Ernie said as he limped to the table and took up a tin plate. "I thank yer, Joe, for yer offer".

"W-w-won't t-thank me if he ups and b-b-busts th' yoke".

"That's on the cards any time", Ernie said.

Romany grinned. "Be a nice birthday present for yer termorrer if we find Darkie dead in the mornin'."

"Don't think about it", Ernie growled. "You're about the only bugger who's goin' to remember it's me birthday anyhow. A man's a year older and no richer, and no bugger cares".

"Yer dead wrong there, Ernie. Yer bloody lucky to have all yer got". There was a note of wistful loneliness in the gypsy's voice. "Me second sight tells me somebody's goin' to remember".

*　*　*　*　*　*

The day was hot, and Katie Lynch walked slowly, carrying the small cardboard box carefully by its binding of twine, changing it from hand to hand ever so often. Far up the track she saw the dust that announced the passage of the waggons. Katie was ten years old, the youngest daughter of Ernie Lynch, and her father's favourite. Her destination was the big clump of box-trees on the Marrimbindi boundary, where the teamsters always pulled up for dinner after clearing the narrow gate that divided Crown land from the station's vast acreage. It was a mile from the dinner camp to McArdle's sawmill, where the loads of logs would be delivered later in the afternoon.

Kate hurried faster, as up ahead she saw the dust-clouds raised by the approaching waggons. On reaching the box clump she hung the box on a low shady bough, then ran to the newly erected gate through which the teams must pass. Joe Tanner, long frame easily recognisable, was walking beside the leading waggon. Some fifty yards behind came Romany's waggon, with her father's team bringing up the rear. Kate ran to Long Joe and with a big smile he lifted her up and deposited her on the back of Chummy, the docile old near-side leader.

"H-h-hang on, don't f-f-f-fall orf, h-h-hold tight", Joe ordered, and Kate clutched the bow-prongs in her small hands. Joe's wagon swung through the gateway, followed quickly by Romany's, then it was Ernie Lynch's turn. The pin-bullocks were almost clear when disaster suddenly attended.

The new gate was a hazard to the teamsters, being barely wide enough to allow the waggon's passage. Scratches and scars showed on both gateposts where wheel-hubs failed by a fraction to clear. Ernie's makeshift leader began to lean away from his partner, swinging team and wagon imperceptibly to the left. Ernie's whip cracked, and his voice rose in a hoarse shout.

"Get orf Lizard! Git ORF!! Git orf Snowy!!"

Had the convalesant Darkie held the position now occupied by the substitute Lizard, he would have swung hard right at Ernie's command, putting the wagon on a straight course again. But the wayward Lizard failed to heed the order. With a dull thud the hub of the near-side rear wheel came up tight against the post, Ernie's yells of "Whoa up, yer bastards, whoa up", coming too late.

Long Joe and Romany had been made aware of the mishap by Ernie's yells. Calling their leaders off the road they quickly screwed on brakes and made haste to assist their stranded mate. Kate slid down from Chummy's broad back and ran ahead, reaching her father first. She drew back at the expression of enraged disgust on his face. Limpy Lynch had taught all his children to stay out of his road if trouble was afoot.

The three men surveyed the jambed wheel with doleful expressions. Long Joe, scratching his long nose, was the first to offer a comment.

"S-s-she's s--stuck bad, ain't she?"

"Yer must be kiddin', Joe", Romany said.

"Hell of a bloody mess", Ernie said savagely. "And

we got the road blocked. If anyone comes along, what are they goin' to do?''

Romany's dark gaze swept the road. "Sure enough, here comes someone now. Looks like Marrimbindi buggy, be the nicklework flashin' in the sun. How bloody unlucky can yer be?''

Mr. Basil Cuthbertson, manager of absentee-owned Marrimbindi station, drew the buggy ponies to a halt. Beside him sat Fenwicke Larkin, an English aristocrat just out from '' 'ome'' on a holiday "in the Colonies", as he was wont to describe Australia. Son of a prominent British banker, he was completely at home in London fogs and high finance, champagne dinners and Ascot race-club balls. But the world of the bullockies was an alien world indeed. Yet he displayed no trace of British superiority as he got down from the buggy and joined the three rough teamsters and the small red-haired girl. Instead his smile was friendly, and his voice warm.

"By Jove men, what a dashed bad show. But easily overcome. You have only to hook the oxen to the rear of the wagon and pull it back off the post. Quite simple''.

"Quite simple", Ernie Lynch said gloomily. "But how the bloody hell are yer goin' to get the bullocks back through the gate?''

"Yer could do it be cuttin' the fence", Romany said.

"Here now let's have no such suggestions like that", Mr. Cuthbertson had alighted from the buggy. "How did a man of your experience get in such a predicament, Ernie? You should be more capable''.

Ernie turned on him savagely. "Go and ask that slatey-coloured near-side leader. He can tell yer better than I can''.

"Gross carelessness", Mr. Cuthbertson said. "Should never have happened''.

"If yer wasn't so bloody stingy, and built the gate a bit wider, it wouldn't have happened", Romany said.

"Are you telling me my job, Romany?''

"No, but I'm suggestin' that yer tell yer directors to get the death adders out of their pockets''.

"You gypsy wretch". Cuthbertson was becoming enraged. "I'll see you do not travel on Marrimbindi anymore".

"Yer can't stop me", Romany jeered. "It's a public road, so dry up".

"By gad, quarrelling won't help". Mr. Larkin made an attempt to pour oil on troubled waters. "Let's be amicable and try to find a solution".

"Only way is cut the fence", Romany persisted. "It's easy strained up again".

"I will not stand for that,", Cuthbertson said emphatically. "That's a new fence. You fellows got in this mess, and it is up to you to get out of it. Let's hear no more suggestions of fence cutting. There must be a way".

"You tell us, since yer so bloody smart", Romany said.

"Dad". Kate's small voice broke in. "I know how to do it".

Ernie Lynch turned heatedly on his daughter, pointing a calloused forefinger. "Go over there and sit on that log, Kate. You've got no right here anyway. Kids should be seen and not heard. Go on when I tell yer".

Obediently Kate made her way to the fallen log, a despondent expression on her face, while the five men debated the problem of the marooned waggon. Larkin was the first to offer a suggestion.

"Couldn't the bally think be pulled sideways off the post?"

"Easy done with twelve ton of logs on it". Romany's voice was loaded with sarcasm.

Mr. Larkin, English gentleman, was strangely not offended. "Well could they be unloaded?"

"Not without blocks and tackle", Ernie said. "And what didn't land on the fence'd block the road".

"Impatiently Cuthbertson consulted his watch. "I'm going to be late for the village store. Something has to be done soon".

"Well do what I reckoned", Romany grinned. "Cut

the fence, take a team back, and pull her backwards".

Cuthbertson's face grew red, and he wagged an aggressive finger at the gypsy. "See here Romany, any more talk about cutting the fence and I'll take action".

Flash Ted's gold caps showed in a loud guffaw. "What can yer do? I'd tie yer be the balls to the waggon pole".

"Jesus, turn it up", Ernie said sharply. "Havin' a civil war ain't goin' to help. There must be a way. But this is somethin' I never seen before in years of bullock drivin'".

It was a sorry mishap indeed. The big gatepost was four feet in the hard red earth. It had been dressed with adzes, and the wheel-hub was hard up against the squared face, leaving the waggon immobile as the post, and the men unpossessed of any solution. Larkin frowned, Cuthbertson fidgeted, Ernie sweated, Romany cursed foully. And Long Joe, who had remained silent throughout, turned away from the breeze to light his pipe, and he saw Kate beckoning to him frantically.

Always kind and considerate to children, Joe went to where the little girl sat, glad to escape for a moment the bickering and abortive suggestions of his fellows. Kate rose and took the bullocky's big, hard work-roughened hand. Her soft voice was confident, sincere.

"Joe, I know how to get the waggon off the post".

"N-n-now how would yer k-know, K-k-kKatie? Y-y-yor oney a l-l-l-l-little girl".

"God has shown me the way", Kate said.

The remark shook long Joe. Like many simple and illiterate men of the time, he was in many ways respectful of a god he knew little about, and as he gazed at the small freckled face between two fierey red plaits, he decided that Kate might possibly have some form of contact with the Almighty. She was a child devoted to religion, in the company of the nuns whenever possible, and her ambition was to join the Order when old enough. Joe decided in favour of God and Katie.

"W-w-what yer w-w-w-want me to d-d-o?"

91

"Take me over to the waggon. Dad will rouse, but if you and Flash Ted stand by me, he'll have to listen".

Still wondering, Joe led Kate to the wagon, shortening his long steps so she could keep up. The group silently studying the mishap turned on hearing Joe's heavy feet approaching, and Ernie's temper rose.

"Kate! I told you to go and sit on that log. Do it now or you'll be sorry".

"W-w-w-ait a while. S-s-s-s-she's got an idea". Joe held fast to Kate's hand.

"I won't have my kids disobey me. Go and sit on that log at once!" Ernie's temper was drawn thin.

Long Joe stood his ground. "G-g-give her a g-g-go, Ernie".

"Whan can a kid know about it? Do as I tell yer, Kate". Ernie stepped toward the girl, his hand raised threateningly. Romany's movement was swift as he scooped Kate up in his powerful arms, and his voice was hard.

"Hit her, and I'll bloody well hit you".

"Hit me!" Ernie's wrath boiled over. "I licked yer years ago and I can do it again. Put my child down".

Romany uttered a derisive laugh. "Yer right, Ernie. Yer licked me at Burke's Shanty, and I was glad, because afterwards I saw that I was in the wrong. But it's you that's in the wrong now, and me second sight tells me yer goin' to see it before long. Now we're goin' to listen to Kate. Nobody else has got any bright ideas, and we're all grown up".

"Jolly well said, old chappie", Mr. Larkin applauded. "Remember what the Scriptures claim. From the mouths of babes comes wisdom. Also that a little child shall lead them".

Kate looked at the slim Britisher with an expression almost of reverence. "You are a good man, Mr. Englishman. God is going to punish Daddy for rousing, and he'll punish Ted Romany for swearing, too".

"Hear, hear!" Larkin clapped his well-kept hands, completely captivated by Kate's remark, and even the displeased Mr. Cuthbertson managed a weak smile. Ernie subsided, realising he was one out against a majority, and Kate addressed Romany.

"Put me down and get the crowbar and shovel, please Ted".

Romany collected the required tools from his waggon, and Kate led the way to the unencumbered off-side rear wheel, all hands following with much hope but little faith.

Kate dropped to her knees and drew a rectangle with her finger in the dust beside the outer edge of the wheel, the inner side touching the shining iron tyre. She studied it for a moment before enlarging it to approximately two feet by one. She rose and smiled at Romany.

"Make that into a hole, Ted. It has to be nearly a foot deep".

In the confined space between wheel and post, Romany plied the bar with powerful strokes, and the red earth broke away. Long Joe shovelled, Romany dug again, and the hole beside the tyre grew larger and deeper. Soon it was to Kate's satisfaction, and she called a halt. Romany wiped sweat from his black ringlets and looked questioningly at the girl.

"Can you see how easy it's going to be now? Dig the dirt away under the wheel now, Ted. And get your bar away quick when the wheel starts to drop into the hole".

"By golly!" Larkin's voice was almost a shout. "I can see now. What a capital idea".

Romany dug again, sharp blows that loosened the dirt under the tyre, and suddenly the waggon lurched as the wheel settled into the hole, Flash Ted jerking the bar away quickly to avoid it being jambed. Like a rabbit Kate ducked under the wagon and out the other side, and her voice was shrill with triumph.

"Come and look, Dad. The wheel's not caught any more".

The men surveyed the near-side wheel with mixed expressions of wonder and relief. The hub was clear of the post now, due to the simple effort of dropping the off wheel down a foot. Kate darted under the wagon again, calling to Long Joe and Romany.

"Dig a little trench in front of the wheel now, so the bullocks can pull it out".

There was no comments as the two men quickly completed the trench, everyone apparently mesmerised by juvenile wisdom. Ernie Lynch yelled at the bullocks, many of which had laid down and were slumbering in their yokes, and they rose and leaned into the bows. The whip cracked and the team buckled down. With a lurch the wagon cleared the gateway.

Long Joe and Romany threw dirt back into the small excavation, while Larkin produced a ten shilling note and handed it to Kate. The girl's eyes grew wide with awe as she regarded it, for in her whole life she had never had more than a threepenny piece at one time. Her thanks were so profuse that the Englishman raised a hand.

"You are a jolly wonderful little girl, and you have earned that money. Tell me, how did you know the way to get us out of trouble?"

"God told me". The devotion in Kate's voice was not lost on Larkin, then Cuthbertson called from his seat on the buggy.

"Come on, Fenwicke, We must be gone".

The buggy took off in a cloud of dust, Larkin waving to the teamsters. The waggons ground their way to the dinner camp, Kate following at a respectable distance. When the teams were stood off and the fire made, she retrieved the parcel from the box bough and placed it on the portable table, then gazed hard at her uncomprehending father.

"What's the hell's that?" Lynch questioned.

Kate smiled. "Have you forgotten to-day's your birthday, dad? That's a cake from Judy and me. And mum and the boys have something for you too, when you get home".

Ernie stood silent for a moment while emotion took charge, then he held his daughter's two small hands. There were tears in the frosty grey eyes as he spoke.

"Ah, Katie I'm sorry for what I said to-day".

He turned to Romany. "And I'm sorry for what I said to you. Ted. I was in the wrong and I can see it now".

"Least said, easiest mended", the gypsy grinned. "You've got a smart little girl".

"T-t-takes after her mother", Long Joe said slyly.

Romany's grin widened as he removed the lid from the cake box and produced a curved knife. "Always remember, Ernie, that out of the mouths of babes comes wisdom. And inter the mouth of this gypsy bastard goes a big slice of yer birthday cake".

Father Rattler

In the early days outback, every little village boasted a church, sometimes two or three, depending on the religious beliefs of the community. In some bush places even yet, churches can be seen, sad tabernacles of warped weatherboard, long unattended. They sag and lean in various states of decay and decriptitude, where there are no other buildings for miles around, giving silent announcement that the doctrine of Christ finds its way to the uttermost frontiers of the earth.

In many of these long abandoned places of worship hang old-world portraits and effigies, their only worshippers the possums that camp in the rafters, and the bush birds that nest under the eaves. Tortured Christs twist in agony on yellowed ivory crosses, faded Holy Virgins hold blessed babies wrinkled by the effect of the heat on cracked, rotting canvas. A garish version of the last supper looks out on a land so dry and arid that one wonders how it would provide sustenance if the disciples in the painting were real. But the spirit of the bearded carpenter who died a martyr still walks the dusty tracks of the bush, just as He walked the paths of the Holy Land two thousand years ago. In the early nineteen hundreds it came in force to the unique and somewhat isolated settlement of Kikkajikalong.

The sawmill was the backbone of the little town, for it employed six men permanently, plus several casuals from time to time. Then there were the teamsters, rough men who hauled the logs to the rapacious saws, afterwards carrying those same logs away cut into timber. Marrimbindi station, owned by rich absentees in England who could not have pointed out their holdings on the map, provided work for a large number of stockmen, and there were free selectors in abundance. Also the village was on a main stock-route, so the drovers were constant customers at Denton's general store and Gilhooley's

Pride of Erin Hotel. And there were always the transients, rabbiters, sundowners, shearers and general bushworkers. **Kikkajikalong** did not grow and flourish, but it struggled and survived.

The residents were predominantly Catholic, and before long the more progressive ones suggested that a church be built. This was met with great support from the female members of the faith, but the men were less enthusiastic, as they were aware that the greater burden of the work would fall to them. The priest who resided in the nearest large town thirty miles away was approached unsuccessfully for financial help. During one of his infrequent visits to the small and sinful village, he had attempted to steer the Donlan girls and Judy Lynch into the narrow path of righteousness. His stirring sermons and pious platitudes were in vain, and he gave up when requested by Judy "to go and bang his bloody Bible somewhere else". A bag containing clerical garb was stolen by Tommy Donlan, while the good father was destroying the devil in Mrs. Denton's parlour. Another happening that invoked his wrath was the day he had lectured Ted Romany, when the big gypsy's oxen were bogged, and profane language was rising like a winter fog. "Flash Ted" had handed his whip to the upright man of the cloth with the words, "here mate, see if God can belt the bastards out. I can't". Father Fitzgerald gave Kikkajikalong up, deciding that the place was possessed of not one devil, but many.

But the truly religious are not easily defeated. Hounded by the women, and the few men who were really devout, the residents in general began the building of the church by personal effort and public subscriptions.

Old Seamus Riley, a carpenter cum selector, agreed to do the building. Jim McArdle the sawmiller donated the timber, despite the fact that he was a confirmed Methodist. Ernie Lynch and Romany hauled the timber to the site with the bullock-teams. The manager of Marrimbindi, a Protestant, gave the iron for the roof, adjusting the station books so that the owners far away in England became the unknowing donors. "Back loadin' for the Lord", Romany announced, when he brought back the iron from town after delivering a load of timber.

It was on this occasion that Flash Ted met the lately arrived schoolmistress, a madly religious lady nearing the thirty mark and unmarried. She was greatly taken by Romany's dark good looks, and soon the gypsy was the leading light in the construction of the church. His intentions, had they been known, were neither moral or religious.

The building was almost complete when Father Brogan arrived in the district. Young and energetic, he did not concur with any religious bigots. He landed at the settlement one Saturday afternoon, and after introducing himself, shouted for the bar. He then challenged Tom O'Malley to a footrace over one hundred yards, for a ten-shilling side wager. Tom, the local champion was considered a certainty, but the priest showed him the way by several yards. Round Johnny Quinn won a considerable amount on the race, and when asked by disgruntled losers why he bet against O'Malley, he stated that he had read about the priest's athletic prowess in a newspaper. He had gambled on the fact that most of the citizens either didn't read or couldn't.

The priest provided entertainment in Gilhooley's parlour that afternoon, singing sad Irish songs in a rich baritone while Romany played the fiddle. Even respectable ladies, who considered the pub a place of evil, were gathered into the congregation. Father Brogan embarked for town next morning, with the entire populace on his side, regardless of their respective religions.

He returned a week later, with the information that the Catholic bigwigs had agreed to provide an altar for the church. Afterwards he gave boiled lollies to the children, then preached a emotional little sermon from the pub verandah, followed by a request that the onlookers join him in singing a hymn. To the amazement of all, Judy Lynch and the Donlan sisters led the singing. Romany remarked that "Father Brogan could convert Old Nick and get him a job as an altar boy".

Father Brogan then retired to Gilhooley's parlour, "to meditate". Here he was accosted by members of the Protestant faith, led by the Reverend Peasley, a very sanctimonious gentleman, and Tim Feeley, and Irish settler who was an Orangeman to the backbone. They informed the good Father that they expected to use the church as well as the Catholics, for they had worked just as hard building it.

Father Brogan surprised them by agreeing at once, stating that "we are all God's children". It was speedily decided that Protestants and Catholic would use the church on alternate Sundays. The men of the cloth shook hands heartily, and Mr. Peasley almost fainted when the Father suggested "a nip of O'Shannessey's Irish". Tim Feeley then announced that the members of his faith would supply the paint for the almost completed church. All were agreed that the painting was to be done voluntarily on week-ends, with Ted Romany supervising the job. The gypsy was a confirmed athiest, who never became involved in religious arguments, despite the fact that the schoolteacher considered she had him well along the road to reformation.

Tim Feely ordered the paint, and it arrived promptly on the mail-coach, with an invoice stating that any unopened cans could be returned and cost rebated. On inspecting it, Romany discovered that it was a deep orange colour, and this gave the gypsy food for thought. He informed Gilhooley, and the ex-bruiser showed considerably displeasure.

"Shure now, 'tis the good green of the ould sod that the buildin' should be painted. And willin' I would be to finance it".

Romany suggested a compromise. Gilhooley scratched his cauliflower ear thoughtfully, and agreed Flash Ted's idea was a suitable one.

Another consignment of paint arrived the following week, and after inspecting it, Romany told the Protestants that work would commence on Saturday. The Catholics would complete the job on the following week-end.

Tim Feeley and his supporters turned up in force, tins of orange paint were opened, and Romany handed out brushes. "Yer do the doors and half of every wall", he ordered. "The top half".

"Why not do one wall at a time?" Feeley queried.

"Don't question the bloke in charge", Romany grinned. "I'm doin' this job on a inspiration I got from the Lord". Miss Anne Luton, the deeply religious teacher, gave Romany her most worshipping smile and held his arm.

The painters went to work with a will. By nightfall the entire upper half of the church, plus the doors, was a blazing orange.

There were suspicious mutterings and expressions of distrust made by the Catholic faction, but Flash Ted informed them in no uncertain terms that all hands would be happy when the job was completed. They waited doubtfully, well aware that it was not good policy to fall out with the gypsy, as past happenings had proved.

The next Saturday dawned warm and sunny, and the R.C.'s were on time for an early start. Romany drove up in Gilhooley's sulky and unloaded the paint. "There y'are boys. Open it up and slap it on any where there's no orange".

The cans were opened, and a ragged cheer went up when it was seen that the paint was a vivid green. Before sunset the church was shining in two-tone splendor, rivalling Gilhooley's Pride of Erin Hotel for brightness, and as Romany had promised, everybody appeared happy.

"I'm a Protestant meself", said Tom Gordon, buck-jump rider of reputation. "But the Tykes here are all good people, my oath".

I'm R.C. and so is all me family", Paddy Quinn said. "But I got real friends among the Prods".

There was mutual agreement, even among the peo-

ple who didn't care if the House of the Lord stood up or
fell down.

★　★　★　★　★　★

"Looks like we've pleased everybody", said
Romany, as in company with Tim Feeley and Gilhooley
he partook of a pint at the bar. "But there was no paint
left over in either colour to get a rebate on. We used the
whole bloody lot".

"Matters little", Feeley replied. "We did a great job,
but it do seem to me that it used up a lot of paint".
Gilhooley nodded agreement.

Nine days later Romany's team came to the mill to
collect a load of sawn timber for delivery in town. The
residents were amazed at the change of appearance
sported by the gypsy's waggon. It had been sadly in need
of paint at its last visit to the settlement, now it glowed
and shone in two very distinctive colours. Even the yokes
on the bullocks were two-tone green and orange.

"Reckoned I'd buy a bit o' paint and smarten her up
a bit", Flash Ted remarked. "Decided to do her the same
as the church".

There were nasty insinuations made behind the gypsy's back, but he cared little. He knew that Feeley and
Gihhooley were too bog-Irish proud to admit that they
had been dusted.

★　★　★　★　★　★

Mrs. Denton and Miss Anne Luton stood at the
counter of Denton's General Store, deep in conversation.
Beside them, making no remarks, was Stella Woodley,
daughter of Kikkajikalong's postmistress, who had been a
widow for several years. Stella was chaste and well
behaved, described by Ernie Lynch as "a credit to
womanhood".

Every now and again Miss Luton's envious gaze
swivelled across the street, to where Judy Lynch was
sweeping the verandah of the Hotel. Still in her teens,
tall, graceful and willowly, Old Limpy's wayward

101

daughter was lovely enough to stir desire in a tailor's dummy.

"She's really beautiful, isn't she?", Stella ventured.

Miss Luton sniffed. "It's a strange thing that the Lord made many wicked creatures beautiful. But who are we to question God's work?"

"The Lord will one day punish her for her dreadful sins", Mrs. Denton said piously. "She is shockingly wicked".

Miss Luton sniffed again. "Just fancy her and the Donlan girls leading the singing when Father Brogan called for a hymn. They are completely shameless".

"Of course", Mrs. Denton agreed. "Such sinners can never be redeemed".

"Judy Lunch is good and kind". Stella spoke hotly this time. "She helps everyone in trouble, and so does her Mum and Dad and her brother Ned. I won't stand by and hear her condemned. The Lords says "Judge not, lest ye be judged. As far as redemption goes, you'd better be very good at it. Because you're going to have your hands full redeeming the man you're so taken up with, Miss Luton". Picking up her parcels, Stella departed.

A shocked Miss Luton regained her sniff several seconds after Stella's departure. "People are always telling me how respectable SHE is. If that is so, why is she defending Judy Lynch?"

"You can judge people by the company they keep", Mrs. Denton said sourly. "And you should heed my remark, Miss Luton. Do not put too much faith in Ted Romany. He is not to be trusted. A dark and dangerous scoundrel".

"I won't listen to any gossip about Ted", Miss Luton said haughtily. "if he has sinned in the past, I am quite capable of leading him to the path of righteousness. The Lord in his wisdom will assist me".

In his office at the rear, Arthur Denton had been listening quietly to the conversation, and he made a mental note. If the soul of Judy Lynch could not be

102

redeemed, there was little chance for Ted Romany, even if the Lord took personal charge of the operation.

* * * * * *

A picnic to celebrate the erection of the church was Miss Luton's suggestion, and it was well received and supported by all. In an era before television, radio and moving pictures, bush people in isolated and lonely places were only too willing to create their own entertainment in an effort to dispel bordeom. Everybody looked forward to the event, that was to be held on a Saturday. The shady creek flat behind McArdle's sawmill was chosen as the picnic sight.

Ted Romany took Friday off, spending his time carting tables and chairs to the sight under the loving eye of Miss Luton. Wood was collected and a stand erected to hold the buckets of boiling water that would be required for the tea. There was to be dancing on the grass to Paddy Quinn's concertina and Romany's fiddle, and the schoolchildren would sing hymns. The gypsy completed a long day of voluntary work, then walked hand in hand with Miss Luton to the house where she boarded, bypassing Gilhooley's pub, as he had done for more than a month.

"Bejabers, but it seems the scoundrel has mended his ways", Mary Gilhooley remarked to Judy Lynch. "Not a drink has he taken for a long time now. 'Tis sad to lose a good customer".

Judy ceased rolling dough, and looked up at the big Irish woman with a shocked expression.

"Surely you don't believe he will change, Mary".

"Faith, but ye cannot doubt what the eyes see, girl".

"It won't last, you'll see". Judy pointed the rolling pin at her beefy employer to emphasise her argument. "Flash Ted's getting something out of it somewhere. Little Miss Perfect Girl is in for a shock. She's going to discover that the fairy prince is still the dirty dago".

"The sooner the better", Mary said. "Our profits have dropped since Romany's been reformed".

* * * * * *

In a belt of scrub half a mile from the settlement, three small boys sat in the noon shade, planning mischief. Tommy Donlan leaned his back on a stout brigalow, looking questioningly at Paul and Peter, twin sons of Ernie Lynch.

"Dontcher reckon it's a good joke?", Tommy queried.

The twins eyed the large and repulsive billy-goat that was tethered to a stump near by. Rattler, as the creature was named, returned their gaze with sinister yellow eyes. Cunning as any fox, Rattler was fit companion in villiany for his three twelve-year-old confederates.

"It's a bonzer idea", Peter said. "But how are we goin' to get the togs".

"Don't worry", Tommy replied airily. "I still got the bag planted. The one I lifted out of the priest's buggy".

"We gotter be at the picnic when he arrives", Paul said doubtfully. "If we ain't, everyone's goin' to say we done it".

"We'll be there when he comes", Tommy said. "Yer know how he chews the tether through when yer not watchin' him".

The twins grinned in union. "We'll do it", Peter said. "Liven the show up a bit".

* * * * * *

The sun was close to the western horizon, a yellow disc fast losing its heat and brilliance as day drew to a close. The crowd at the picnic were gathered in scattered groups before the table where Ted Romany fiddled, and Paddy Quinn pumped the concertina to the tune of a popular hymn. The men sang lustily, the women and children rendering plaintive accompaniment. Speeches were to follow, then the revellers would disperse. Miss

104

Luton sat on a cane chair, her adoring gaze on Romany as he completed the last notes with a flourish. Mr. Arthur Denton rose and gestured for silence. His voice was syrupy and sanctimonious.

"Fellow Christians, we have cause to be proud of our new church. Sadly neither Father Brogan or Mr. Peasley were able to attend our celebration to-day. However, the willing workers and donors are present in force. I will ask Miss Anne Luton, our schoolmistress, to offer sincere thanks to these good people who worked so hard in honour of the Lord".

"Faith, 'tis a sad thing that no man of the cloth is present", Mary Gilhooley whispered to Judy Lynch.

Judy made no reply, for she considered there were enough hypocrites present as things stood. Like her brother Ned, she was a confirmed atheist, but she was too clever to make any remarks that would incur the wrath of Heaven's local representatives.

Miss Luton arose, and gazing at the sky with arm flung wide, addressed the gathering.

"Good Christian people, let us give thanks to all the devout and honourable citizens whose efforts made our church possible. Let us praise God, who is with us here to-day. Good Christian souls, I can feel the presence of the Lord. He is with us. Even now he comes to my side".

The congregation stood open mouthed, but it was not the words of the seemingly mesmerised woman that held their attention. Rattler had appeared suddenly from the brigalow suckers at the rear of the speaker, and moving to her side began to nibble at a large plate of leftovers on the table. It was not the goat that caught amazed eyes, but the garb that the creature wore.

Around Rattler's neck hung a short piece of rope, the end frayed and sodden. A white clerical collar accompanied the rope, and on the goat's head, held in place by his horns, was a priest's black hat. A broadcloth coat, fastened securely to the goat's front quarters, completed its religious attire.

But Miss Luton evidently thought that the crowd
106

was held in thrall by her speech. Her voice became louder and more shrill, the uncontrolled cant of a religious fanatic.

"God is here. He is beside me. He guards us all from vice and sin. Repent ye sinners, for the Lord is at my side".

She became suddenly aware of Sally Casey gesticulating wildly, and pointing a shaking finger. Looking down she beheld Rattler, who had abandoned the plate of food, and was nibbling at the hem of her skirt. With a scream of fear Miss Luton collapsed, just as Tommy Donlan dashed through the crowd and siezed the goat's neck rope. Tommy's voice shook with passion.

"I'd like to know who pinched our goat. I been lookin' for him everywhere."

Doubt was clearly registered on the faces of all present, then Judy Lynch stepped forward, a convincing smile on her beautiful face.

"It's quite true. He came to the pub this morning, terribly upset because someone had stolen his goat".

"That's true". Terry Riley spoke up. "He come to the mill askin' if we'd seen Rattler anywhere".

"And I'd like to know who put them clothes on him", Tommy said savagely. "It's an awful thing to do".

"Tis a fearful sacrilege", Mary Gilhooley said. "So wicked and sinful".

Judy caught Terry Riley's gaze, and closed one violet eye, offering the young sawmiller silent thanks for supporting her in her lie. She remembered how Tommy and her twin brothers had arrived very late for the picnic, and she had put two and one together.

Silently the group dispersed, for further speechmaking seemed rather out of place now. There remained only a few well-wishers surrounding Miss Luton, who had recovered, no longer thinking that the Lord stood beside her.

On reaching town the ladies gathered in dignified groups before Denton's store, their one subject the despicable happening at the picnic. The men, more amused than offended, made furtive entry to Gilhooley's bar. But the scandal was not to end with Rattler's escapade.

* * * * * *

A week later Ted Romany disappeared, leaving Ernie Lynch in charge of his team and waggon. A rather disturbed Miss Luton questioned Old Limpy as to the gypsy's whereabouts, only to find that Lynch "Didn't know for sure, but Flash Ted said he was goin' to Roumania to visit his mother's people".

Decidedly agitated now, Miss Luton resigned and left the village for good, stating that she was too upset by the incident at the picnic to continue at her job as teacher. There were conflicting opinions among the residents as to the real cause of the religious lady's departure, much slander and many sinister rumours, but only one person was totally aware of the truth. Maudie Quinn, the local midwife, had little knowledge of the finer points of obstetrics, but was well aware of any signs of pregnancy, even in its early stages. She held her tongue, not wishing to be the propagator of gossip that involved Ted Romany.

Time went by, and one day the mail coach rolled to a stop in front of Denton's store. Ted Romany, looking hale and hearty, climbed down from the box and made a beeline for Gilhooley's pub, greeting the onlookers with golden smiles and flambouyant gestures.

The bar was deserted except for Judy, who presented the gypsy with a flashing smile and a foaming mug of beer.

"It's good to see you back, Ted", the girl remarked. "We thought you were gone for good. Did you know we have a new schoolmaster, a Mr. Jones. The department must have decided that there are too many cruel temptations here for a lady".

"Beer's good", Romany remarked.

I suppose you have kept in touch with Miss Luton?" Judy enquired.

"Hell of a hot day", Romany said.

"There's something I could never work out", Judy said. "Perhaps you can help me. Do you think religion is stronger than natural desire, Ted".

"Why ask me?" You should have a bloody good idea yerself", Romany said artfully.

Judy silently conceded a point to the gypsy. "Anyway, people will be glad to see you back. You played such a big part in building the church. The priest hasn't forgotten you".

Romany smiled. "D'yer mean Father Brogan?"

"No", Judy replied. "Father Rattler".

The Good Samaritan

Sue Frawley was a little bit surprised when the lanky stranger entered the bar. The early winter morning was still young, and she had expected no customers until a later hour. Sue ran the bush hotel in partnership with her husband. A childless couple reaching middle age, they had successfully carried out their business for more than a decade, and in doing so had encountered a very mixed bag of people. But this gaunt and tragic-looking newcomer was to all appearances something out of the ordinary run of outback transients. She watched silently as he deposited just inside the door a lean swag neatly rolled, and a worn saddle blackened by grease and perspiration. Masking her surprise she gave the man a welcoming smile as he approached the bar with slow, ungainly steps.

"What will it be, mister?"

The stranger's long face and sad spaniel eyes displayed no expression. he reached a thin hairy hand inside his threadbare broadcloth coat and produced a small amount of silver, which he dumped on the bar.

"Just a raspberry cordial, please, Missus. Too early for grog". The voice was a drawn-out drawl, seemingly requiring a maximum of oral effort.

Sue prepared the drink and placed it before the man, her eyes making careful appraisal as he rolled a slender cigarette, his entire attention concentrated on the small undertaking. He was painfully thin, his skinny frame and long legs reminding Sue of a brolga. A growth of ebony whiskers announced that he had not shaved for several days. Sweat grime festooned the collar of a blue cotton shirt, and moleskins that had once been grey were now white and threadbare from constant wear and washing. The old Ashburton felt hat was broken around the crown, and a tuft of black hair jutted out like the forelock of a brumby horse. He was, Sue decided, less than thirty. With a soft thanks he drank the cool red liquid, his

110

Adam's apple jerking in concert with his swallows.

"Have you come far?", the woman asked after refilling the glass, and the stranger nodded silently, then realising a more explicit reply was expected he spoke softly, the sad drawl slow and almost exaggerated.

"Down from central Queensland. Two blood mares for a bloke named Collinson. Been five days on the train".

"What a long trip. Been in Victoria before?"

"Naw, first time down".

"It's a wonder Bill Collinson isn't here to meet the train. Where are the horses?"

"Truckin' yard.

"How do you like our little town?"

"Looks nice".

It was evident to Sue that the stranger was not a talkative type, and the fact made her all the more determined to draw him out.

"You work as a stockman up in Queensland, I suppose".

"Yair".

"Our school picnic is to-morrow. Did you notice our neat little school right near the trucking yard?"

"Yair".

"Everybody is welcome if you like to come. But I suppose you will leave on the train to-morrow night".

"Yair. Thank yer". The man seemed detached, far away.

"And there's another exciting event during the afternoon. A drover named Parkin, "Professor" Parkin they call him, has an outlaw horse that he claims nobody can ride. There is a crack Queensland rider who has been working out at Bill Collinson's place for a fortnight. Bill is so impressed with the man's ability that he has backed him for fifty pounds to ride Parkin's outlaw. At three o'clock to-morrow the ride takes place, down in the trucking yard. Everybody around this little place will be there. It's the topic of the town".

111

The stranger took a sip of his drink. "This Queensland rider. Would yer know his name?", he drawled.

"Why yes. His name is Carmody, Jack Carmody. He says he is known in the north as "Black" Jack. Perhaps you know of him, as you are a Queenslander?"

"Yair, I know of him". There was the ghost of a smile on the whiskered face.

"And can he really ride?"

"Well, a lot of good judges reckons he can". The man drained his glass, scratched his shiny whiskers. "Tell me, missus, is there a place here where a bloke can get a feed?"

"Why, yes. Just along the street on your right. I'll show you". Sue ducked under the bar-flap and led the stranger to the door, squinting as the bright sunlight struck searingly at her eyes. On either side of the narrow ribbon of gravel that served as a street the buildings crowded each other, no life evident except for three men who stood conversing under a sign that said "Southern Star Restaurant", a hundred yards to the right. Then suddenly the sound of many child voices was plain on the still morning air, and around a corner beyond the eating place came a crowd of children, led by a short, stocky woman wearing the uniform of the Salvation Army. Unconsciously Sue gripped the stranger's arm, the lively and voluble group of juveniles a sudden sad reminder of her own childless existence.

"Oh, look at the lovely children. Millie is taking them down to the park for some religious stories. The Army has no Church here".

The stranger lifted a foot, scratched a vesta on the sole of a worn riding-boot, and ignited his cigarette, his entire manner announcing a complete disinterest in everything around him. Good Lord, Sue said to herself, here's a real drone. Got a job to open his mouth, and looks as if he could lie down and die at any second. A dead loss.

The Salvation Lassie came on, surrounded by her noisy entourage, leading a small girl with either hand. She

112

acknowledged the raised hats of the three men, and was drawing close to the pub when the waggonette drawn by two galloping horses came round a corner to the left, without a driver and completely out of control, heading straight into the crowd of children.

In the confined space of the narrow street there was little chance of complete escape, though the children scattered like quail, the girl trying desperately to drag to safety the two whose hands she held, and two other small ones who clung to her skirt, terrified as the runaway bore down on them. Then the tall stranger left the pub verandah like a streaking snake, long legs covering the ground as though they were equipped with seven-league boots, skinny arms removing the tattered coat with the speed of an escapologist. Straight into the path of the bolting team he sprang, flourishing the garment like skilled matador. The yell that burst from his scrawny throat would have wakened the dead of long centuries.

"YAH-HOO-OO!!! R-RING 'EM IN THE GIDGEE!!! WUP-WHOA-O!!!"

The horses slowed, and propped almost to a stop as the tail of the coat snapped like a whip in front of their faces, then the weight of the rolling waggonette drove them forward again, the pole-straps lifting the collars up to their flattened ears. But the tall man's hands gripped the winkers now, and though forced to run backwards for several long awkward strides, he fought the plunging pair to a standstill.

From doorways along the street people erupted, brought to life by the yells, screams and thudding hooves. A sweating man dashed through the crowd, his face displaying fear and agitation, his voice hoarse with relief.

"Jesus, mate, good on yer! I only left 'em for a minute to go inter a bloke's place, and a bloody stray dog nipped one of 'em. Quiet horses, you'd never reckon they'd take orf".

"Get up on yer trap and grab the reins". The stranger's slow drawl was suddenly sharp. "Next time yer

113

leave 'em, tie the bastards up to somethin' and drop the tugs and pole straps. That way yer won't have any corpses on yer hands, or a smashed-up gig".

Still mouthing apologies the farmer swung his team around and departed, the chastened pair moving at a controlled trot. The tall man found himself accosted by a lean individual in khaki shirt, jodphurs and leggings, looking every inch the man on the land. He offered a sinewy hand and a sincere smile.

"I'm Bill Collinson. Mrs. Frawley tells me you are the man in charge of my mares. That was a really smart bit of work that you just performed. Tell me, did the mares arrive in good shape?"

"Yair". The tall man's attention was on the rolling of a cigarette. The Salvation lass waited several yards away, while the children, evidently recovered from their fright, ran noisily up and down the street in fine imitation of the bolting horses.

"Well, can we go now and inspect them, and I will take delivery? I realise I'm a bit late, but there is always so much to be done on a stud farm that it's hard to be on time". Collinson's excuse was a valid one, as the tall man well knew.

"Didn't reely expect yer to be early. Look, I'm so bloody hungry me guts is startin' to eat one of me ribs. Could yer pick the mares up without me? When yer see 'em you'll be satisfied they been well cared for. I'll be here for the buck-jumpin' termorrer, anyway".

"So you've heard about the wager. If you're a Queenslander, you must know Jack Carmody. He won the big buckjumping contest at Rockhampton show four years ago. Told me all about it".

The tall man dribbled smoke through his nostrils, a tight smile splitting his black whiskers. "He won it all right. People reckon he's a hard bloke to know. Funny bugger. I'll be goin' now, and if I don't see yer before, I'll see yer at the buckin' ".

Collinson hesitated. "I didn't get your name".

"It's John Patrick'.

Collinson moved off, as did the remaining onlookers, with the exception of the Salvation lass. She moved to the tall man's side, a wide smile on her small, plain face. She was so short that she was forced to tilt her head far back to look the tall stranger in the eye. Her tone was soft and endearing.

"My name is Mildred Blaine. I wish to thank you for your brave act. Surely the hand of God guided you".

"Didn't notice anyone near me except Mrs. Public House".

The smile became more endearing. "God is everywhere".

"Some day I might have the luck ter run inter him". Humour lurked in the doglike brown eyes and the long sad face.

"Anyway you were really brave. Some of the little ones could have been injured".

The stranger took a long pull at his cigarette before grinding it under a boot. "The Lord said, suffer the little children to come unto me".

"Why, that's lovely". There was rapture in Millie's voice. "Have you read the Scriptures?"

The sad face grew sadder. "There ain't any way, miss, that I could read the Scriptures".

"Then you do not have a religion?"

"Yair. I'm a godless Christian".

"Oh dear, I don't undertand. Could you explain what you mean".

"Well not just now, maybe later. I'm tuckered out, and even blokes guided be the hand of God have to eat".

"I'm sorry to detain you. I must collect the children now, and to-night I will say a prayer for you, as well as praying that this man Carmody will ride the outlaw and win the wager".

"The wager mean anything to you?"

"Why yes. If Mr. Collinson wins, he is going to donate half the money to the Salvation Army".

"That's great. The Sallies are one mob I believe in and always support". There was sincerity in the man's

115

slow drawl now. "One thing yer can count on. Black Jack Carmody won't let yer down".

He strode off abruptly, moving with long awkward steps through the door of the restaurant. Millie stood silently viewing his departure, her mind recalling a picture she had seen in an old religious periodical. An artist's conception of the Good Samaritan.

*　*　*　*　*　*

The tall man completed his meal, ordered seconds and another pot of tea. With these disposed of he silently paid the waitress, returned to the hotel and collected his swag and saddle, then at the grocery store purchased bread, cheese and a tin of bully beef. A line of gums marked the river a quarter of a mile away, and shouldering his load he walked steadily. Under the willows he found a grassy, sheltered spot, and there he spread his swag. With the saddle for a pillow he stretched out comfortably. It was a long wait that confronted him, but his hard journey on the jolting train had not been conductive to peaceful sleep, and the rest was welcome. Soon he was snoring.

*　*　*　*　*　*

Millie Blaine was twenty-eight years old, and had never known a serious love affair. Her mother had died shortly after Millie's birth, and her father had turned her over to a spinster sister who was a firm and dedicated member of the "Sallies". The religious aunt had passed on when the girl was fourteen, and she had returned to her widowed father, a schoolteacher on a meagre wage. Peter Blaine was a kind, forthright and good man, who wished heartily for his daughter to marry well, but it soon became evident that Millie's only interest in life was the creed and beliefs of General William Booth. Religion had claimed her, and for fourteen years she had been housekeeper and cook for her father. Now as she cleared the tea-table, she was more than normally quiet, a fact quickly noted by Peter.

116

"You appear to have something on your mind, Millie", he remarked as he filled his pipe.

"I keep thinking of that man I told you about, Dad", the girl replied. "The one who stopped the bolting horses. He seemed so different, as if he didn't belong to the present day and age. He looked like.... well like a sketch of the Good Samaritan that I saw in a book. When the subject of religion came up, I couldn't decide whether he was making fun of me or whether he was sincere and devout".

"As you know, I once taught school in central Queensland, when you were a baby". Blaine's face displayed a knowing smile. "I can assure you that Queensland stockmen, or ringers as they are called up there, are in the main the most wild and ungodly men you could find anywhere".

"This man didn't look wild or ungodly to me", Millie said. "He looked sad and gentle, and sort of....well....understanding. The kind of man who gets things done and doesn't say much. Like the way he stopped those horses, and didn't say a boastful word".

Peter smiled. "By their deeds shall ye know them. He really made an impression on you, didn't he, Sister Mildred?"

Millie flushed and dropped her gaze. "Yes, dad", she replied. "He really did. I keep picturing him in a turban and a long gown. And sandals".

"You'll be believing soon that he is a reincarnation of the Samaritan", Peter said.

"Stranger things have happened, dad. Like the birth of the Saviour".

Peter made no reply. A realist all his life, he could never quite understand or accept extreme religious fervour.

"It's time for prayer and then bed", Millie said, eyeing the clock on the mantlepiece. "Tomorrow will be a tiring day, but I wouldn't miss it for the world".

"You're looking forward to seeing your friend the Samaritan again, of course", Peter said.

117

"Yes dad". Millie flushed again. "And I'm hoping that the Queensland rider will win the bet for Mr. Collinson".

"I share your hopes", Peter replied. "But to be frank, Millie, the man does not appeal to me. He is too ingratiating, too flashy. In fact he carried all the earmarks of a confidence man, and he has really worked his way into Bill's good graces, with in my opinion, an ulterior motive in mind. I do not trust the fellow".

You're only guessing, dad", Millie said confidently. "The Samaritan says that Black Jack Carmody can be trusted. That's good enough for me".

* * * * *

The school picnic and its athletic events had taken longer to finish than the sponsors had expected. It was shortly after four o'clock when the crowd adjourned to the trucking yards where Professor Parkin and his challenge horse waited. Parkin was a big blond man, personable and smiling, his hearty manner hiding a corrupt and avaricious character. He stood in the centre of the big receiving yard, holding aloft ten five-pound notes. Beside him, bridled and blindfolded, stood a lanky chestnut horse, held by "Dummy" Simmons, Parkin's faithful assistant. The deaf mute was the type of man that suited the Professor. He was unable to give the show away when skullduggery was the order of the day. The stage was set for a financial killing, and the tableau had been enacted many times before. Parkin watched Bill Collinson climb through the rails, in company with a small, dark ferret-faced man who walked with the springy step of a horseman. On one arm he carried a high-backed kneepad saddle. Parkin's voice was courteous and friendly.

"Well, Mr. Collinson, I see your rider is ready to perform. Do you wish to nominate a stakeholder and judge?"

"If you are satisifed", Collinson replied, "I would suggest Peter Blaine, our schoolteacher for stakeholder, and Constable Allbright for Judge".

"Agreed. I do not doubt they are men of integrity".

Blaine stepped forward and collected the stakes, while Allbright produced a watch and checked the winder. The policeman was a sour and morose-looking man, a hard customer but noted for dedication to fair play. He spoke loudly.

"Let's get things pat. If Carmondy stays on for ten seconds Bill Collinson collects the stakes. If he's thrown inside ten seconds Parkin collects. Am I right?"

"Dead right", Collinson said, and Parkin nodded agreement. The rider moved to the horses side, and Dummy Simmons caught an ear and took a firm grip on the bridle as the saddle was adjusted. In the forefront of the crowd Millie Blaine's eyes searched in vain for the tall stranger. Then the rider swung up and Simmons pulled the blindfold clear. With a snort the chestnut exploded.

The rider rode out three vigorous bucks, then suddenly he was gone, sprawling on hands and knees in the dust, while the horse, relieved of its burden, came to a halt and stood snorting. The rider rose and dusted himself, then leaned on the nearest rail for support, his tones sad and apologetic as he addressed him mentor.

"Sorry, Mr. Collinson. He's the hardest bucker I ever took on. I didn't reckon the horse was foaled that could throw me, but I was wrong".

Collinson's face was a study in dejection, but Parkin moved forward, hand outstretched to Peter Blaine.

"As the horse threw Jack Carmody within the ten allotted seconds, I now claim the wager", he said. "Hard luck, Mr. Collinson".

It was then, as Peter Blaine was in the act of handing over the stakes, that a voice rang out sharp and clear above the babble of the onlookers.

"Wait a minute! The horse didn't throw Jack Carmody".

Millie turned at the sound of that voice, recognising it at once, for though it had quickened, traces of the drawl still remained. All eyes were on the tall stranger as he seemed to flow between the rails like a snake. Calmly he drew himself to his great height, his left hand gripping his tobacco pouch, his right pointing a long finger at Peter Blaine.

"Don't pay anything". The soft voice had regained its calm slow tempo, and the finger swung to indicate Parkin and the lately unhorsed rider. "This pair of birds have been havin' yer on. They've pulled this act a dozen times between here and the Queensland border. The rider's Nifty Winton, and he goes on ahead of Parkin and cons somebody into backin' him to ride the horse. He's fell off it so often he could take the spill in the dark and never get a bruise. Yer a good rider, Nifty, and a good con man, but yer didn't expect to see me here, and neither did Parkin. But be sure yer sins will find yer out. The game's up."

Parkin and the rider were speechless, seemingly rooted to the ground, and Allbright spoke sharply.

"How do you know all this? Any proof of your accusations".

"How I know", the tall man's gaze rose from the cigarette he was rolling, and met the police officer squarely, "is because I happen to be Black Jack Carmody. And here's the proof".

He drew from the pocket of his coat a shining pair of spurs, the long shanks bent into a deep gooseneck that ended in two flat discs that were part of the unit, taking the place of rowels. Silently Allbright accepted them, and read aloud the inscription on the gleaming discs.

"J.P. Carmody, buckjump champion. Rockhampton Show, 1907",

"You told me your name was John Patrick", Bill Collinson said. "Why didn't you put me wise to these jokers?"

Carmody raised a foot, the movement reminding Millie of a brolga about to dance. He ignited a match on the bootsole, lit his lean cigarette and puffed, taking his time before replying.

"I wanted 'em to catch themselves, because I don't

120

like blokes usin' me name and reputation to pull off a swindle. And John Patrick's me name alright. John Patrick Carmody. Beware of imitations".

There was a sudden short silence, broken by Allbright. His face displayed anything but an affectionate expression as he addressed Parkin and his accomplice.

"What have you pair of heroes got to say for youselves?"

Winton's demeanour was one of fear and trembling, but the drover offered a stubborn belligerant attitude, and his reply was defiant.

"It was good game while it lasted, but all good things have to finish sometime. There's not much you can do about it anyway".

"Don't be too sure", Allbright said savagely. "If I take you and your flash little friend down to the station, be bloody sure I'll find a charge of some sort to hit you with. Possibly more than one. But instead, we will let the contest go on as scheduled, providing Bill Collinson agrees. And of course, Jack Carmody, the man you backed your horse to throw".

A twitter of excitement ran through the crowd, growing to a cheer as Carmody nodded. "Yer on", he said. "If Collinson agrees".

"You can be bloody sure I agree", Collinson said, and the cheering broke out again. Parkin realised he was being given a chance that he hardly deserved, and he caught the horse's bridle and led it to the centre of the yard, signalling Dummy Simmons to take hold. Carmody spat out his cigarette bumper, tightened his belt and moved to the rails. Reaching through them he collected the worn poley saddle.

"Never rode in a kneepad yet", he announced. "Better pull that tub of yours off, Nifty. Before long yer goin' to need it to raise a bit of finance."

With a bad grace Winton complied, and Carmody adjusted the crupper and girthed up tight, then buckled on the presentation spurs. All his lethargy gone now, he sprang up and jerked away the blindfold as Dummy Sim-

121

mons leaped clear. The blunted spurs dug in, gavanising the chestnut into instant action, and it produced a half-dozen savage, twisting bucks that caused pebbles to fly and dust to roil. Carmody rode high and loose, left hand giving the animal a free rein, right brandishing the tattered Ashburton. Bill Collinson had witnessed many bucking exhibitions, but never had he seen a man with a seat so careless and relaxed. It was all poise and balance with Carmody. Collinson was reminded of a tired worker enjoying the comfort and luxury of a padded chair.

The horse reached the rails and traded ends, coming back across the yard with another explosive burst, and now Carmody shook his feet free of the stirrups and drew the spurs down the sweating shoulders, producing a shower of violent grunts as the horse put everything into a major effort to dislodge the tormenting rider, but to no avail. Suddenly the bucks subsided into pig-jumps, and above the applause of the crowd rose Allbright's loud yells signifying that time was up. Carmody swung a leg over the pommel and leaped, landing catlike. Dust was heavy on his clothes and thick in his whiskers, but his sad smile was wide. He went quickly to the rails where Millie Blaine stood, her face a portrait of adoration, as the tall ringer spoke.

"There y'are. I told yer Black Jack wouldn't let yer down".

"Thank the Lord you came", Millie's eyes were wet with tears that cut channels through the dust on her face. "You really are the Good Samaritan, I am sure, and God sent you".

"No, young lady". Again humour lurked in the sad eyes and painful drawl. "A stock-agent in Queensland sent me".

"Yes, but God was with you".

"Don't recall him bein' around. Only two blood horses'.

"Oh, why do you make fun of me". Millie was really in tears now.

"I ain't makin' fun of yer. Just stickin' ter facts". Carmody's long fingers were fashioning a cigarette. A hand fell on his shoulder, and he turned to face Bill Collinson, who brandished a hand full of paper money.

"I can't thank you enough, John Patrick. How I fell for that polished little rat I will never know. He really had me up a tree, but things turned out all right, thanks to you. Allbright just told them to move out and keep going. They'll think twice before they try their monkey tricks again".

Carmody shook his head. "Losin' out to day won't alter things. They'll den up for a bit and lick their wounds, then it'll be on again. They're the kind of leopards who never change their spots".

"Here's the donation I promised, Millie". Collinson had turned his attention to the girl, handing her a roll of money, then he addressed Carmody again. "What about something for you, Jack. You've earned it. How about a fiver?"

"I wasn't thinkin' of profit when I made the ride". Carmody's smile was turned on Millie. "But the Good Samaritan must have had to take a quid sometimes to keep operatin'. I'll be glad of it".

He accepted the proffered note, put it in the greasy tobacco pouch and extended his hand. "I wish yer luck. Train leaves at five o'clock, and time's movin' on. I best soon be movin' with it".

"I can keep you in employment if you like to stay", Collinson said eagerly. "Good wages and plenty of tucker".

"Oh, please couldn't you?" Millie's voice was a desperate plea.

"I'm committed", Carmody said. "Drover bloke named Rusty Ned Cook's waitin' up in Dalby. We got to go north and lift a thousand bullocks. But I won't build false hopes for yer. This part of the world is too close settled for me. I belong where yer talk in miles, not acres".

"Well, all I can say is, good luck Mr. Carmody. If you ever come back you know where to drop your swag".

Collinson turned to where Peter Blaine waited among the few loiterers who had not dispersed.

Carmody shouldered his swag and saddle, while Millie still waited, an expression of anguish in her eyes. With her sandy hair jutting awry from under the blue hat, and her duty tear-stained face, she appeared to Carmody like a bedraggled, frustrated schoolgirl. The tall ringer's voice was soft, comforting.

"Yer can walk to the station with me, if yer like".

Too full of emotion for words, Millie fell into step beside him, hurrying to keep pace with his long strides. Bill Collinson spoke knowingly to Blaine.

"She's fallen at last, Peter".

"And with a terrible thud", Millie's father replied. "But nothing will come of it. He isn't the kind who wants a serious woman. A vagabond whose home is under his hat".

"Like the wandering Jew", Collinson said.

"No, more like the good Samaritan", Blaine replied, smiling.

★　★　★　★　★　★

"I wish you'd stay", Millie said. "Why go back to all the lonely places. Here you could make a new life. You could find God".

"Ain't got time to look for him". Carmody fired up a cigarette. "Hard enough to find a livin' when a bloke's got nobody only himself to fall back on".

"Have you no family, no people".

"Not a one". Carmody trickied smoke through his nostrils. "Me parents were Irish. Mum died bringin' me into the world, and the old man died when I was fourteen".

"Oh, I am sorry. Please tell me about your past life, and perhaps I can help you. I feel I could do so much if you would only stay".

"I appreciate yer concern, believe me". There was no doubting the ringer's sincerity. "Now I'll tell yer somethin'. When yer fall for a bloke and lose out, it hurts

a hell of a lot, but yer get over it. When yer go overboard the second time and miss again it still hurts, but not as bad as the first time. And be the time yer lose the third time, yer already lookin' for the fourth one. Keep up the good work yer doin', and one day the right bloke will turn up. Yer ain't found him yet, but yer will. Remember that the meek shall inherit the earth''.

Far down the line the train whistled. Carmody shifted his gear closer to the platform's edge, and with a sudden thought Millie reached into her spacious handbag and produced a small copy of the Bible. Turning, she offered it to the ringer.

"Please take this and read it. It may help you to find God, and then you may return".

"Not a hope". Carmody's long face was sorrowful. "Yer see, I can't read or write, and anyway it was read to me when I was a boy".

The train rumbled to a halt, and Carmody pitched saddle and swag through the door of the guard's van, then reached out and took Milie's hands.

"I wish things could be different, fair dinkum I do, but they can't".

"It's hard to say farewell". There were tears in Millie's eyes again. "May God watch over you, Mr. Carmody".

"Black Jack Carmody. The funny bugger. The Christian who doesn't believe in God".

A long stride took him into the van, the whistle shrieked and the wheels hummed as the train gathered speed. Millie watched it out of sight, a terrible sense of loneness enveloping her. She turned to see her father approaching at a quick walk, concern on his face.

"You are overdue for supper, daughter. For a moment I thought you had eloped with the Samaritan".

"I wish I could have, Dad. But I couldn't get him to believe or care".

"If he is the kind of man I think he is, he did what he thought was best for you", Peter Blaine said. "It would be your welfare he held at heart, not his own'.

"Like the Good Samaritan", Millie whispered.

"Yes", Peter said. "Like the good Samaritan".

*　　*　　*　　*　　*　　*

With his horse feeding on a loose reign, Carmody sat slouched in the saddle, quiet as the big silence that surrounded him. The open country was boundless and without barrier. Rusty Ned Cook had dismounted, and was filling his pipe. Far up the plain at the lead of the slowly spreading cattle rode Crocodile Jones, a barely mobile speck in a sunlit infinity.

"Yer a long way away, Jack", the boss-drover said. "I'd bet Coolgardie to a trey that yer thinkin' on that religious woman yer told me about".

"Yer right on me, Ned", Carmody drawled. "She was too bloody innocent and good for this hard old world".

"Yer could hve brought her back. A girl like that might have been the makin' of yer".

"Bring her back here!" Carmody's voice was shocked. "She'd find no God here, Ned. Anyway, blokes like you and me ain't got any time to spare on gods".

"Yer could have stayed down there and made a home with her. Yer never had one yet".

"Not in all them little cramped places. If I laid down and stretched out, me head would be in the Murray and me boots in Bass Straits. Anyway, a woman like her, well, she's worthy of a better cove than me. And she's too close to this God I don't believe in. I don't want to go to Heaven, Ned".

He made a sweeping gesture with a long arm at the vast expanse of country. "That's my Heaven out there, Ned, and I don't like the thought of leavin' it".

Shinin' in the Sun

The spring in Western Queensland is always a wondrous season if preceded by beneficial rain, and to-day the land was beautiful in its vivid brilliance. Flowers thrust out their blooms in every garden along the narrow street, each varied colour vying for prominence, the petals titillated by the increasing heat of the mid-morning sun. No cloud formation etched the pale, almost colour-less dome of the sky, and no current of air stirred. My companion and I were alone, leaning indolently on the knife-scarred wooden bench under the pub verandah.

The old man beside me had been silent for several minutes, his pale, fading eyes taking in the beauty of Nature, a beauty that no construction conceived by the hand of man can ever hope to equal. Slowly he ignited a cigarette, his hard and calloused fingers crushing out the match with complete indifference to the flame.

"It's a bloody bonzer day", he remarked at last.

"It is", I agreed. "You wouldn't find many places in the world that could look any better this morning, Ned".

The old eyes studied me intently. They were shrewd and ruthless orbs, savage and feral in a scarred and brutal face that bespoke a youth steeped in reckless physical violence, when desperate need for survival had eclipsed all else. Quite a few old hands had told me that Rusty Ned Cook had "the heart of a lion, and more guts than a slaughtered bullock". Ned's appearance, the craggy countenance, the twisted and smashed fingers and knuckles, all gave evidence of a man to whom courage and determination were watchwords.

This little street's a bloody pretty place", he stated. "But I can show yer a place that leaves it fer dead".

"Just where would that be?", I queried.

Ned's reply was somewhat indirect. "This place is gettin' too civilised. Modern ways and styles, well I just can't cop 'em sweet any more. Time and changes pass a man by".

128

"You're right", I agreed. "But where would you find a nicer little spot?"

The old man raised a hand, wagging the burning cigarette up and down, as if to inject proof into his argument. "I'll tell yer, boy. Out on the Cooper. Out on the channel country, in a spring like this. When all the trees and plants and flowers are bloomin', and the big plains are shinin' in the sun".

"I went through there the winter before last", I said. "When the big dry was on. Awful lonely land. Lot of secrets hidden there I would think."

"Lot of secrets, lot of lonely graves", the old man replied. "Bloody little law when I was a young bloke, and no God. Lots of blokes with a dead past, broken reeds lookin' for a new place to take root. Went there to fergit, and were soon fergotten".

The old man shivered suddenly, and I jerked erect in surprise for the day was hot. His smile begame grim.

"Don't let it worry yer. That was only the Reaper makin' a practice stroke with his scythe. I'm eighty-three, lad, and he's had his eye on me for quite a while. One day soon he's goin' to make the final swipe, and I'll be off to join me old saddle-mates, quite a few of which are buried out in the place we was just talkin' about. Them big plains that are shinin' in the sun".

"You told me once before about a stockman named Tragget*, who was killed out there", I said.

"That's true". Ned scratched his white whiskers, rough as the bristles on a nylon brush. "But it wasn't Wally Tragget I was thinkin' about just this moment. It was an Englishman we called Limey Tom. Ex-officer and broken gentleman".

* (For the story of Wally Tragget read "The Funny Bugger" Keith Garvey)

* * * * * *

I first met Tom Margnan in a pub in Mitchell, in the winter of eighteen-ninety-nine. That was the name he used. I was to find out later it was somethin' a bit different.

"I was drinkin' with "Bulla" King, who'd just

delivered, and was lookin' for men for another job. I was tied up with old Bill Warden, shiftin' six hundred steers down via Hebel to a delivery at Walgett. Just as we were downin' the second drink, up comes this Englishman, and bones Bulla for a job.

Christ, but he looked bad. Small bloke, red face bloated from grog, heavy fair moustache. Thin and wiry as a lignum sucker. The biggest part of him was his bloody dignified manner.

"Mr. King", he opens up, "I am in dire need of employment with a droving outfit. I completed a job with Mr. Rickers last week. Due to a common human weakness, I am at present unfinancial. Mr. Rickers does not commence work again for two weeks. Would you consider me as an employee?"

Bulla didn't seem real keen. He was one boss drover who didn't like drunks. "Are yer a capable man?", he asks.

"I am sure Mr. Rickers will recommend me", the Pom says, and just as if he'd been ordered, a bloke as tall as a brolga steps ups.

"Yer can take him on, Bulla", the bloke says. "He's alright". Not much, but a hell of a lot from a cove who knew the game like Long Tom Rickers.

"Yer look like a drunk to me", Bulla says.

"Sir", the Pom says. "You are to some extent correct. But I assure you that while I am in your employ, sobriety will be my watchword".

"Yer on", Bulla says. "Bring yer swag to the common in the mornin'. I hope yer a man of yer word."

The Pom straightened up sudden like, and the look on his face told yer he was both hurt and bloody surprised. "Mr. King", he says, "I am an Englishman".

"Alright", Bulla says. "The common in the mornin'. And my name's Bulla. Mr. King died a long time ago".

"My sincere thanks, Bulla", the Pom says. "My name is Margnan. Tom Margnan".

He turned to go, and the way he eyed the glasses of

130

grog would have broke the heart of a saint. Really cravin', the poor coot was. I fished out a ten bob note and offers it to him. "Here, have a drink", I says. "Yer look as if yer need one".

"My good friend", the Pom replies," as I am financially embarrassed, and it is doubtful if we will meet again, I must refuse your greatly appreciated generosity".

"Go on, take the bloody thing", I says. "You'll see me again, and if yer don't the loss of it ain't likely to break me".

His hand shook as he took the note. "May I request your name", he asks.

"It's Ned Cook", I tells him, and he offers his hand. "I will not forget your Samaritan act, Mr. Cook", he tells me. "You will be repaid".

"Call me Rusty Ned", I says. "Mr. Cook died a long time ago".

It was ten years before I saw Tom Margnan again.

★   ★   ★   ★   ★   ★

"Ten years", I said. "Surely you heard of him again".

"Out there where them big plains are shinin' in the sun, lad, it's awful wide and lonely. I never met Margnan in all that time, but I used to hear of him. What a hard drinker he was, and how his posh English manners and style went over big with the wimmin'. And how he could hold his own with the best of bloody stockmen around. When I finally got me lamps on him again, I was in jail at Quilpie, broke as a woman's promise, and no bastard around to pay the lousy ten bob that was on me head.

I'd done me money at a swy game, belted a bloke who had the mistaken idea he was a pug, and got meself lumbered. I'm sittin' in the chokey, with a sad regret and a shirt full of sore ribs, when the copper comes to the door of me cell.

"You're free to go, Cook", he says. "There's a Pommy cove outside who just made bail".

I collects me watch and empty wallet off the trap, and

131

out I goes to find Margnan waitin'. Lookin' older and more worn, but there was no mistakin' that English courtesy.

The outback roughens and toughens most blokes, but it had only toughened Limey Tom. He still had them high bred English manners that showed when I first met him.

"I want to hand yer a hell of a big thanks", I says, "for bailin' me out. Me plant's at Cheepie, and I forgot to bring me cheque-book along. Came over here on the coach for the week-end and landed in strife. Headin' south to a musterin' job when I get organised. Got to find some men. Need five of 'em".

"My services are available if you consider me worthy", Limey Tom says. "I am financially embarrassed, as I was when we last met. It was fortunate that I had sufficient left to secure your release. I now stand completely impoverished, and your offer of employment is more than welcome. Just as your offer of a small unsecured loan was more than welcome long ago".

That really got to me, my oath it did. When a man remembers a piddlin' debt ten years old, and puts his last few bob into gettin' yer out of the clink, it means a bloody lot.

"I need four more blokes", I tells him. "Let's go down to the pub and see if we can scare up some ringers. The landlord's good for loan".

I was a bit lucky. A tough old wattlebender named Duncan McCourt and two of the Commerford boys from Boulia were lookin' for a start. McCourt was one of them reliable and steady old hands yer don't see to-day, good camp cook as well as an experienced stockman. The other two were hardly out of their teens, but they'd cut their teeth on a greenhide fall. Wild and woolly boys, I tell yer. Cecil was the quieter of the pair. Clarrie was a great man for the gins, and the biggest fancy Dan with a stockwhip that I ever seen.

I'm still a man short. I got a starter off the publican, and I'm settin' up a shout when in comes this Irish feller, young bloke about twenty, with a brogue as thick as a Cobar dust storm, and more confidence than a billy goat in a garden.

"Are ye the drover named Ned Cook?", he asks. " 'Tis a job I seek, and a reference I have from Mr. Cunningham of Brockton station".

I read the reference and it was a good one. Old John Cunningham wasn't the sort to recommend a dud. The name on the brief was Patrick McDermott of Londonderry, Ireland. I liked his style, so I takes him on.

The Commerford brothers had young horses that needed workin', so they reckon they'll ride to Cheepie and take a pack-horse. The Irishman joins 'em, with a shiny-fat saddle-horse and pack animal. Like his gear they were well looked after, and old Duncan remarked on it when he boarded the coach with Limey Tom and me. "The Mick's goin' to be all right", Dunc says. "Yer only got to look at his outfit see that".

We picked the plant up at Cheepie, and out we goes to this wilderness sixty miles from anywhere. It was a joint that was bein' sold up for debt, and hadn't been mustered for three years. Only a caretaker at the homestead, and he gives us directions to the three big paddocks that had to be cleaned out. The holdin' paddock we had to work into was only a small Queensland back-yard, ten thousand acres. It was a bloody good time, plenty of grass and water. It was me guess that there was cattle there that had never seen a white man, and it turned out pretty right.

Old Dunc was the travellin' cook. I call him that because we were movin' so much and so quick that he bloody near had to put a feed together on the run. The cattle was wild as hawks, and I was glad I can tell yer, that the Commerford boys and Paddy had brought the extra horses along. We was havin' some hard ridin' but we were gettin' there.

At night we were always dead beat, no time much time for socialisin'. Nine days straight we put in, and I decides to call a halt for a day, to let men and horses rest.

133

That night Dunc gets his old mouth-organ out, and grinds out a few tunes. He gets on an old Irish number, and Paddy starts to sing.

Holy smoke, what a voice he had. Sweeter than cold beer runnin' into a glass. All hands was sort of mesmerised, old Dunc sittin' with his mouth open like a heat-stunned galah, Cec and Clarrie, always silent blokes, more silent than ever. And Limey Tom, so help me he's as white as an angel's waistcoat, and I see that he's nearly in tears as Paddy sings on like a bloody lark.

I'm biddin' ye a fond farewell
My Mary kind and true
And I'll not forget ye darlin'
In the land I'm goin' to......

Limey Tom gets up from the fire and walks a bit away. He really was shook up. He was a bloke who never spoke about his past life, and I wondered what old memories Paddy's song was bringin' back. Then the song ends, and the Commerford boys, whose mother was Irish, started clappin'.

"With a voice like you got Paddy, yer should be makin' a quid in the London music halls", Cec Commerford says. "What made yer come out to this wild bastard of a place where the pigs have gotter root for daylight".

'Tis not good enough for the stage I am", Paddy replies. "And besides, 'tis hard under the British rule in the ould sod. No people I had once mother died, so for a better adventure I looked".

"No brothers or sisters?", Cec asks, and Paddy shakes his head.

"And no father either", he admits then, quite bloody open about it. "Me father was an English officer, stationed at Belfast durin' the troubles. Now why should a big brave British soldier worry about a little Irish farm girl named Mary McDermott, who he took down and deserted, so he did".

Limey Tom had come back to the fire, and was pourin' a pint of tea. He looks up and asks, "did you know the English officer's name, young man".

"Aye, I surely did. Major Terence Markham. Just another member of a race that enslaves its fellow men. Gentlemen, they call themselves! Cut throat robbers with violence would be a better name, so it would. Bloody oppressors and tyrants".

We were all waitin' for Limey Tom to take Paddy up on his outburst, but the Pom never said a word. Walks over to his swag and starts arrangin' his blankets. Dunc swings into a lively tune on the mouth-organ, but it fell a bit flat, and soon we was all in our swags, sleepin' the sleep that comes to the unjust as well as the bloody just.

Like I've done all me life, I woke a bit before daylight. Clarrie's swag was empty, and I knew he'd gone for the horses. Limey Tom was hunched over the fire, drinkin' tea. He never spoke when I filled me quart. Just sat starin' at the coals as if his mind was miles away. "Are yer a bit off colour, mate", I says.

"Just a bit upset in the tummy, Ned", he replies. "Something has evidently disagreed with me". I was pretty sure that it was somethin' in his mind, not his guts. The bells were gettin' close, the rest of the gang rolled out and we caught up a mount for the day. Dunc had the tucker spread out as day broke clear.

Old Ned paused in his oratory, rolled a thin cigarette and lighted it, then took up the strain again. "You ever see them big plains when day is breakin', young feller?". When the world is wakin' up, and all the livin' things are wakin' with it? There ain't a more bonzer sight on earth. And then the sun comin' up over the scrubline and puttin' a shine on every thing. That's how it was that mornin'. No hint of the tragedy that was waitin'. We saddled up in good spirits and off we rides, the tension of last night forgotten by all. All except Limey Tom.

I took Cecil and Dunc with me, down the east side of the paddock where the scrub was thickest, and sent Clarrie, The Pom and Paddy west where the open country lay. "As soon as yer come onto cattle, start back with 'em", I says. "Don't try for a big muster. They're goin' to run like hell".

"They can run, but they can't escape", Clarrie says, full of bloody confidence, then they canters off. Three real good ringers, but only two of 'em was due to see the sun go down.

We went about three miles before we found cattle. About thirty broke out of the timber to the right. Cecil was on that side, and he swings 'em over towards Dunc and me. A bloody mixed grill of beef, old cows and calves, a few mickey bulls and calfy heifers, tails up and gallopin'. We got 'em headed the right way, knowin' they'd soon run out of puff. I hears whips goin', well over to the west, and I knew the other boys had struck oil too.

We got to the open country, and about a quarter mile away there's about fifty head, trottin' in front of the riders. Even at that distance yer couldn't help spottin' the piker bull. A big slatey-coloured bastard with horns stickin' out like the points on Lord Kitchener's moustache, only longer and a bloody sight sharper. Ever so often he'd turn and face the riders, paw the ground and then trot after the mob. A nasty bit of beef, take my oath.

The cattle we are holdin' kept tryin' to break back, and Clarrie notes this and starts canterin' over to us. Just when he's about half-way across, our mob spots the others, and goes racin' towards 'em. Well and good. We reins in, and Clarrie pulls down to a walk. That was when it happened."

Old Ned's cigarette had smoulded out, forgotten as he relived the wild days of his youth. His pale eyes were bright, alive with memories.

"A lot of years have gone, young feller, but I can still see it plain as ever. The big sweep of open country, the dust rollin' red behind the cattle, and all of a sudden the old piker bull takin' off back towards the timber.

An old hand would have let him go and kept the rest movin' ahead, but Paddy was young and game, and he didn't see or know of the danger. He rode right into the

136

bull's path, crackin' the whip. The piker charged, quick as yer could wink yer dexter eye.

That old bull upended the horse like a garbageman emptying' a can of slops. Paddy was pelted clear, got onto his pins, tried to run and fell. If he'd laid still the bull mightn't have noticed, but his movements drew its attention, and it left the horse and made for this new target that's flappin' about on the ground. Right then was when Limey Tom rode his mount straight into the bull.

Us other four men were ridin' as hard as we could to get there as quick as possible. Clarrie had a start on the rest, the heavy persuader with the short fall streamin' out behind him, spurrin' as if the devil kicked him endways. But I could see he's goin' to be too late.

When Tom's horse hit the bull broadside on, the rider was slung clean over the piker, and landed on all fours. The horse took off riderless, and the bull lines Paddy up again. Dead set on a bit of Irish blood, he was, but Limey Tom had other ideas.

Now I can tell yer lad, the Pom had plenty of time to escape. There was a low box-tree not twenty yards away, and here's Limey Tom on foot, no whip in his hand, nothin'. But he doesn't make for the tree, he runs straight for the bull's head and grabs it by the horns, just as it was about to mow Paddy down.

Clarrie got there just about five seconds too late. The piker had pawed Tom underfoot and was gorin' hell out of him. Like a shot Clarrie pulled his horse in and started layin' that short fall across the bull's eyes. You ever see a real top ringer usin' a whip with a short greenhide fall? He can blind yer with one stripe, and Commerford was a real gun. The piker packed it in and made for the scrub, and we let him go with a mental note to attend to the bastard later. We turns to the mess he left behind.

It was easy to see that Paddy's right leg was either broke or sprained, because it wouldn't hold him up. But he was all right apart from that. The man in a mess was Limey Tom. Tryin' to draw the bull off Paddy had cost him the big price. He was bleedin' out of the nose and

137

mouth, and it was easy to see he was busted up bad inside. His breath was comin' in groanin' gasps, but his speech was clear.

"Ned", he says, "I would speak privately with you".

I motioned the other boys aside, and knelt down beside him. He was havin' trouble gettin' the words out, but I could understand him. Christ, when my time comes, I hope I can go out as calm and dignified as Tom Margnan did. Even at death's door, he never lost that courteous old English. He grabbed me hand as he spoke. Took his time with the words, even as the light was goin' out.

"There is a key on a chain around my neck. It will open the door of my dwelling at Roma. It is my wish that you take what is there, and reveal no secrets you may discover".

'I'll do it mate", I says. "Sure as there's shit in a cat".

"A rather ignoble end for one who was once an officer and a gentleman", he whispers. Then the light faded out of his eyes and he was gone.

I covered his face with his hat, and turns to the boys. Clarrie and Cec were lookin' pretty white and peaky, but old Dunc wasn't upset a bit. He was a return man from the Boer War, and he'd looked on death a lot of times. But Paddy! Holy Smoke!

He's sittin' flat on his arse with his gammy leg stretched out in front of him, and the tears are runnin' down his face like a waterfall. You know how emotional the bog Irish can get. Our boy was breakin' all records.

"Holy Mary", he sobs. " 'Twas me loife he saved be givin' his own. May the Saviour forgive me for what I said last noight".

"Hold up, boy", old Duncan says. "He's on a road we all gotter foller some day. Perhaps it's the way he wanted it".

I sent Clarrie for the horses, and be the time he got back Paddy was gettin' in control of himself. His foot was

138

swelled up and turnin' black. Bones broken for sure. We caught Dago, a black half-blood that was a horse that had plenty of bottom, and a bay mare that was a good 'un too.

"You'e the lightest man here, Cec", I says. "Get on Dago and ride for town. It's seventy mile, but yer on a horse that'll carry yer. Report to the police, perhaps they'll come back with yer. You go with him as far as the homestead, Clarrie. There's a buggy there, and harness horses. Bring it back so we can get Paddy to town. And bring a bar and shovel, and a rifle if yer can get one".

"What for?", Clarrie asks.

"The diggin' tools are for a grave", I tells him. "A body goes rotten in a few hours in this temperature. The rifle's for the bull when we meet him again".

The brothers rode off, men yer could depend on to the last ditch, but there was still a lot to be done, Dunc and me carried Paddy to the shade of a big krui that was growin' close by, just near a little gilgai with water in it. Then I sent the old hand back with the horses, to our main camp to pick the gear up. Next I carried Tom's body to the shade, and covered it with raincoats, and saddlecloths off our horses. Neither of the horses that had mixed in with the bull seemed to be hurt. A strange thing.

I sat in the shade of the krui and talked to Paddy. He was in a good bit of pain with his foot, but he was crackin' hardy. All of a sudden he missed his watch, and I goes lookin' for it where the tragedy took place. I looked for quite a while, then I sees the chain stickin' out of the sand. It was still goin', and when I opened it I finds the picture of a women inside the lid, under a glass facin'. A strikin' lookin' girl she was. I takes the watch back to Paddy, and he was real pleased.

"I thank ye, Ned", he says. " 'Tis a portrait of me mum there is inside. All I have to remember her by. And join her I would have this day, had it not been for Limey Tom. A brave man he was".

I got a quart off me saddle and made tea, and Paddy seemed to brighten up a bit when he had a drink. I forgot all about the picture in the watch. I had cause to remember it later.

The sun was about an hour high when Clarrie got back with the buggy. The old caretaker was along too. His name was Leo. They had the diggin' tools and a thirty-two rifle, also a tarpaulin that would be all the coffin Tom would get. We wrapped the body in it, and got busy in the shade of the krui. The ground was sandy and soft, and we kept diggin' long after dark, with a lantern lighted.

At last we had it deep enough, and we lowered the corpse, already startin' to smell, into the dark and lonely bloody hole. "What can we say", I asks. "Somebody ought to say somethin'."

"I'll pray for him", Clarrie says, and he kneels down at the graveside. Sweet Jesus, but I couldn't believe that a rough and rowdy bloke like Clarrie Commerford knew how to pray. But he recited the Lord's Prayer word perfect. I found out later that his old mother was real devout Tyke, and she brought up her boys to respect their god. Perhaps he was lookin' on, I don't know. If he was, he was lookin' at a pretty crude burial.

There was Clarrie, kneelin' by the grave, the spewey lantern light reflectin' the sweat on his black curls, and shinin' on the shanks of his spurs. Dunc and Leo, old bush rats made hard be a hard life. Paddy sittin' with his leg stretched out and the waterworks turned on again. And your's truly, with his many sins ridin' heavy on his head. It wasn't what yer could call a dignified funeral.

We harnessed the buggy again, loaded Paddy in, and Leo starts back to the homestead with him. I'd wanted 'em to leave earlier, but Paddy had been determined to see Tom off. It was after midnight when we got in our swags.

Next day we saddled up. The job had to go on. We ran into the old piker bull, and gave him a lead injection, so he was no more trouble. The day after that Cec turns up with two ringers who were out of work. The police officer in town had taken his statement, and wanted the rest of us to call in when we got in. In the meantime he was

140

lookin' to find any relatives Limey Tom might have. He never found any.

When we finished and got to town I found Paddy had gone to Mitchell, to stay with some friends until his foot got right. I posted his cheque on, and left his outfit with the policeman. Later I heard he'd gone to the Territory. I never saw him again.

A week later I picked up a job takin' cattle to Roma, and when I delivered I finds the humpy where Limey Tom used to hang out. It was only a one-room hut with a padlock and chain on the door. The key I had unlocked it, and I goes in to find that there ain't much there of value, except for a few sentimental things. There was a sheaf of letters that I reckoned was none of me business, and a little square tin that had held coffee grounds once upon a time. I tell yer, lad I got a bloody shock when I opened it and found the medal and the Army discharge. And the locket.

Old Ned ceased in his rhetoric, and pointed down the street, beyond the farthest houses, where the heat haze shook and shimmered against the scrubline. After a long pause he spoke again.

"Even away out there, where the land's measured in square miles, the world is a bloody small place. Small enough to bring together a father and son that never knew each other. Out there, where the big plains are shinin' in the sun, Paddy found his father, but he never knew it".

The old scoundrel became silent again, and I knew his still keen old mind had retreated over the long hard years. He was seeing again the dust clouds over the plodding cattle, hearing the tinkle of the horse-bells in the star-studded velvet darkness, living the sanguinary battles in bar-room and back alley. Dreaming of lost loves and desires, and the fortune that never came. "Go on", I prompted, and he resumed his tale.

"The medal was a D.S.O., won for bravery under fire at the big Sudanese dust-up. There was a cuttin' out

142

of a London paper, tellin' how Major Terence Markham won it, and there's a picture on the cuttin' too. A much younger edition of the man we knew as Tom Margnan, or Limey Tom. It was him alright. And when I opened the locket I finds more proof. There's the photo of a young woman, the same one as was in Paddy's watch. I knew then why Limey Tom tackled that piker like a meat-ant takin' on an elephant. It was plain suicide, but the load on his conscience was bigger than any fear. Beat that, young feller".

"The belongings", I was moved to ask. "What did you do with them?"

"I told no bugger what I knew, just as I promised Tom. I went to a lawyer, and he told me to send the stuff to Army Headquarters in England, with a view to findin' any kin of Tom's. And as I told yer, I never saw Paddy McDermott again. Half a bloody century gone, boy. No harm can come if I talk about it now".

"It's a wonderful human interest story", I said. "I can't thank you enough for telling it".

The old man licked dry, leathery lips, and pointed to the open door of the bar-room.

"If yer want to show some appreciation, fill me up a big schooner. All the enjoyment I get these days is a few grogs. And a few old memories about old saddle-mates. Men who were the backbone of Australia. Fellers like the Commerfords, Dunc McCourt, Tom Margnan. The blokes I laughed and suffered with. Out on them big plains, shinin' in the sun".

Black Jack's Oversight

The cool afternoon wind, blowing southward, ruffled the surface of the creek, carrying the smell of water to the plodding horses half a mile distant. Heads were lifted and the walk became a trot, causing the three riders following the plant to break into a canter. Jones and Carmody spurred up to the lead, ready to grab the halters on the three pack-horses should they decide to roll in the water with their burdens.

Quickly the thirsty animals were sated, and with muddied legs and bellies, went floundering up the bank to the creek flat where young tender summer grass sprouted. Rusty Ned Cook's desiring gaze was rivetted on the grog shanty that stood at the top of a rise two hundred yards distant. He licked dusty lips as he spoke.

"We camped here to-night. Sun'll soon be gone. Let's grab the pack-horses and unload. Then it's our turn to have a drink".

At once the drovers became busy, Carmody hobbling the horses while Crocodile Jones unpacked and Rusty Ned gathered wood for the fire.

"No need to rig the fly", the boss drover said." "It's goin' to be a fine night".

"Goin' to cook anything?", Crocodile queried. "Not much ready. We cleaned up the damper and junk at dinner time".

"Let's think about a liquid supper", Rusty Ned grinned. "There's a couple of tins of bully beef, and we can soon knock up a johnny-cake later".

Carmody threw down the bumper of his cigarette, and cast a suspicious glance at the shanty. "Rough lookin' joint", he observed.

"We're used to rough places", Ned said. "Let's try 'er out".

The closer the drover got to the shanty, the less appealing it appeared. It seemed to lean in several directions at once, due to rotting blocks sinking ever deeper into the sandy soil that could never be a sound foundation for any building. The windows, long ago broken in drunken brawls, gaped glassless. A large dog of many breeds, every bone in its emaciated body straining at its dehydrated pelt, eyed the drovers with a savage, famished expression. Two large cats, rivaling the dog in condition, added to the fact that an acute shortage of animal sustenance existed.

Above the doorway was nailed a piece of rust-pitted tin, on which had been painted the words, "CHEEP GROG HERE". It hung so far over the sill that Carmody had to bend his great length almost double to enter the gloomy bar.

Behind the scarred counter stood an unshaven fat man, in a shirt that had once been white, but was now multi-coloured with grease and liquor stains. Mine host hawked and spat into a large biscuit-tin that was half filled with sawdust, then turned a suspicious gaze on his customers. His croaky voice was no more engaging than his appearance.

"Wot yer drinkin?".

"Three beers", Rusty Ned ordered. "Hope they're cold".

"Where d'yer think yer are, the North Pole". The publican's voice was an offended whine. "Nothin' on tap. Only bottles".

"Well, give us three bottles", Ned said resignedly.

"That'll be fifteen bob", said the fat man, making no effort to fill the order. Ned's face fell.

"Fifteen bob!! Why it's only one and nine a bottle anywhere in the bush!".

"This ain't anywhere in the bush, mate. It's right 'ere, and right 'ere it's five bob a bottle".

Ned hesitated, then thirst overcame thrift. Gloomily he dropped a pound note on the counter, three bottles of beer were produced, and change slapped on the bar.

"Hey, look 'ere", Ned snapped. "You only gimme four bob change".

The fat man peered at the money and added another

shilling. "So I did mate. An honest mistake. It's a terrible handicap to have weak eyesight".

"Good thing there's nothin' wrong with mine", Ned said pointedly. "How about openin' the bottles?".

Mine host remained unmoved. "That's one and six extra. Uncorkin' fee is sixpence a bottle."

"We can handle it ourselves, mate". Carmody produced a scratched and dented tobacco tin. A gleam of what could only be disappointment showed in the publican's eye as Black Jack expertly sprung the caps of the bottles. Footsteps sounded on the unsound floor, and a gaunt and faded-looking woman appeared in the hallway at the rear. Carmody appraised her with sad, shrewd eyes, and decided she was the cook, and possibly wife or mistress to mine host.

"Supper is on in half-an-hour", she said. "Do you men wish to stay?"

"Thanks, but we got plenty of tucker at the camp", Ned said quickly, remembering the cost of the beer. The woman retreated, and Carmody handed his almost empty bottle to Crocodile Jones.

"Guard it with yer life, mate. It's worth more than gold", he said, then addressed the publican. "Where's the dunny, mate?".

"Out the side door and down past the kitchen".

Carmody went through the door and headed along the side of the building. Ahead the leaning outhouse sagged like a boxer on the verge of a knockout, its splintered door hanging on a single hinge, acute evidence of the decay that surrounded the place. The only sign of life was the ribby yellow dog, trotting in the direction of a dense clump of trees. Then as Carmody drew level with the open kitchen window, a tantalising aroma smote his nostrils. Furtively he thrust his head through the aperture and surveyed the room's interior.

The kitchen was deserted, but on a table near the window sat a large enamel dish containing the biggest and brownest meat-pie that the ringer's eyes had ever beheld, and from it rose the appetising smell that had first caught

146

his attention. Ears alert for any intruder, he reached a
long arm through the window and siezed the pie.

★　★　★　★　★　★

"I just get a bare livin' here", the fat publican said
sadly. "The blokes around never have much money, so a
bloke has to sell the grog cheap to make any profit. You
coves think me prices are dear, but just remember I got to
maintain the buildin', keep it lookin' spic and span. A
tidy pub with a clean appearance is what I try to have, my
oath".

"Just at present you ain't havin' much success",
Rusty Ned said.

An aggrieved expression crossed the fat man's bloated face. "All the place needs is a few minor repairs", he
stated sourly, then his attention was claimed by a sudden
hurrying of footsteps outside the bar, and Carmody re-
entered at almost a run. He waved a long spidery arm at
the publican, his voice rising to a yell.

"Hey, boss!! A big yeller dog just jumped out the
kitchen winder with a pie in its mouth. I sung out for him
to drop it, but he kept goin' inter that patch of scrub over
to the left".

With a savage oath the publican bolted through the
door, and could be heard uttering yells that grew fainter
as he drew further away. Carmody disposed of his remaining beer in a long, glugging gulp, then slid silently
behind the bar and obtained three bottles from the goodly
supply under the counter. The sawdust in the spittoon
neatly covered the three empties, also the stoppers from
the full ones.

"Bargain price", Crocodile cackled. "Didn't take
yer long to cut the costs, Jack".

When the fuming landlord returned, he found the
three drovers seated on the long bench near the door,
happily sipping. Mine host dried his sweating forehead on
a dirty bar-towel. His voice dripped self-pity.

"Trouble is I'm an animal lover. Too bloody fond of
animals. That there dorg's got no bloody gratitude. I look

after him, feed him on the bloody best, and plenty of it. And what does he do? Steals me pie off the table. That's me reward for lookin after him and keepin' him in good condition".

"He's in good condition alright", Ned said acidly. "Good racin' condition".

"No chance of gettin' it back now", the fat man moaned. "You blokes want another beer? Yer awful slow drinkers".

"I've had plenty", Crocodile said, grinning. "Any more and I'd be drunk".

"Me too", Ned agreed, while Carmody nodded and smiled his slow smile.

A light patter of feet sounded on the verandah, and the yellow dog appeared in the doorway, a living portrait of abject poverty and starvation. With a howl of rage the publican lumbered from behind the bar, waving the bar-rag at the offending canine, sending it yelping to the rear of the building. "Orrible ungrateful bludger", he panted. "I oughta shoot him".

"He looked pretty empty", Carmody observed. "Pie didn't fill him up much".

"I'll fill him with a charge of shot one day. Trouble is I'm an animal lover. Can't bear to hurt 'em. Always kinds to 'em and they don't appreciate it".

Rusty Ned finished his beer and stood up. "Time to go", he announced. "Thanks for the cheap beer'.

The sarcasm went over the publican's head. "Don't fergit to tell yer mates", he requested. "Yer can recommend me place for cheap booze and quick and clean service."

"We can do that", Crocodile cackled, "if yer pay us sixpence a head recommendin' fee".

With an affronted look mine host watched the drovers move off in the direction of their camp.

* * * * * *

"Think he'll miss the three bottles we lifted?", Crocodile queried.

"Don't think so", Carmody replied. "Look how he swallered the yarn about the pie".

"The pie!" Rusty Ned exclaimed in a puzzled voice. "Didn't the dog get the pie?"

"No chance", Carmody said, drawing on his thin cigarette." I shoved the pie up on the roof of the kitchen. After dark I'll sneak back and capture it. Teach the fat bludger not to overcharge".

"Jesus, what a beaut move!" Ned stared at Carmody with open admiration. "Was the pie a good 'un?"

"It looked bloody bonzer", Carmody replied.

The camp was reached, and Crocodile built up the fire and swung the billy." No need to cook nothin'," the old man decided. "The pie'll be a feed on its own. I'll warm 'er up in the camp oven. And let me tell yers, I'm reely lookin' forward to it".

"My oath, you ain't the only one", Rusty Ned said as he licked his chops in anticipation.

The sombre darkness of the bush closed in as the drovers drank tea and smoked, then Carmody lifted his long length like an emu arising from the nest, and throwing his cigarette butt into the fire, went off silently towards the shanty.

There was a light shining through the glassless windows, and a babble of voices announced that several drinkers were at the bar. Noiseless as a snake Carmody slid along the wall until he reached the kitchen window, where a low-turned lamp shone dimly. Reaching over the broken guttering, Carmody's exploring hand found the pie-dish, lifting it carefully. It seemed extremely light to his touch, and with sinking heart he realised it was empty. There was an almost inaudible sound on the roof, and looking up he saw a pair of green eyes regarding him balefully. There was a soft thud, followed by another, as the gorged cats sprang to the ground and scuttled into the night.

* * * * * * *

"I brought the dish along", Carmody said sadly.

150

"But that's our share of it. It was an oversight of mine, not rememberin' the cats".

"How unlucky can yer be", Crocodile said mournfully, and began fishing potatoes from a pack-bag.

"Bloody cats", Rusty Ned said dolefully. "I'd like to drown the bastards. Honest men ain't got a chance these days".

"That's right", Crocodile said. "It's rogues like that publican that get on in the world. If you blokes can wait a while I'll knock up a ragout of some sort". He began dropped peeled potatoes into the pot where the bully beef simmered. Suddenly Rusty Ned cracked a dry mirthless laugh.

"Yer know, Jack, it ain't often yer take on a job and fail to do it. But yer can't expect to win all the time, so let's not worry about it. We got the fat bludger's pie-dish, and we got him for three bottles of beer. So why worry over a small oversight".

Carmody lit a thin cigarette, his long face more gloomy than ever as he recalled the tantalising odour that had risen from the pie." "It was a big oversight", he remarked sadly. "A bloody big oversight. My oath it was".

So Hard the Pavement

As Ned climbed down from the mail-lorry the baby awoke and began to cry. It was wet and smelly, and it urinated suddenly, the thin, sour torrent running over Ned's arm and spilling on the dusty red ground. Ned swung the worn suitcase and small Gladstone bag down with his free arm, then dug in his pocket and produced three florins, which he handed to the driver.

"Thanks, Chicka", he said, smiling through a grimy stubble of red beard. The train-trip from Sydney had been long and exhausting, capped by the thirty mile journey on the bumping mail-lorry. The tall shearer and his tiny charge were both in need of prolonged ablutions.

"Thanks Ned", "Chicka" Lewis pocketed the coins, his eyes on the howling baby. "Little bugger's got bloody good lungs".

Ned made no reply. Catching up the cases he moved in the direction of the hotel, and Chicka resignedly put the lorry in gear and rattled off noisily towards the post-office. Wonder what's the strength of it, he thought. Long bastard was awful close all the way in. I'll find out soon enough anyway. A secret can't be kept in a place like Kikkajikalong

Ned crossed the road to the hotel with long, unhurried strides, the baby yelling with all the power of its small lungs. The noise drew the attention of several women who were gossiping in front of the grocery store, and their faces registered amazement as Ned disappeared into the bar.

Pat Fagin looked up as Ned's long shadow darkened the doorway. The publican's jaw dropped with surprise at sight of the gun-shearer's small burden.

"Faith, Ned!". Pat's Kerry brogue was strong. " 'Tis a family ye have, so it is!"

"I'll leave me port with yer for a while, Pat", Ned said. "Pick it up later".

"For sure. Lave 'em both here. 'Tis safe they will be behind the counter".

152

"Only the suitcase", Ned replied. "I'll take the Gladstone with me".

He deposited the heavy case, then left so quickly as he entered, to be immediately accosted by the group of ladies he had noticed earlier. Foremost was Mrs. Susan Kincaid, wife of a local stockman, a notorious busybody referred to by the locals as "Sue Stickybeak". Accompanying her was the schoolmistress, Miss Joyce Trew, an ageing and angular female who had long ago abandoned hope, and Mrs. Jackson, whose husband was the local police-officer.

"Why, Ned", Sue Stickybeak gave her impression of a motherly smile that was in reality a deceitful smirk. "What a lovely baby! Whose is it?"

"It's mother's", Ned said shortly. "And I have to be on me way, good ladies. I'm runnin' late. Haven't time to gossip".

"Oh, Mr. Lynch", Miss Trew's horse-like countenance cracked in an appealing smile. "Won't you tell us who owns the little darling?"

Ned grinned, a hard grin like that of a full-fed fox. "I found it under a cabbage".

"Oh, Mr. Lynch, please don't be so childishly deceiving".

"That's what yer tell the kids at school", Ned replied. "And the deceit doesn't worry yer then. Now I'll tell yer what I got this little feller for. To make people ask questions about somethin' that's none of their business. D'yer savvy?"

There was an abrupt silence, and Ned, his grey eyes hard, stepped past the trio of offended females and strode off in the direction of old house half a mile distant, its roof just visible above the line of dense sandalwoods that glittered green in the noonday swelter. For his two questioners he cared little, but he knew that Mona Jackson, who had remained silent, would report the matter to her husband. The trooper would certainly wonder why Ned Lynch, a bachelor of forty years, had brought a baby in

153

arms back from the city. A visit from Constable Johnny Jackson could be expected shortly.

Ned was sweating hard when he entered the old weatherboard kitchen. He deposited his burdens on the wide table, removed the stove ring and placed the kettle over the open heat. The baby's howls had subsided, and from the inner house sounded the whir of a sewing machine. He called loudly, his voice echoing in the long hallway.

"I'm back, Mum, and I've got a surprise for yer".

Maggie Lynch entered from the hall, and her shocked gasp at sight of the infant brought a wry grin to Ned's face. "Little beaut, ain't he? And he's all yours, Mum. Judy even put it in writin'."

"Holy Mary!" The small grey-haired woman's Irish accent was charged with sudden emotion. "Are ye yellin' me that Judy had a baby after all these years?"

"It's fair dinkum". Ned's voice was earnest. "Take a dekko at him. The spittin' bloody image of Paddy Doonan".

"Was Doonan at the funeral, Ned?"

"Only in spirit", Ned said callously. "He died more than six months ago".

"Lord above". Maggie crossed herself. "What more is there to tell about it, Ned boy?"

"A hell of a lot". Ned rose as the kettle began to bubble loudly. "I'm famished for a feed, Mum. Take care of the kid, while I make the tea and dig out a bit of tucker. Then I'll tell it all".

There was silence as Ned ate and Maggie filled a tub and bathed the baby. It cried little, and soon was feeding from an improvised bottle and teat, its small flushed body reminding Ned of a well-cooked yabby. Maggie fondled it lovingly as she spoke. "Napkins I don't have. It's so long since there was a baby here. I'll have to be cuttin' up a flour bag".

"Plenty of dirty ones in the port at the pub", Ned said. "I kept changin' him, but it ain't a job I'm good at, and water was bloody scarce".

154

"Why did ye not bring it with ye, and leave the bag".

Ned slurped a mouthful of tea and grinned, "That little bag happens to be very bloody important, Mum".

There was the sound of approaching hooves, and Blinker, the old cattle-dog, began to bark. At the gate Ned saw Trooper Jackson dismounting from his well-groomed horse. Maggie moved to the door, the baby in her arms. "Ye may come in, Mr. Jackson", she called. " 'Tis hot in the sun".

The trooper entered and stood awkwardly, cap in hand, eyes on Ned. Johnnie Jackson was a good police-man, impartial, understanding, and never a bully. He knew Ned respected him as a man, and he was also aware that there was too much rebel Fenian blood to ever allow Ned to respect the law. Maggie broke the short silence.

"Tis wishin' to thank ye I am, for bringin' word of our daughter's death. 'Twas quick ye were last week when the wire came through".

"Just part of the job, Mrs. Lynch", Jackson replied.

"Sit down, Constable. No need to stand", Ned had risen and produced a worn kangaroo-hide wallet. "I now what yer here for, so I'll read this to yer, then yer can inspect it yerself. Mum will want to hear it".

Ned unfolded a heavy sheet of paper, and read slowly.

"I, Judith Eileen Lynch, spinster of Darlinghurst, New South Wales, do herewith declare my mother, Margaret Kathleen Lynch, widow, of Kikkajikalong New South Wales, the guardian of my illegitamate son Edward Ernest Lynch. His natural father, Patrick John Doonan, police-officer of Darlinghurst is deceased.

Signed Judith E. Lynch
in the presence of
Maria Kelly, Housewife
John A. Robinson J.P."

Jackson took the missive and scanned it slowly, then

returned it to Ned. "it's good enough for me", he said. "I wouldn't know if it complies completely with the law, but for me it's good enough".

"Thanks", Ned said. "Now the old busybodies who ran to yer will really have their noses out of joint".

Jackson flushed and dropped his gaze. His own wife had been one of the informants, and he knew that the term "busybody" fitted her well on occasions. There was nothing deceitful about Johnnie Jackson, nothing cheap or underhand, and he quarrelled frequently with his wife over her careless tongue and lack of discretion. Maggie moved to the stove, took the kettle and added hot water to the teapot.

"Will ye be havin' a drop, Mr. Jackson, before ye leave"?

"No thank you. I have a few jobs to attend to, you see. You both have my sympathy. Be sure that I will put a stop to any malicious rumours I hear".

He turned to go, and on an impulse Ned rose and offered his hand. "I thank yer and wish yer luck. I know a policeman's job ain't always easy".

Jackson shook hands warmly, then smiled broadly. "But you don't like police, do you, Ned".

"No, I reckon I don't. It's the bog Irish in me, the Fenian strain on both sides. But I reckon you're one trap that's fair dinkum".

Ned's sincerity had an obvious effect on Jackson, and his reply carried no hint of flattery. "And you're a good man Ned. As highly respected in the district as yer father was, and that's saying a lot. Never be afraid to call on me in a time of trouble".

Ned watched the trooper depart, then turned to his mother, who was fastening a flour-bag napkin around the baby's small rump. The gun-shearer smiled at the insignia on the rough cloth. "He's goin' to be a bloody advertisement for Brunton's flour".

"Ye wore the same brand yeself, Ned when ye was little", Maggie said. "it's happy I am to have a baby in the house again".

156

"Jesus, Mum! Thirteen of yer own, a grandchild reared as well, and now yer want another."

"The Irish are never happy Ned, without somethin' to strive for. Now tell me what happened in Sydney".

"It's a pretty long story, Mum". Ned began to roll a cigarette. "She looked peaceful in the coffin. The bullet wound in her temple was covered".

"Bullet wound?" Maggie's voice displayed shocked amazement.

"She shot herself, Mum. She was riddled with cancer, and the load must have got too heavy".

"Holy Mary! Twelve long years since she ran off with Doonan. Lost to us now forever". There were tears in the old woman's eyes.

"There wasn't many at the funeral". Ned lit up and blew a banner of smoke. "A pretty rough lookin' crowd. We got to face it, Mum. We know Judy was never moral, and what with poverty and the need for drink, she got pretty low down at the finish".

"Davey, me clever boy. Was he there?" There was pride in Maggie's voice as she spoke of her youngest son, who was a bank manager in Sydney, far removed from toil and harship in the bush.

"Davey was there, and he was bloody great. Paid for everything. But success has changed him a lot. As well yer know, the bankin' corporation he's in is a big one, and he's the youngest man ever appointed as a manager. He's goin up the social scale in leaps and bounds, and he didn't want it made too public that Judy was his sister. Yer can't blame him. He's got a wife and family".

"And Judy's bad name didn't worry ye, Ned".

Ned grinned. "Yer pretty hard even thinkin' it might have, Mum".

"Ah, Ned boy!" Maggie moved forward and threw her arms around her eldest son. "Would that all the men in the world were like ye. And tell me, how did ye find out about the baby".

"A woman come to me at the funeral and asked was

157

I Judy's brother, Ned. She owned the place where Judy boarded. Told me about the baby and a letter Judy left for me. Hearin' about the baby knocked me rotten, but I went with her and collected the letter. It was in a sealed envelope. There was the paper I just read appointin' you the baby's guardian, a cloak-room deposit slip from Central Railway, and a letter for me givin' a few instructions. It's goin' to upset yer, but I know you'll want to hear it''.

Ned took the letter from his wallet. What little schooling he had made his task difficult, and he read slowly, while his mother cried silently, overcome by the emotion so common to her race.

Dear brother Ned,

By the time you get this I will not be around any more. I am far gone in cancer, and growing weaker all the time. The pain is almost unbearable. But enough of self-pity. A year ago Doonan died from a heart attack, brought about by alcohol. He was always kind to me, and although I loved him I was not always faithful, and to my shame I admit it. But I reared his two children, and learned to love them greatly. Immediately after Pat's death his wife came and took the children. I couln't do anything about it, as I had no legal claim. Then found I was pregnant. It seemed unbelievable that at thirty-eight I was to have a baby, but it was true. I developed cancer soon afterwards, and soon after the birth it reached an advanced state. I was broke and the only way to keep afloat was to sell what charms I had left. It was the final degradation, but I couldn't look Mum in the face, and in a way I am glad Dad's gone and doesn't know of my downfall. It meant turning to you, Ned, for the baby's sake. You were the one we all leaned on when things were bad. You were the one who made the sacrifices. Take the enclosed cloak-room ticket and release a bag that belongs to me, and it has in it something for the baby. Be sure to get it, Ned. It is terribly important. Don't fail, whatever

158

you do. Look after the little fellow. I had him christened Edward Ernest, after you and Dad.

It's time for good-bye. The pain is pretty bad, and getting worse. I know you will do your best. Love to Mum and all the family. Your loving sister
                                    Judy.

Maggie stifled her sobs, but her voice was thick with emotion. "Lord above! Me beautiful daughter, who could av married more than once a wealthy man".

"We got to face fact, Mum". Ned's voice was grim. "Judy had a ton of beauty and brains, but no common sense. Anyway you've got the baby, and it won't go short. Judy looked after that, too". He indicated the Gladstone bag that reposed on the table.

"The bag", Maggie said. "What's in it?"

"Get ready for a surprise". Ned was smiling again. "There's three thousand quid in the bag".

For a long moment Maggie was speechless. Long inured to shortage and hardship, three thousand pounds seemed to her something that could only be acquired in a dream. Ned went on.

"Once the funeral was over I had no reason for hangin' around, so I gave Mrs. Kelly, that was the lady's name, some money for lookin' after the kid and the letter. Then I grabbed the little donkey, released the bag at Central, and got on the first train home. The bag was locked, but it wasn't hard to cut a slit in it and work the spring from inside. I had a carriage to meself for most of the way, and when I got it open there's all this dough in loose tenners".

"Lord above, Ned! How did Judy get so much money".

Ned gazed long at his mother before he replied, the cigarette drooping from the corner of his mouth. "That's somethin' we're never goin' to find out. It's plain she didn't want us to know. You know how close she always was when it came to keepin' secrets. The thing is, we've got the money, and we can invest it for him, so we don't spend it".

159

"Faith, Ned, 'tis a grand idea. But I'd surely like to know how Judy came by it".

"We might have a chance to find out in the next world, Mum. But like you, I'd like to know how she came by it".

* * * * * *

The pavement was hard, and Judy could feel the heat of the sun-blasted concrete through the worn soles of her shoes. Campbell Street was busy in the late afternoon rush, but men seeking to spend money on illicit mating were in short supply. A tide of pain rose in her stomach and receded, leaving her weak and dizzy when the spasm passed, and she knew she would shortly be forced to return to her lodgings in Darlinghurst, a walk of more than half a mile. It's getting worse, she told herself. Soon I'll be like a drought-struck bullock. Get down on this hard old pavement and never get up. I'll have to call on Ned before it's too late. I can't go home and face Mum after what I've done for a living lately. I know she'll take the baby if Ned comes and gets him.

She moved slowly down the street, pausing at a shadowy doorway where a woman leaned indolently. In a cheap dress and run over shoes, peroxided hair and heavy make-up, Lillian was a walking advertisement for her profession. No application of cosmetics could hide the long razor scar on her right cheek. Her smile was warm, a contrast to the brittle voice. "Judy. Wotcher know this happy day?"

"Not much, Lil", Judy replied. "Life gets harder".

"Hard as the bloody pavement we got to walk on to get a quid, but we'll get by". Lil was always cheerful despite her degraded existence. "I wheeled a pretty good captain this morning. He felt sorry for me on account of this". She indicated her ravaged cheek. "Sometimes the scar pays off. I told him I got it in a motor accident, and the mug believed me".

"But you got it from Bluey Doakes", Judy said. "I don't know why people like him are allowed to live.

Somebody ought to murder the low bludger".

"It's got to come", Lil said. "Either him or Roths-tien's got to go. The underworld isn't big enough for two top dogs. As far as we count, one's the same as the other. Pay your cut or take the consquences".

"He's never come near me yet", Judy said.

"He will". Lillian's laugh was bitter. "You've only been on the game for a couple of months. He's saving you up for something".

"He'd better hurry", Judy said. "I won't last much longer".

"But, Judy what's going to happen to the baby?"

"I've got a brother I can depend on. He'll come. And I want to thank you, Lil, for the baby clothes you sent when you found out about him".

Lil made a deprecatory gesture. "Forget about. The devil looks after his own. All the girls on this beat threw in when they knew you'd booked a one-way ride".

Pain struck at Judy again, and she leaned against the wall. "I'm off home now. I'm pretty sick".

"Sure you can get there?" Concern showed on the scarred, raddled face.

"I'll be all right. It's not far to the bus-stop, and I've got a few bob left. Good luck, Lil".

"Don't give up Judy. And don't leave it too late to get in touch with your brother. Here comes hope". Lil made off up the street to where a group of Lascar seamen were approaching, and Judy shuddered. God, what have I come to, she thought.

★　　★　　★　　★　　★　　★

When Judy arrived at her lodgings she found the baby bathed and sleeping, and his newly-washed gar-ments hanging on the line. Mrs. Kelly was a typical slum woman, kind in trouble, but unrelentingly hard in money matters. Her husband worked in a brewery, and invested most of his wages on his employer's product. The old woman was the strength of the partnership. She greeted Judy in voluble tones.

161

"I've take care of little Ned, and his clothes are washed. So you can take a rest, for you look something that's just escaped from a coffin. And I must remind you that your rent is overdue, so please think about it. Also, a man came and asked for you to-day. Not a very nice man".

"Who was it", Judy asked.

"None other than Hobo Bates, watchdog for Bluey Doakes. Said to tell yer to be in the Tradesman's Arms tomorrow at ten o'clock".

So it's come, Judy thought. On top of everything I've got gangsters to worry about. Lil was right, when you get this far down there's no escape.

"I wonder what he wants", Judy said aloud, and Mrs. Kelly's reply was swift.

"I don't know, Judy. And I don't wish to know. Bluey Doakes is bad news, and I'll say this much, girl. Tread carefully".

Judy went to her cheerless little room, taking care not to wake the sleeping baby. Taking the bottle of cheap wine from under the commode, she poured a glass and drank quickly, then sank down on the bed. After a short time the pain grew dull, and she was able to concentrate on the matter that was too swiftly coming to hand. I'll go to the pub tomorrow and meet Doakes, she decided. He's sure to find me if I don't and at best I can live only a little longer. I'll stand up to him like Dad would. He can't kill me any deader than the cancer's going to. And there's the baby's future to be thought of.

She rose as night was falling, saw that the baby was awake and kicking his small feet in the air. She carried him down the rickety stair to where Maria Kelly prepared tea for her husband, who was doubtless dallying at the Evening Star Hotel. Judy prepared a bottle, fed her restless charge and watched him sink back into sleep. After returning him to his cot, she took a heavy sheet of notepaper and a pen, and wrote slowly and carefully. Satisfied with the result, she decended the stair again, and

162

handed the missive to her landlady. "I need a witness for this, Mrs. Kelly", she said. "Would you sign it, pleases?"

The big woman read slowly, and a smile broke on her hard face. "It's a good idea,", she said. "And we better make a sure thing of it. Old Robertson in the store across the road is a J.P. We'll get his signature as well".

"A wise move", Judy said thankfully. "Now it's a matter of getting word to Ned".

* * * * * *

There were no customers in the shabby parlour of the Tradesman's Arms when Judy entered, but several broken lives lined the public bar in a sick parade. She had scarcely sat down when Doakes joined her at the table, his feral countenance under a head of coarse red hair reminding Judy of a hungry tiger-cat. The lapel of his loose fitting jacket bulged slightly on the left side, denoting the presence of a gun, and Judy knew the razor would also be in easy reach. Doakes wasn't going to be left at the post if Lew Rothstein, his gangland rival, decided to introduce battle tactics. He was careful to sit where he could keep an eye on the door. He wasted no time.

"You ain't been payin' yer protection dues, young lady. Why?"

Judy had been mesmerised by the gangster's presence at first, but a stab of pain rocked her, and she realised that anything the hoodlum might do could not make the situation any worse. She looked him straight in the eye as she spoke.

"Nobody told me I had to pay anything".

"All the girls pay Bluey". The gangster grinned like a starved shark. "Sooner or later they all pay".

"Except Rothstein's girls", Judy said.

Doakes flashed an ugly scowl. "Rothstein's goin' to be taken care of soon".

"By who?" Judy taunted. "He's a dead shot. I don't think you'd be game to have it off with him unless you had your watchdogs along".

163

A homicidal light sprang up in Doakes' eyes. He leaned forward and pointed a hairy forefinger at Judy. "You're a cheeky little trollop", he grated. "Now let me tell yer somethin'. I know all about yer. Yer dyin' with cancer, so yer think yer can afford not to be scared. Now just remember the kid yer got by that drunk copper. There's a lot of things a baby can die from. Bite on that".

A cold terror gripped Judy then. Doakes had read her like a race-book. "You wouldn't dare", she whispered. "You wouldn't dare to kill a baby".

"Don't bet on it", Doakes said grimly. "But yer don't have to fear anything if yer prepared to do a simple little job for me. If yer do it, fifty quid in yer hand and the protection dues wiped. It's dead easy".

"Why me?" Judy asked, her scared voice almost inaudible.

"Because you'll soon be dead", Doakes said brutally. "Anything yer know will die with yer. And if yer say anything in the time yer got left, the nipper might disappear. But if yer do yer part, the kid remains safe and yet get fifty quid and no face decorations".

"All right. I'll do what you want if I can". Judy's hatred was strangled by fear as she thought of little Ned. "What is it".

"All yer got to do is go to Central and get a bag out of the cloak-room. An ordinary Gladstone bag. I meet yer on the corner of Castlereagh Street, near the Tivoli, and give yer the release ticket. Yer go up and get the bag and bring it here to the Tradesman's Arms. Hobo Bates will be follerin' yer to see yer do things right. Yer wait in front of the pub here until I come out. Yer hand me the bag, I hand yer fifty, and everyone's happy. Half-past seven yer meet me here. The bar will be closed, but I'll be in the foyer".

"But why", Judy said, "can't you get the bag yourself?"

"Curiosity can kill babies as well as cats". Doakes' scowl grew uglier. "What yer don't know can't hurt yer".

"All right", Judy said. "What time do I go to the
165

Tiv to get the ticket".

"Tomorrer at six o'clock".

"Why not to-day?"

"Tomorrer's more suitable. Now remember to hold yer tongue".

"Just one little thing", Judy said. "I'm flat broke, and I'll need money for bus fares".

Doakes produced a large wallet and drew out a ten-pound note. "Take this now. Yer get the other forty on delivery".

Judy took the money, gripped by a terrible loathing. She watched the big mobster step into the street, cruel as an alley cat, rapacious as a jungle beast. She trembled as she thought of the threat to little Ned, realising that a child's life meant no more to Doakes than that of a stray dog. For a fleeting moment she considered going to the police, then she rejected the idea, knowing she would receive the stock answer for her type of complaint. "We can't move until he does something". That, and the knowledge that many senior police-officers battened on the harlots, caused her to change her mind quickly. By taking money from Doakes she had placed herself in his power. There was no escape now. A soft step sounded, and she looked up to see Lillian approaching her table. The scarred face wore a look of cheerful defiance, a shield against blows delivered by an unkind society. Judy wondered how Lillian consistently mustered the courage to fight unequal odds.

"Judy. Watcher know this happy day?"

"I saw Doakes come out the door", Lil said looking behind her furtively. "Did he want you?"

"He did", Judy nodded. "Told me from now on I have to pay up".

"I knew he would". Lil's tones was positive. "But Rotherstein's waitin' his chance. The fight gets closer every day".

"It's a wonder they don't join forces", Judy said. "But let's hope the bastards kill each other. What caused all the hatred in the first place?".

"They both want the lot", Lil said. "But the real hate started when Chow Blake pulled off the Haymarket robbery. He was one of Rothstein's gang, and he got clean away with three thousand. The cops didn't have a lead, didn't have a suspect. Two nights later Chow was shot dead in Orwell Lane. He didn't have a razoo on him when the cops got there".

"I remember", Judy said. "The papers were full of it".

"Then the rumour started". Lil was warming to her tale. "Chow is supposed to have deposited the loot in a Gladstone bag at Central Station".

"Wait, Lil. I'm dry. Let's have drink". Judy's heart had begun to thump.

"Gin", Lil said, and Judy went to the bar and returned with two glasses of the clear liquid. Lil sipped and continued her tale.

"I don't know how true this is. But the loot hasn't turned up. And there's a big chance that if the cloak-room ticket hasn't got lost, somebody's got it and is waitin' for things to cool off to collect. And it could well be one of the coves we just mentioned. And rumour says our protector shot Blake. You can bet the Jew knows it. What's wrong Judy? Yer look awful pale".

"I've got the pain again", Judy said untruthfully. It was Lil's amazing story that had jolted her emotions. She gulped the gin, and the fiery liquid sent a flush to her chalky face. "I'll be alright in a moment".

"Well take care. I have to leave now. Haven't got a sprat, so I better find a starter quick".

She went through the door into the man-made jungle that provided her survival. Hardly aware of her departure, Judy moved to the bar and bought another gin. She had almost confided in Lil, but fear of Doakes had tied her tongue. Now she was glad that she had kept silent. It has to be true, she thought. Doakes must have murdered Blake and taken the cloak-room ticket from him. Now I'm to be the cover. Rothstein is sure to have a man watching Central, but who'd suspect a down and out

167

whore to be the contact. Once Bluey gets all that money he can do a flit.

She took a cab to her lodgings and paid the rent owing, which was accepted without question. How it had been acquired did not trouble Mrs. Kelly. She had lived most of her life in peace, the fact due to her ability to mind her own business. Never look a gift horse in the mouth was a safe motto in the slums.

Judy went to her room and sank down on the ricketty bed. The pain was minimal, and she rested uneasily, her mind on the task that faced her on the morrow, the money a tantalising thing foremost in her mind. All for a man who was too bad to be alive, and I'm the poor mug who gets it for him, she thought. Then the worn Gladstone bag on top of the doorless wardrobe caught her eye, and she pictured its duplicate in the cloak-room at Central. One filled with her late lover's old clothes, the other holding a small fortune. The glimmering of a plan began to grow in her mind, and soon the possibility registered clearly, giving her new hope. I'll do it she decided, but I'll have to wait until dark.

She undressed slowly, her wasted arms reminding her of two thin carbeen boughs. The pain came, and a dizziness gripped her. She took out the wine bottle, took a long drink and then stretched out on the bed. There was ladanum in a jar under the commode, but she was aware that the task coming to hand forbid the use of the drug. The room grew dark as rain-clouds gathered over the city, and she slept.

Night had fallen when she awoke, and a dull, slow rain misted the grimy window. The baby was crying, and she dressed quickly and carried him downstairs to the kitchen, the weakness in her muscles more apparent than ever. Maria Kelly was washing up while her husband snored in the old armchair near the gas stove. A pot of stew steamed on the grid, and Judy suddenly realised it was more than twenty-four hours since she had eaten. Moving to the stove she filled a plate and ate slowly, the warm hash giving her a false feeling of renewed strength,

168

while Mrs. Kelly surveyed her with shrewd, searching eyes.

" 'Tis in hospital you should be, girl", the big woman said in a sympathetic voice.

"Not while ever I can stand", Judy said. "I have to go out to-night, Mrs. Kelly. Will you look after Ned, please. I'll bath and feed him before I go".

"You can leave his needs to me. And have you got word to your brother yet?. 'Tis a walkin' skeleton ye are, with a face like a ghost".

"There's something important I have to do yet", Judy said. "If anything bad should happen, you have Ned's address. I'm putting complete trust in you".

"And safe it is". Mrs. Kelly was smiling now. "Good luck, girl".

Judy ascended the stairs, searched the clothing in the worn Gladstone for identification marks, then dropped the bag though the window, hearing it land with a soft thud on the gravel of the small backyard. She returned to the kitchen, bid her landlady good-night, and went out the back door. Quickly retrieving the bag, she followed the narrow lane to Riley Street, keeping to the shadows as much as possible. As the rain increased in tempo, she hailed a cab, and gave the Hotel Sydney as her destination, disembarking unnoticed in the late rush. She paid the fare from the dwindling money supplied by Doakes, and began the furtive approach to Central station, mingling unobtrusively in the hurrying crowd.

There were two women in the cloak room, and they paid her no attention as she deposited the bag, took the ticket and departed. The pains were increasing as she made her way back to the Sydney, and a sickening weakness flooded dizzily over her, but the thought of little Ned and his helplessness bolstered her will to go on. She got to Campbell street as a cruising cab turned the corner from Pitt.

She reached her lodgings as the rain became heavier, the drops bouncing on the pavement. The old house was in darkness, and it was with extreme difficulty that she climbed the stair. Once in her room she saw that the baby was sleeping peacefully. Taking a big dose from the laudanum bottle, she collapsed fully clothed on the bed, completely at the end of her tether now, aware that time was running out too quickly.

* * * * * *

Day broke sullen under a cloudy sky, and she woke from a slumber filled with drug induced dreams. The rest had given her strength, but she knew that any exertion would bring on a recurrence of the pain and weakness that were close to devouring her for good. She attended to the baby's needs, drank a glass of wine laced with laudanum, and lay down again, husbanding her strength for the ordeal that was to come at nightfall. Slowly the long day passed as she slept fitfully, weird nightmares invading her mind in a phantom parade. It was the baby's cries that woke her minutes before the old alarm-clock jangled at a quarter to five. Descending to the kitchen she placed Ned in Mrs. Kelly's care. The old woman took charge without question, and Judy stepped forth on to the unrelenting pavement, calling down a cab to carry her to her date with destiny.

* * * * * *

There was a large crowd waiting for doors to open at the Tivoli, despite the adverse weather conditions, for the current show was a popular one. On the outskirts of the gathering, hat pulled low and coat-collar turned up, Bluey Doakes lurked as unobtrusively as possible, his henchman Hobo Bates standing in the shadows close by. It was a few minutes past six.

A block away on Elizabeth Street, Judy Lynch paid off the cabbie, then entered the nearby telephone booth. Lifting the headset she called the Gaiety Club, a night spot where Lew Rothstien could be found every evening after five o'clock. A female voice answered.

"Gaiety Club. Yes, Mr Rothstien is here. He's pretty busy. Who is calling?"

Judy steeled herself. I mustn't fail now, she thought,

170

this is the important part of the plan. "Please tell him quietly that one of the girls wants to speak to him about a bag of money".

There was a silence of more than a minute, then a sibilant voice came over the wire. "Rothstein here. Who are you?"

"I'm one of Doakes' girls". Judy spoke slowly and clear. "I'm sick of being beaten and ill-used. I got it from one of the other girls. She's just released a bag from Central with a lot of money in it. She's meeting Doakes at the Tradesman's Arm's at half-past seven to give him the bag".

"Who are you?...Wait...Wait on..." Remaining anonymous, Judy dropped the instrument on the hook, and set her shaky steps in the direction of the Tivoli. He'll come, she thought. He's too money-hungry to let a chance go by.

*　*　*　*　*　*

Doakes was becoming increasingly impatient as the minutes fled by. This little caper was one that he couldn't afford to lose. He had been lucky to have a tail on Chow Blake when the hoodlum had deposited the bag, and he knew without doubt that it must contain the proceeds of the Haymarket robbery. He had murdered Blake in the darkness of Orwell Lane. He had been lucky to find the release tab on Blake's body, and to make a quick getaway. But somehow the rumour had got around that the money was in Central clock-room. Perhaps the police were waiting for the bag to be collected, perhaps Rothstein was waiting too. Chances he had to take. If the chromo got picked up, he had lost. Fear for her brat would make the woman hold her tongue, but the prize would be gone. At least he had better than an even chance. He jerked up from his slouch as he saw Judy hurrying across Castlereagh Street. She halted outside the perimeter of light flung by the street lamp, and Doakes moved to her side.

"Yer late", he growled. "Here's the ticket. Now yer

know what to do. Dont try any monkey tricks. Bates will be right behind yer".

Wordlessly Judy took the ticket, her whole being filled with a monstrous loathing for Doakes and all his kind. She made off down Campbell Street, turned left at Pitt and began the slow climb up the hill to Central Railway. And she knew without looking back that twenty yards behind her, Hobo Bates strolled.

The pain gripped her as she reached the crest of the rise, almost doubling her over, and for a long minute she stood gasping. Then she found the strength to go on, the hard pavement stones jarring her feet with every step. She reached the cloak-room counter and stood trembling as an attendant moved forward. Under his enquiring gaze she took from the pocket of her shabby coat the ticket that represented the bag of old clothes deposited the night before. Without a word he handed the bag over the counter, and Judy surreptitiosly tore off the duplicate ticket that was glued to the worn leather. Heart beating like a drum, she went out and made for the taxi rank, Bates keeping his distance behind her. Suddenly she noticed that the clock was chiming the hour of seven. No cabs were on the rank, and for ten long minutes she waited before a taxi drew to a halt. Turning, she called to Bates.

"Come on, or we'll be late".

The hoodlum came at a lumbering run, pushing into the rear seat beside Judy, who held the bag firmly on her lap.

"I thought we were goin' to walk", Bates growled.

"I'm not up to it, besides I don't want to be late", Judy replied.

The rain descended in a sharp, blinding shower, and the traffic slowed to a crawl. Progressing at a snail's pace they reached the corner of Oxford and Palmer Street, where Bates stopped the cab and paid the driver. "We walk from here", he said, dropping back several yards behind Judy. A block ahead the lights of the Tradesman's Arms shone dully through the thin mist of rain. The bar

172

was closed, and the street almost deserted, except for a big Buick that was parked on the opposite side to the pub, where a lane ran at right angles to Palmer Street. Judy knew the car belonged to Bluey Doakes. Her heart sank. Rothstein hadn't taken the bait after all. She stepped into the dimly lit foyer.

Doakes appeared from behind the staircase, big and terrifying. She handed him the bag without a word as Bates appeared at the entrance. "It's O.K.", he said softly, "She done it fair dinkum".

With a trembling hand she took the money offered by Doakes, watched him step from the foyer. What will happen now, she thought. When he finds what's in it. Terror gripped her. Then she saw Rothstein.

The Jew had stepped from the dark cul-del-sac at the rear of the Buick, and he had a levelled revolver. His hat was pulled low, throwing the thin Semitic face into shadow. The sibilant voice was clear.

"Drop the bag, Doakes!"

For a fraction of a second Doakes hesitated. Then he dropped the bag.....and reached inside his coat for a weapon.

From the safety of the foyer, Judy's terrified eyes saw the semi-darkness in front of Rothstein riven by a stripe of fire. She heard the splat of the bullet, saw Doakes go down like a heart-shot kangaroo. Rothstein lowered the pistol and stepped forward, and suddenly Doakes was on his knees and firing, the shots a staccato roll. The Jew was flung against the door of the Buick by the force of the bullets. Doakes rose almost to his feet, staggered, then pitched forward on his face. His fingers twitched, released the smoking gun. The long awaited battle for the Czardom of Sydney's underworld was over and there were two losers.

From doorways on both sides of the street people were appearing, staying close to the walls, not eager to approach too closely the scene of the affray. Then the pound of heavy boots announced the arrival of two police officers. Of Hobo Bates there was no sign, and Judy realised

173

that the hoodlum had lacked the courage for a confrontation with firearms. He had fled.

She saw one of the policemen pick up the Gladstone bag with it's worthless contents, and she pressed the small handerchief in her pocket, drawing strength from the knowledge that in one corner was tied the ticket that opened the door to fortune. The crowd was growing larger, and slipping silently through the motley gathering, she began to walk slowly in the direction of Oxford Street, her legs almost too weak to support her. She reached the long avenue just as the lights of a cab showed through the rain.

When Judy left the taxi it was only a maximum effort of will that she was able to remain on her feet. The old dwelling was in darkness but she felt her way silently to the stair and began the painful ascent. Half way up she was forced to rest as the terribie crab closed its claws on her stomach. She leaned grasping against the bannister, then the spasm passed. Weakly she climbed to her room and switched on the light. Taking out the wine bottle she took a long drink then sank down on the bad while across the room little Ned slept soundly in his cot. A half hour passed before she could rise and it was then only with great difficulty. Taking pen and paper from a draw she seated herself by the lopsided dressing-table and began to write.

* * * * * *

"What I can't work out", said Police-sergeant Reddy," is what sparked the fight".

"Shure now, its been comin' for a long time", replied Constable Corrigan, his eyes on the lights of the departing ambulance. "'Tis well rid of such trash the world is".

"It saves a lot of trouble when gangsters kill one another", Reddy said. "I can't see where the bag comes in. It's full of dirty clothes". He hefted the shabby Gladstone.

"I'd surely say it has no bearin' on things", Corrigan said with dogmatic confidence. "Here comes the paddy-wagon. Lets be off and makin' our report before the vultures from the press get here."

★ ★ ★ ★ ★ ★

Judy placed the note for her landlady beside the carefully sealed envelope addressed to her brother. On top of it she put the four ten-pound notes she had received from Doakes. She had no regret for her treachery. They're better dead, she told herself. They're gone, but others will take over. Crime will go on, girls like Lillian will be walking that hard old pavement while ever the world is what it is. She read the note again, written by a shakey hand, but legible.

> I am saying farewell, dear Mrs Kelly. The pain is too great for me to wait any longer. The money is yours for looking after the baby. Please take care of him until my brother gets here. I know he will come. Make sure he gets the letter. Good luck always.
>
> Judy.

She rose, drank long from the wine bottle, and leaned over the cot, bidding a silent good-bye to the sleeping child. Thinking back to the days of her own childhood, she forced back the tears. "I've got to go through", she said aloud. "Limpy Lynch reckoned he never reared a squib, and I'm his daughter, through if he was alive he'd have no cause to boast about me".

Moving to the commode, she took from the drawer the small calibre pistol that had been Doonan's. She seated herself, still hesitant, then pain racked her cancerous body, almost causing her to cry out, and the agony added to her resolve.

The small sound of the shot was muffled by the downpour on the roof, the heavy clouds bringing a deeper darkness to the dark unyielding city. Hard was the pavement, and soon the only sounds were the noise of ceaseless traffic, and the steady beat of the rain.

175

Uncle Harry Returns

Keith Garvey

The Oxen Operators

Just recently when a patient in Manly hospital, I read in the Sydney paper several reports about an unknown person (described rather dramatically as "A fiend") who was shooting stray dogs and cats in the Lewisham area. I was greatly amused at this emotional and likely exaggerated blather by the press regarding the destruction of a few useless and possibly starving animals. It caused me to think back to the bushmen of my father's generation, the hardships they endured, and the harsh treatment perpetrated on their working animals in order to survive. Some of their actions would send R.S.P.C.A. devotees to the razor of the river. I will quote an example, an unusually humourous though brutal experience when I was a schoolboy in the north-west of New South Wales.

My Uncle Harry was a bullocky. So was his brother-in-law George ("Stevo") Stevens, but they attempted to bring some form of elegance to the profession by referring to themselves as "oxen operators".

Harry's two "polers", (the pair yoked one on each side of the waggon-pole), were bulls. Their names were Fiddler and Bandy, and Fiddler, the big red bull was well known in our village for his remarkable docility. When Harry unyoked the team he would lift any children present on to Fiddler and give them a ride. It was a common sight to see Harry leading the tractable old bull along the road with a halter, four or five children sitting one behind the other on his broad back, so there was great anxiety in my juvenile when one morning I heard Fiddler was taken ill.

The North-West was in the grip of a severe drought. All animals, particularly the working-stock, were in poor condition, and Fiddler seemed possessed of some internal malady. His stomach was swollen to an enormous size, and he would rise to his feet at short intervals, emitting painful groans. Harry and Stevo, with several other "oxen operators", were trying to diagnose Fiddler's complaint. I stood well back, for when Uncle Harry and Stevo mounted any form of operation, fireworks were likely to result.

"It ain't his appendix, mate", Stevo announced. "I just give him a jab in the right flank with me whip-handle, and he took no notice".

I was greatly awed by Stevo's wisdom. At that time of my life I firmly believed a bull could suffer from appendicitis like a human.

"It ain't ploorer" (pleuro-pneumonia), said Big Jim Moffet. "His nose ain't runnin'."

"There's somthin' crossways in his guts", decided Jack Nolan.

"I think yer right, Jack", Stevo agreed. "Looks like he's constellated".

"You mean constipated", Uncle Harry corrected.

"Same thing", Stevo said. "His insides are bound up. We better give him a boogee, mate".

"Boogee" is a slang term used by bushmen to describe a bowel enema. I knew what it was, and wondered how it could be administered to a bull weighing more than a ton. I was soon to learn from Stevo. He was a short, powerful bear-like man, noted for his ruthless approach to any difficuty pertaining to his profession, and for his artistry with with bullock-whip in a tight pinch when the team was bogged and it was necessary to resort to force. Like the old British generals, a few casualities never worried him, and he at once began to give Fiddler medical aid, Stevo fashion. It was useless to think about a veterinary surgeon. There wasn't one within fifty miles.

Under Stevo's supervision a forty-four gallon oil-drum was half filled with hot soapy water, then hoisted by means of block and tackle to the limb of a nearby box-tree some ten feet high. Stevo insisted on the height. "To give the water enough pressure to go through him, mate". Stevo then attached a length of garden hose to a tap that had been conveniently fitted in the drum, and was about to commence

the operation when it was discovered that the hose was not long enough to reach the prostrate Fiddler.

"We got ter get him closer, mate", Stevo informed Uncle Harry, who placed a halter on the bull, but Fiddler was so resigned to his fate that he refused to co-operate, and lay groaning and rolling his eyes. Stevo applied a stimulant in the form of Tiger.

Tiger was Stevo's cattle-dog, a treacherous, unlovely, unsociable canine feared and hated by everybody but his owner. At a word from Stevo he slid silently to Fiddler's rear and fastened his teeth on the bull's hock. Like Lazarus rising from the dead Fiddler came to his feet and allowed himself to be led to the tree, when after a careful look behind him to see if Tiger was in attendance, he sank down groaning louder than ever.

Stevo began the preliminary performance of the operation, which consisted of inserting the hose in Fiddler's anus and thrusting energetically until a good three feet of hose-pipe had disappeared into the bull's lower intestine. "He's pretty tight in the tucker-chute, mate", Stevo announced. "Turn the tap on".

Uncle Harry complied, and the hot water began to invade Fiddler's digestive system. As his poor old stomach grew tighter, he produced groans that were supersonic beside his earlier complaints. "For Gawd's sake don't bust him, Stevo", Uncle Harry said apprehensively.

"He's right, mate. He's in the c'rect position. That's how they give it to yer in the hospital. Layin' on yer side". Stevo had once had a carbuncle lanced by a doctor, and was afterwards regarded by his mates as an authority on all matters pertaining to surgery.

Suddenly Fiddler began to resent the undignified treatment. Emitting a slobbering bellow he lurched drunkenly to his feet and staggered forward, pulling free from the hose. At that instant, without any authority from his master, Tiger rushed in and grabbed Fiddler by the leg. Whether the dog's disobedient action assisted Stevo's medication is difficult to say, but Fiddler's bowels acted quickly and on a grand scale. Stevo had sprang forward to grab Tiger by the tail and pull him off, and the geyser-like stream of water ejected by Fiddler's tortured digestive organs narrowly missed the chief surgeon as he dragged the dog away. The water was followed by a great quantity of foul-smelling excreta containing twigs, leaves, lumps of earth and undigested pieces of prickly pear. It was evident that during his desperate struggle for survival in the drought, Fiddler had eaten anything that looked like sustenance.

A prolonged string of agonised yelps announced that Stevo was taking disciplinary measures with Tiger for his lack of self-control. The instrument used to impart psychology to the canine mind was a heavy greenhide strap, applied externally with much vigor. Any dogs Stevo owned learned obedience sooner or later, and contrary to the belief of modern psychiatrists, grew up without inhibitions and loved their master.

By this time Fiddler had deflated to his normal size, and was his old docile self. Stevo then administered a mammoth dose of Epsom salts, "to clean him out properly, mate". Fiddler survived the ordeal, and a few days later, heavy rain fell. The stock grew strong and fat, and soon our old pet was back beside his workmate Bandy, doing his small share in the development of a young country.

Uncle Harry and Stevo and their fellow bullockies are gone from the scene, and the bullock teams are a distant memory to a few elderly people. And though they were hard brutal men, they were not callous or sadistic. Cruelty was repugnant to them, but at times it was necessary to their survival. Compare them with the scientists of our modern age, who in the name of progress have harnessed atomic power capable of bringing agonising death to millions by pressing a button. Are these men any more enlightened in the cause of Christianity and humane kindness than the "oxen conductors" of my boyhood?

MORGAN

I met him in the 1957 drought, and we finished up doing a droving job together. He was a lean sinewey bloke from somewhere on the Atherton Tablelands. You hear great old tales of how Dad and Dave behaved in the city. Morgan had never been away from the outback in his life, and when I took him to Sydney, his performance made Dad and Dave look pretty dull. And by the time we got to our lodgings at a King Street pub, my mate had formed a pretty poor opinion of city people.

"Higgerant lot of buggers, mate", in the thunderous voice he used for wheeling a breakaway. "Real higgerant. Like a mob of bad bullocks, mate. Run clean over the top of yer. Not civilised, mate".

Feeling like a lion-tamer who has allowed a particularly unruly beast to escape, I hied him off to Kings Cross, where a few schooners helped to produce his best form. "We been too long in the bush, mate", Morgan decided. "Where's these lanes yer read about where the sheilas are waitin' on the doorsteps?"

I led him down to Chapel Lane, after warning him to tread softly. On arrival the ghetto seemed deserted, except for one hefty and rather unhygenic young female, who was seated on a doorstep. "How much?" I asked.

"Two quid", she announced, running cold and predatory eyes over us. It was evident she could smell gum-leaves and hear horse-bells.

"Don't you reckon you're selling yourself short?" I kidded her. "Down in the Cross tonight you'd get more".

"Listen, mister", she said icily, "advice won't pay the rent. If you or your pal want to help me, get in here and spend a few bob".

We moved out of earshot, and I looked questioningly at Morgan, who shook his head. "Don't think so, mate",

184

he said doubtfully. "Bad class of cow. If there was a gilgai hole handy where we could take her and wash her first, I might be in it, but the country looks a bit dry round here. Can't yer find a yard with a few cleanskins in it?"

I remembered a flat in Bourke Street, where a better class chromo hung out. After knocking repeatedly for several minutes, the door was opened by a young blonde girl I had not seen on a previous visit. In a gaudy floral dressing gown she was a living advertisement for her trade. I asked for Linda the girl I knew well, and was informed that Linda was asleep, she had been working hard at dressmaking. I wondered.

"What do you do, lady", Morgan asked bluntly.

"I'm a vocalist", was the reply.

Morgan looked a bit stunned, but he stayed upright, and while he was recovering I made arrangements to meet the girls in the Mayfair lounge at eight o'clock.

Morgan was slightly intoxicated by the time we arrived early at the Mayfair. "Keep a bit quiet in here", I warned him. "This isn't the public bar at Bandywallop".

Morg was obviously amazed at the splendour of the lounge, and he shuffled his feet on the pile like a boxer using the resin-box. "Lovely soft carpets here, mate", he thundered. "Lovely soft carpets. Ain't they lovely soft carpets."

With difficulty I steered him to a table and beckoned a waiter, whose dinner suit Morg eyed with admiration. ' Yer look real tidy, mate. Just like a penguin", he informed the purveyor of drinks.

We had a beer, and I informed my mate that it was customary to tip the waiter. "We'll have another", he roared. "Call the penguin over. Hey, mate! Two more, and give us big 'uns this time. Give us big 'uns, and get one down yer own black guts".

The waiter must have had a good temper, because he served us with a knowing smile, but our table was the target of all eyes. It was easy to see that everyone considered Morgan a very unique type of Australian. To cut a long

185

story short, he finally went off with the blonde vocalist, but luckily I managed to get most of his money off him before we split up. He arrived home next morning hung-over, penniless, and obviously contented. "How did you make out with the vocalist", I asked. "Could she sing?"

"Couldn't sing, mate, but she could act", was his cryptic reply. "And she'd never been taught to tie up. She took me to her flat, and some time in the night she broke the bridle and cleared out. Glad I gave yer me roll, mate, I had none this mornin'. Come on, lets see if we can get a beer somewhere in this horrible ants nest".

As I quoted earlier, Morgan was a unique type of Australian.

The
Religious Horse-Breaker

"Do you believe in Darwin's theory of evolution", I asked Uncle Harry, or do you think the Bible is true?".

Uncle Harry hawked and spat a nicotine flavoured oyster of phlegm. "I'm a Darwin man", he announced. "You've only got to look around yer to see that a lot of blokes haven't come far since man evolved from apes. If yer doubt me, pay a visit to Canberra".

"Now I remember a cove once who went mad on religion. Every spare bob he got was donated to religious organizations. He was a big gun horse-breaker, took a lot of risks, and seemed to have no fear. He claimed if you were generous and God fearin', you could always call on the Lord for help and he'd be right on the job.

"Now this bloke, we used to call him Joggy Jackson, was breakin' in at a place near Inglewood, just above the border. One day he tackles a pretty bad horse. It could buck a house down, but Joggy soon took the kinks out of him, then yells for us to open the gate. Out in the open they race and it was apparent that the horse had a mouth as hard as a harlot's smile. Soon he was gallopin' at his top, and Joggy could neither hold nor steer him. He's headin straight for a big gum-tree with a limb stickin' out level with Joggy's head. Joggy saw he was in real trouble. It was a case of jumpin' off and possibly breakin' his neck, or stayin' on and gettin' his head knocked off.

"Just as he gets close to the limb, Joggy starts callin' on the Lord to save him". "Save me Lord, I am your servant. Save me!", he yells.

Uncle Harry paused for another spit, then continued. "It wasn't any good, nothin' supernatural happened. Joggy

188

copped the limb on the forehead and spread himself out as flat as piss on the road. He put in three weeks in hospital, and it was two months before he was back on the job. And he seemed to have changed. Whenever anyone talked religion he walked away, wouldn't discuss it at all. Then came a day when a man of the cloth comes along. I forget what church he represented, but he hit Joggy for a donation. Believe me, that Bible-banger got the shock of his life".

"Just listen for a bit, mate", Joggy says, pointin' at the sky." All me life I been supportin' the bloke who is supposed to be up there. Never knocked him back once, never asked him for anything. Now I was a good hundred yards from that tree when I called on him for a bit of help. He had plenty of time to put aside what he was doin' and come to me aid. But he didn't take a bit of notice, didn't care if I got me brains knocked out. So if that's gratitude, or Christianity, I don't want any more of it. He'll have to get along without me from here home".

Uncle Harry sat down and lit his pipe. "What became of Joggy?", I asked.

"Don't know", Uncle Harry replied. "Last I seen of him he was still horse-breakin', and puttin' in all his spare time studyin' Darwin's theory".

A Serious Breakdown

' Motor-cars", said Uncle Harry, "can be very deceivin' things. That is if yer don't understand 'em".

"They can give a lot of trouble at times", I agreed.

The old boy chewed his moustache reflectively. ' Yes, but not half as much as the hire-purchase payments", he said. "Or a serious breakdown. I well remember when I first bought me trusty old Chev Four. Back in the days when I had the bullock team, and didn't understand motors."

"I paid cash for it and drove it home, cruised about the place for a few days, then drove it into town again. We starts home about dark, and when we gets about a mile from the dwellin', the Chev gives a long splutter and rolls to a stop. We gets out, your Aunty Emma and me, and walks all round the vehicle wonderin' what can be wrong. We decides it must be a pretty serious breakdown for it to stop like it did, so we decides to walk the mile home, and come back in daylight".

"I gets up early next morning, and me two old leadin' bullocks, Plum and Pilot, are feedin' right near the house. I yokes 'em and hooks on a bar-chain, and down the road we go, drivin' the two bullocks in front of us. I hooks 'em on the Chev and they take her slowly home with the missus steerin'. We get the car to the house, but I wasn't game to try and start it, for fear I might do further damage. I sent word to town for a mechanic to come out".

' When he arrives I tell him it must be a pretty bad breakdown to cause her to stop dead. He takes a look at her, grins like a carpet snake in a fowl-yard, and pours a couple of gallons of petrol into her innards. He treads on the starter, and away she goes." "That was your serious breakdown", he says. "You drove her til she ran out of petrol".

"I was so bloody disgusted that I felt like sellin' the thing and gettin' another horse and sulky. But I decided it was better to study the mechanical monster, and try to

understand it. But I kept Plum and Pilot handy for a few weeks in case I needed 'em again".

"Do you think the fast motor-car is a benefit to the younger generation", I asked.

"Of course it is, boy", Harry announced promptly. 'Think of how it's given more scope to the medical students to study damage to the human body. And consider the jobs if provides for young blokes who aspire to be ambulance drivers, coroners and undertakers. And don't forget the girls who want to be nursing sisters. And every weekend it plays a part in keeping the country from getting over-populated".

The Saga of Bully

Many years ago when I was a schoolboy, I remember a dog Uncle Harry owned named Bully. It was a huge, unlovely canine, fierce as a panther and almost as big as a small pony, comprising a mixture of many breeds. Why the old boy was enraptured by this unspeakable hound I will never know, for it was one of the most accomplished sheep-killers I have ever encountered. But Harry, for some unstated reason, always found an excuse for Bully's sanguinary misdeeds.

One day we went fishing on a property close to the village. We had not long commenced to fish when we missed Bully, and on searching we found him eating the liver of a stud ram that he had killed. We were not game to return to the locality for weeks.

When walking beside his master near a mob of sheep, Bully would pretend not to notice them, but as soon as something caught Harry's attention, Bully would disappear, and the inevitable result would be a sheep killed or badly mangled. Harry always forgave this blood-thirsty creature, until the day we went up to Stevo's place to collect a lamb to kill for the larder.

Stevo had several fat crossbreeds running in a small paddock, and Harry and I drove up in the old Chev, with Bully sitting in the back looking demure and harmless, but no doubt fashioning his murderous plans. On arrival we captured the lamb and tied it up in the back seat of the Chev, then accepted Stevo's offer of 'a cuppa tea, mate'. We had forgotten Bully, who had walked off to visit Stevo's dogs.

We were just finishing off the cup of tea when Stevo sat up with an alarmed expression and pointed to the car. "Look at the way the Chev's shakin' mate", he said. "That sheep must be kickin' a lot".

The old car was swaying up and down on it's springs, and Harry bounded to his feet as he realised what was

194

happening. Displaying great speed for a man of his years, he raced to the car. Sure enough, Bully was in the back seat eating prime hogget. The rear seat of the vehicle was splattered with blood, and the dead lamb almost mincemeat. Harry dragged Bully out, still hanging to the sheep.

"Get yer rifle, Stevo", Harry yelled. "I'll shoot the bludger".

"Rifle's out at the camp with the waggon, mate. I can knock him on the head with the crank-handle", Stevo offered as he flourished the instrument.

This was a bit too brutal for Harry, but he compromised by holding Bully by the scruff of the neck while Stevo administered chastisement with a piece of chain, the heavy wallops having little effect on the wayward hound, for a week later the local dairy farmer caught Bully devouring a poddy calf he had killed. Unforturnately for the dog, the farmer had a rifle and was a good shot. Vale Bully, to the benefit of stock-owners.

This repulsive hound must have possessed a striking personality, for Uncle Harry always hated sheep-killers, but could find no fault in his pin-up dog. For years afterwards he lamented the death of Bully, always overlooking his many faults while extolling and exaggerating his completely non-existant virtues.

The Fox and The Fleas

"How is it that you never find fleas on a fox?", I asked Uncle Harry. "He's about the only canine creature that doesn't have them".

Harry lit his pipe and gave me a knowing look. "My boy", he announced, the fox has a very skilful way of disposing of his fleas. And I am one of the few men who witnessed the cunning little fellow at the job. I don't often tell the story, as it seems impossible, and people would disbelieve me. I would hate to be thought a fibber".

"Come on, tell me", I requested, knowing the lie couldn't be any bigger than others Harry had told me.

"There was a terrible drought on", the old boy began. "It was in 1902, when I was a young fella doin' a bit of fox huntin'."

"One hot day I was walkin' through a belt of lignum near a creek, and up ahead of me I sees a fox in terrible discomfort, twistin' and rollin' and scratchin', and I realised he was covered in fleas. He was out of range of the old shot-gun, so I waited and after a while he got up and trotted towards the creek. I sneaked up usin' a tree for cover, and peerin' over the bank, I saw foxy go to the carcass of a dead sheep and pull a big mouthful of wool out. Then he goes to the water's edge and starts backin' in an inch at a time.

"Soon he was half submerged, and the part of him that was out of the water was swarmin' with fleas, all racin' forward to excape drownin'. At last there's only foxy's head stickin' out, and the fleas have all run onto the wool in his mouth. He keeps sinkin' down until only his nostrils are showin', and every flea has climbed to what they thought was safety. Then presto!!. Foxy drops the wool, swims out, and all the fleas drown! A great bit of work.

"And I suppose then you shot him", I said.

Uncle Harry puffed a cloud of smog, and showed his only two teeth in a grin that was hard and cunning.

"No mate, I didn't. That little fox was so resourceful that I decided to spare his life. I thought how great it would be if mankind could work out a way to rid the world of certain fleas that swarm and are immune to eradication. You get me, boy".

Amazing Acceleration

"The modern motor-car is a big improvement on earlier models", I remarked to Uncle Harry as he polished the duco on his old 1926 Chevrolet. The vehicle looked like it's owner. Rather dated.

"I don't agree", the old boy said as he felt in his pocket for his pipe. "It's only a fallacy. Modern drivers think they go faster, but they really don't. This Chev of mine without doubt had greater acceleration in it's hey-day than all your modern jobs".

"On what do you base your supposition?", I queried.

"It ain't supposition, it's fact", Harry said dogmatically. "I well remember a day many years ago when I was coming home from Moree to Pallamallawa. As you know, the Railway Hotel is the last pub on the road to Pally, and four miles further on, where the highway swings in close to the fence on the right, is the Weebolla Stud Bull paddock."

Harry took time off to ignite his fumigator, then continued.

"I decided to have a rum at the railway, and when I came out of the bar a bloke I knew was on the lookout for a lift to Pally. "Hop in", I says, "and hang on. This old bus takes some holdin' on the road home".

"Thanks, Harry", the bloke says, and he jumps in the passenger seat. I rev the old engine up, drops her into bottom gear, and then it happened!. Just as I let the clutch out, the bloke's wife rushes round the corner, and he leans over the door to kiss the lady good-bye, and believe me boy, he got the shock of his life".

Harry became silent, and began to dig wax out of his grizzled ear with a safety match. I became impatient. "Go on", I requested. "The suspense is killing me".

"The old Chev", Harry said at last, "got so much pace up when she took off, that instead of kissin' his wife good-

bye, he kissed a Weebolla bull on the arse at the four mile. Now if that wasn't amazin' acceleration, what is?".

"Your imagination", I replied. "It has amazing acceleration as well as your car".

Uncle Harry put on a pained expression. "Just like all the modern blokes", he said sadly. "Full of doubt when they hear an authentic story".

Unhygenic Bushmen

I have encountered in my youth many many old timers who were very dirty and unhygenic in their habits. And it is rather disconcerting to note that most of them lived to a ripe old age, thus giving the lie to the old adage that cleanliness is next to godliness. These old sinners lived hard and uncomfortable lives, but possessed a survival value that appears to be sadly lacking in the overwashed and overmedicated people of modern times.

Stallion Joe was a weird old scrubber who travelled in and lived under, a dray drawn by two horses. I have seen him fill his camp oven with water, allow his dogs to drink out of it, then drop his corn meat in what remained and boil it for tea. It took a bushfire to kill Joe at the age of seventy eight.

Stumpy was a lover of galah soup. A foul looking old wretch, he always put the galahs in the pot feathers and all, and after boiling for several hours, strained the soup off through the tail of his shirt and drank it. He was eighty three when he killed himself by falling off a haystack.

Kaiser was an old ex-blade shearer who refused to wash, claiming that water always destroyed the "natcheral hoils on yer skin". He would buy a new flannel and wear it until it fell off him. I don't know what became of him. Possibly he smothered in a smog of "natcheral hoil".

Barney was a Boer war veteran who liked to make dampers. He would mix the dough while he smoked, and large blobs of spittle would run down his pipe and drop into the mixture. He didn't seem to mind, nor did weevils in the flour cause him any concern. Vale Barney at ninety-two.

Bogan Jack was a believer in a light swag and plenty of dogs to sleep among. The fact that they had been rolling in offal didn't matter at all. On a cold night he would curl up with the dogs all around him. He died from drink and exposure at seventy-six, on a freezing night when his faithful

hounds were not present to act as heaters.

Lofty was an emu-bobber who never cleaned his two sets of dentures. When in close proximity his breath was remindful of a dinosaur that had been eating offal for a week. Sometimes he removed them, to reveal a coating of green slime and particles of decaying food, and his mouth gaped dark and terrifying as the home of a toad. He entered the old peoples' home in his eighty-first year, and it was reported later that he died of shock when a tube of toothpaste was presented to him with instructions for use.

As you will note, all the old reprobates I have recalled in my tale lived to be very old. What I would like to know is would they have lived longer if they had been clean and hygenic in their habits. Or are we present-day people a mob of pill-happy, washed-out weaklings?

It's a pretty moot point, but the health authorities and their highly paid employees are making a big industry out of hygiene. I am doubtful if they will live as long as the tough sinners I knew who were extremely dirty and extremely healthy.

But one small thing you can be sure of. The bureaucratic boys will finish up a long way in front financially.

205

The Chinee Cook

"The stockmen in the Territory used to live lives of terrible hardship and privation", Uncle Harry said as he studied a copy of Walkabout.

"I don't reckon they do too bad", I said, "they have all the modern comforts these days".

"I was thinking of the time I worked on a cattle station near Birdsville", Harry replied. "I was a young fella then, full of life. It was the last hole on earth. Nothing there only a lot of black ringers, a few white bosses, and a wizened up, ugly old Chinee cook. I felt pretty lonely away out there in the West where some men are men, but an old ringer we called Rusty befriended me and gave me a lot of good advice".

"After a few weeks I got in the mood for a bit of female company, but there's none available. I says to Rusty, "listen mate, how do you release yer natural emotions about here, where there's no women around. I'm gettin' frustrated".

"Easy done, boy," the old ringer says. "There's the Chinee cook, and his services cost fifty quid".

I nearly fainted.

"Fifty quid for the Chinee cook!" I says in a shocked voice. "That's bloody ridiculous, and besides, it's an unnatural act".

"You ain't fully informed, son", Rusty says. "Thirty quid goes to the boss. He is a very clean living moral man, and he doesn't like that sort of thing to happen".

"It's robbery!" I replied heatedly. "There's professional girls in Sydney who're glad to get a couple of quid. And whatever the boss gets, twenty quid is too much for the Chinee cook."

Rusty stroked his whiskers and looked at me in a pitying way.

"You ain't in Sydney now, boy. You're out where the dead men lie, and yer gotta take the best that's offering. Also out of the twenty quid yer talkin' about, a tenner goes to the overseer. As you may have noticed, the overseer is a deeply religious and forthright man. He doesn't like that sort of thing to happen either".

By now I had cooled down, and after givin' the matter a bit of thought I decided that a tenner was still too much money to give the Chinee cook, and I told Rusty my opinion.

"There's a point you don't understand, boy", the old villian said. "Five quid goes to the head stockman. Immoral and unnatural antics are very painful to the head stockman, as he is a kind and gentle Christian soul. He doesn't like that sort of thing to happen either".

"Look, Rusty," I says, "it strikes me that all these blokes who want a cash salve for their wounded feelings are a mob of bludgers. And anyway, a fiver is too much to give the Chinee cook!"

Rusty gave a cunning smile.

"There's a point I haven't enlightened you on concernin' that fiver, boy. There's a quid each for five of us able bodied ringers to hold the Chink down. He doesn't like that sort of thing to happen either."

Uncle Harry got out his pipe and lit up.

"You see, mate," he concluded, "those old territory stockmen were really rough citizens."

The Big Yellow Belly

"The yellow-belly is the best fish around here", said Uncle Harry, as he wrung fish-fat from his moustache.

"Their right name is Golden Perch", I remarked. "I don't reckon they're as tasty as a jewfish, and they don't grow as big as a cod".

"You're wrong there", the old boy replied. "I remember a yellow-belly that was as big or bigger than any cod".

I could tell by the expression on Harry's face that he was dreaming up an enormous lie.

"It was in the Whalan Creek, near Garah", he began. "Me and Steve were waterin' the bullocks, when we sees a fish's fins stickin' about the surface. We chucked a few stones at it and nothin' moved, so Steve gets a rope with a meat-hook on it, and swims out to the fish. He dives under, and after a while he comes up gaspin'."

"Haul away, mate", he says as he swims out. We both gets hold, but the fish was too heavy for us, so I hooks me two polers on to him, and they lead him out after a hard struggle. He was stone dead.

Harry paused to light his pipe, then ejected a black geyser from his skinny chest.

"We had no scales to weigh him", he went on blandly, "so Steve gets a small step-ladder and his hack-saw, and climbs up level with the fish's back, then he cuts off a spike from the dorsal fin. He used it as a spare pole for the waggon for years after. That'll give you an idea how big the fish was".

"Did you try to cook him", I queried, hoping Harry would make some blunder in his story.

"He was startin' to decompose, so we couldn't eat him, but we got the cross-cut saw and took his head off for a trophy. Rigged a block and tackle to load it on the waggon, and a few days later we sold it to a squatter who happened along".

Denny
Hutton

"What did he do with it", I asked innocently.

"He dried it out and used it as a kennel for his dog", Harry informed me.

"What breed of dog", I enquired. "A pekinese?"

"It was a Great Dane", Harry said calmly. "That fish-head was just the size required for a Great Dane's kennel".

"Are you sure it wasn't a whale", I asked sarcastically.

"No, boy", the great liar replied. "It was a yellow-belly. Or Gold Perch, if you want to be scientifically speechified".

I lapsed into silence, having no comeback to beat Harry's latest effort, but he wasn't finished. He continued.

"A few months later he was comin' back past the spot, and here's the fish's skeleton. All the flesh had rotted off it, and the framework was covered with pieces of tarpaulin, hessian and scraps of tin. On investigation we finds five bag-men were livin' in it. And they've trimmed the tail into a rectangle, and are usin' it for a table".

I walked off quickly, as Harry sounded so sincere that I almost believed him.

Uncle Harry - Gardener

"Your's cooking enough spuds for ten men", I told Uncle Harry as he filled the camp-oven.

"I like to fill the pot up", the old boy replied. "An empty pot is the sign of poverty."

"That one's too big for two men", I said. "We need a smaller oven."

"This one is really quite small", Harry claimed as he stoked the fire. "I recall a camp-oven that Stevo had. It held twenty five turkeys at one filling. And when they shrunk up a bit from the heat, you had room for a bag of spuds".

"How did you turn the birds to cook them properly", I asked.

"Stevo used to put on a pair of wading boots", Harry stated blandly. "Then he'd walk out into the middle of the oven and turn the turkeys with a pitchfork. The spuds were a bit harder to handle, as they were a special type spud that I grew up on Mosquito Creek. Four of the smaller ones would just fill a wool-bale nicely".

"Must be pretty fertile soil up on Mosquito", I remarked doubtfully.

"It certainly is", Harry said. "I remember some carrots I grew up there too. Slicin' 'em up for a stew was quite a job. We used to lay 'em along the ground and cut rings off 'em with a crosscut saw. That saw was six feet long, and when you got down into the middle of the carrot there was only about five inches of the saw stickin' out on each end. But those carrots made a delicious stew. I grew some good spinach too, only me bullock team was a hell of a nuisance when it was full grown."

"Did they eat it off?", I asked.

"Not on yer life", Harry said indignantly. "A herd of elephants couldn't have eat it off in a year. When the sun

212

got hot the bullocks used to come up and stand in the shade of the spinach stalks, so now you get an idea how high it was. But I worked up a way how to keep the team off it".

"I had some pumpkins growin' in among the spinach, so I cut a hole in the side of one of 'em, and took out the fillin' until only the shell was left. The team used to camp inside it and leave the spinach alone. The hardest part was findin' em all if yer wanted 'em in a hurry. There was a lot of gloomy corridors in that pumpkin-shell where a bullock could hide. In fact I lost one bullock who got away from his mates, the cause of his death bein' me cucumber vines. He got entangled and strangled in their rapid growth. We found him hung up in the air dead".

"How did you water all these veges?" I asked. "Water is pretty scarce on Mosquito Creek".

Harry assumed a pious expression as he loaded his fumigator.

"I trusted in God", he replied. "The Lord watches over truthful and forthright men always. Come and get some dinner, boy. The spuds are cooked".

Bush Drunks
and Hangover Cures

Australians have always been regarded as being among the world's best drinkers, and after seeing some of the pot-sinkers around my boyhood home, I cannot deny the fact. In the hard old days, (I refuse to call them good old days) some terrifying concoctions were swallowed.

Rum was a great favourite with the old bushmen, and to give it a greater kick, essence of vanilla were often added. The old teamsters believed that the addition of two cakes of black tobacco per keg of rum gave the spirit more body. One old rabbiter I knew would take a seven ounce beer-glass, half fill it with rum, and top the glass with Holbrook's sauce. I was always of the opinion that this old cove had no intestines, and was filled with non-corrosive steel pipes. He lived to be nearly ninety.

Cheap draught wine, referred to as "Plonk" or "Red Ned", was available at two shillings a bottle. I remember one dedicated drinker claiming that he didn't need any first class tickets, he could go round the world for two bob. Plonk was a great favourite at all bush dances. The bottle would be surreptitiously hidden outside the dance-hall, and after every dance the owner would fortify himself for further effort.

Another deadly brew was "rock-melon grog". A hole was made in a large ripe rock-melon, and a quantity of brown sugar was inserted. The mixture was allowed to ferment, and was ready for drinking ten days later. A small nip had to be broken down with a large quantity of water, as the percentage of alcohol must have been at least forty percent.

A favourite and easily prepared drink among certain of the aboriginal populace was "the mission cocktail". A spoonful of methelated spirit was placed in a long glass, which was then filled to the top with lime cordial. For a variation

condensed milk was often added.

The old pack-horse and waggonette drovers were a mighty force at the taps, and after delivering the stock they often went on benders that lasted several days. One old character I knew was called the Pirate, because he sank so many schooners. These men had a wonderful resistance to alcohol, possibly owing to their hard physical constitution and the rough condition they lived under.

I well recall a humourous incident concerning an old shearer who went to sleep after placing a bottle of rum under his bed. He awoke through the night, and reaching under the bed, got hold of a bottle of sheep drench that had been placed there earlier in the day by his son. He drank a couple of mouthfuls before he realised his mistake, and he was very ill for a few days afterwards. But he claimed it killed his stomach worms for all time.

But then of course, shearers can drink anything. I speak from experience, for I practised this punishing profession for ten years, and when I look back on some of the devilish and crude concoctions carelessly consumed all I can say is, thank the Lord for our modern civilised drinking habits, and unlimited quantities of foaming beer.

The Dog Fanciers

The hometown of my youth has long been noted for it's stray (and useless) dogs. It is an old saying there that the children and the dogs must never be chastised. The children are not quite as important as the dogs, in the sluggish minds and distorted opinions of the residents. Sheep-killers and egg-eaters abound, also spiteful thieving curs and all-night barkers and howlers. These are always referred to by their moronic owners as watchdogs, smart dogs, child protectors, valuable dogs or simply good dogs. With most members of the male population, to threaten a dog is an instant invitation of fisticuffs.

They are always allowed to roam free, and breed at will, producing a polyglot group of canines that are neither use nor ornament, and make the small hours unbearable with their baying, and the shire officials who are responsible for dog registrations can seldom be stirred from their places of imbibement to do anything. So sooner or later some civic-minded citizen scatters poison baits around.

This is a brutal and ruthless procedure likely to cause the death of some valuable working dog, but as Uncle Harry always claimed, "you got to get a few good ones to get the bad ones".

The dog owners show great grief when the stiffened corpse is discovered, and with tears and maudlin sniffles claim, "he belonged to our children. Fancy anyone being cruel enough to poison a little kid's dog". Strangely, the children show no grief like the parents. I will always remember a humourous incident one Christmas Day.

Sandy, a mate of mine, owned a large dog of all breeds, a useless canine criminal that everyone for years had been trying to poison, shoot or trap, but it had survived to a great age by roguery and cunning.

Sandy had just consumed a huge Xmas dinner with

218

plenty of wine, and was heading for the pub when it became evident that his dog had swallowed a bait. He seized the twitching hound by the hind legs, and began to swing it in a circle, revolving on his boot-heels.

"If yer swing 'em round and round they get sick and bring up the bait" he informed the onlookers.

Faster and faster he went, and dreadful howls and groans were emitted by the dog.

"He's gettin' sick", Sandy panted. "They'll be some vomit flyin' in a minute". The dog's howls began to subside, and suddenly Sandy dropped the unfortunate canine and collapsed to his knees as his prophecy became true. While the dog gave up the ghost, Sandy lay gasping on the ground as he vomited up his Xmas dinner.

A few charges of Penfold's Rich Red brought our hero back to normal, and the dog was soon forgotten, as there were plenty of pups growing up to take it's place. And this fact causes me to ask a very debatable question. Would the country benefit if the law took sterner measures with criminals other than those of the canine class?

Uncle Harry - Sportsman

"Bowls", said Uncle Harry, as he cleaned his pipe with a piece of fencing wire, "is not a game for elderly men".

"Why not?" I argued. "It's quiet and relaxing".

"It's too strenuous", the old boy replied. "When those rickety old blokes get down on one knee to bowl, it takes 'em half an hour to get back up again. Too much physical strain. What I would suggest is a good game of cards, in a nice warm room, with nips of hot rum served."

"Did you ever play bowls?" I enquired.

"Didn't have time", Harry said. "I was too busy breakin' records as a bike-rider. I won that many cycling events that they put me on a pretty severe handicap. I had to compete with one pedal removed from the bike. Of course I still managed to win me share of races".

"I thought cricket was your long suit", I said.

"It was until I killed that wicket-keeper", Harry said sadly. "I could stand under the goal-posts on an Aussie Rules football ground, and pelt the cricket-ball over the cross-bar at the other end, on the full. It's only a matter of skill".

"How did you shape at tennis?" I asked.

"I only played once", Harry said in a sincere tone. "The first ball I served went through the netting behind my opponent and broke the hip of an elderly spectator in the back seats, then passed through a brick wall behind the court. That was just before Ken Rosewall went into temporary retirement. He heard about me."

"Was the ball ever found?" I queried.

"I don't think so", Harry replied doubtfully. "I think it might still be in orbit. But I was pretty good at golf, too. I never needed a set of clubs. Only used to carry the driver".

"Why was that?" I asked.

"Because I used to hole in one every time", Harry grinned. "But I think revolver shooting was me speciality. I perfected the old Yankee wild west style, and used to practice the fast draw in front of a mirror. I became so swift that the mirror failed to reflect me movement when I drew. I used to set up a knife with the blade towards me edge on. I could split the bullet on it at fifty yards, every shot. And the two halves of the slug were identical in weight every time".

"Were you any good as a footrunner?" I questioned.

"Me best performance was in a one hundred yards sprint on the blacksoil plain at Brewarrina", Harry replied. "There was an inch of rain the night before, and I had to run in me bluchers, as the bindieyes were bad. But I still cut her out in a tick under ten seconds".

"You should have been a rugby winger", I suggested.

"I don't like football", Harry said. "It's too brutal. Here's some poor harmless coot runnin' with the ball, and it's your job to try and break his neck by buryin' him in the dirt. It's a sadistic and un-Christian sport. Anyway, I soon get tired of the company of athletes".

"Why?" I asked innocently.

"Because they tell ridiculous lies about their past performances Harry replied seriously. "Come on, boy. You waste too much time talking".

New Chums I Have Known

The old type of new-chum that our early scribes wrote about is not seen anymore. Nevertheless, the back country still draws a few inexperienced migrants. My old mate Paddy Austin, top of the tree in bushmen, used to tell a story about an English gentleman who was visiting a station where Paddy was rabbiting. This Pommy was in no way a snob, and he visited Paddy's camp early one morning.

"And how is the jolly hunting, old bean", he asked cordially. "What sort of a catch did you get this morning, bai Jobe".

"I got sixty-three rabbits, a manshee and banuette", Paddy replied very seriously.

The Pom was not at all perturbed. "Doubtless some of your remarkable Australian fauna, by Gad sir", he replied.

"That's right", Paddy informed him very soberly. "The Manshee is the father of the banuette".

The Pom was pretty gullible, and he strolled off wearing a puzzled expression, without asking for further details.

Another new-chum I well recall was a Scottish boy who was abandoned in our village by a travelling vaudeville show. He was known as Tim the Drummer for he was something of a musician. He found employment on a station as wood-and-water joey and milkman, and there was a pretty tough cow to be milked. Tim was not having much success, so one of the ringers gave him a bit of advice as follows.

"Yer got to imitate a calf, Tim. Get down on all fours and bleat, and butt the cow in the udder with yer head. Tim did his best to imitate a hungry calf, but it didn't avail him much.

Later on he was conned into imitating a dog when mustering the killers and was often seen on all fours barking furiously at the small mob as they entered the yard. He also sat for half the night near a shed, playing a guitar in hopes of

224

charming out a non-existent snake that reportedly lived under the building. At long last he left the district, little wiser than when he came.

I also recall an Irish new-chum who worked with Uncle Harry and Stevo on a tank-sinking job, and was subjected to many tall tales and jokes by the bullockies. Harry had him fully convinced that it was a punishable offence to wear green in Australia, as we were under a strict law by a Protestant king. This bogtrotter was pretty dumb, and wasn't game to leave the camp at night for fear of the man-eating kangaroos that Stevo told him about. He had little idea of scooping, and on several occasions was thrown in among the bullocks when the scoop bucked. But he always came back bulldog game and willing. Harry and Stevo respected him for his good humour and determination in the face of hardship, and this is something we should make a note of.

Our forefathers, who conquered a wild and brutal land, were all new-chums at the beginning, whether they came to the colony wearing a leg-iron or a title. Let us give full consideration to them, whether they be the old timers who are a memory or the modern long-haired mechanised models who seek an understanding.

Morgan on Religion

For many years now, I have been criticised by the neighbours in my home town for the fact that I eat meat on Good Friday, though many who condemn me are more hardened sinners than myself, which is hard to imagine. The cause of my flouting this Christian custom is the fact that I was converted by a wild North Queensland stockman named Morgan.

It was the Easter of 1957, and I was in trouble with a mob of cattle, believed to be mine, but in reality the greater equity belonged to a stock firm.

There was a prolonged drought at the time and Morgan was my assistant in the search for feed on the stock routes.

On the Thursday night we were fortunate enough to acquire an unwary sheep from a station paddock. We had been living on tinned food for a week, and I looked forward to a meal of fresh meat on the Saturday. I was amazed to see Morgan commence grilling chops in the camp oven on Good Friday morning.

"You're not going to eat meat", I asked in a surprised tone.

"Why not mate", he replied. "We been a week on tinned stuff".

"But it's Good Friday", I said.

"What matter mate. It says nothin' in the Bible about noteatin' meat on Good Friday".

"It's an old Christian custom", I said.

"But Jesus never mentioned it in any of his teachin's" Morgan argued. "I was reared in a Convent, I know. Jesus wasn't the kind of bloke to see anyone go hungry. A big hearted bloke like Him would want yer to bog in and have a feed, no matter what was on the table. Some cunnin' religious rat started this. He was most likely tryin' to sell a lot of fish one Easter time years ago, and wanted to get a quick quid".

Although Morgan sounded a bit too practical I had to concede a point, as I couldn't remember anything in the Scriptures about the custom either.

"You'll see everyone eatin' fish, but they won't eat meat", Morgan went on. "Why, I'd like to know". "A fish feels and bleeds and dies just the same as a sheep or a cow, what's the bloody difference".

"It could have something to do with the story in the Bible of how the multitude was fed on a small number of fish" I suggested.

"Don't think so, mate" Morgan said sceptically. ' I'll bet if yer could a been there to see it, a lot of the multitude went short. Which convinces me that a man wants to make use of any tucker he's got while it's available. Don't worry about the day and date".

Morgan's rugged logic was taking a big effect on me, plus the fact that I was ravenous for a bit of fresh meat. When the chops were removed from the oven, and placed before me with a flourish, I decided that Morgan's logic couldn't be denied. Also I considered the fact that my former sins were enough to keep me out of heaven in any case. The last traces of conscience disappeared with the departure of my hunger, and since that day I have never worried about what I ate on Good Fridays, and I am not devoted to religious principles.

But, there is one thing I must admit. The good Sisters of the Convent must have been truly devout Christian souls to go to the trouble of rearing Morgan.

Fleecy Lined Stew

"Why is it", I asked Uncle Harry, "that shearer's cooks are mostly sour, cranky cows?".

"Dunno", the old boy replied. "They're a queer mob of cattle. Some are clean, some are dirty, and most are drunks".

He began to fire up his villianous pipe.

"I remember a time", he began, "when I was pennin' up at a shed in the West called Rutamuree. The cook was an awful dirty, stinkin' cow of a bloke, always half-stonkered on cheap wine. One day we fronts for dinner, and all he's got on is a pair of underpants. Those old fleecy lined type that the Yanks call Long Johns. He hadn't washed 'em for a week, and the blowflies were swarmin' all round 'em."

"It was the last straw. We hold a meetin' and sacks him on the spot, and he takes it pretty hard.

"What's up with you blokes?", he asks in an insulted tone. "What have I done wrong?".

'We can't put up with the smell of yer stinkin' underpants", says the rep. "I wouldn't let me dorg sleep on 'em".

"The cook goes off mutterin', while the overseer cranks the Ford T up to take him to town and find a new cook."

"We knocks off for afternoon smoko, and the cook's ready to depart.

"No hard feelin', boys", he says with a big grin. "I left a big bucket of stew on the table for yer tea".

"We wish him luck, and away he goes to town.

When we front for tea there's a three gallon bucket of stew on the table, and the smell is bloody delicious. We bogs into it, not thinkin' that there might be a reason for the cook's sudden good humour when he was leavin'.

"It was the best feed the dirty old bludger ever turned

230

on. The men kept doublin' up until we get down near the bottom of the pot. One of the loppies starts fishin' deep after a bit of meat, and suddenly he gives a yell of horror and staggers back lookin' sick and turnin' pea green in the face. He points a shakin' hand at the stew. The rep rushes over with a fork, and what d'yer think he comes out of the bucket. The cook's underpants, boiled to a nice shade of brown from the gravox in the stew.

"The men all rush outside, some vomitin', some cursin', and some callin' on God or the devil. A couple of 'em grabbed their horses and galloped into town in hopes of catchin' the departed poisoner, but the train was just pullin' out when they got there, with the cook on it.

"There was no shearin' next day. The team was prostrated with a whole lot of imagined stomach ailments. It was nearly a week before things started runnin' smoothly again. And the rep insisted that the new cook eat a plate of any stew he made, before the meal was served."

Uncle Harry knocked out his pipe.

"It's like I told yer, boy. Some cooks are clean, some are dirty. And there's some that be bloody revengeful".

The Plague of Yabbies

"Yabbies are pretty hard to get", I said to Uncle Harry. We had just made an unsuccessful attempt to obtain some yabbies, or freshwater crayfish by dragging a portion of the bore-drain with a piece of netting.

"They don't grow very big around here", the old boy replied. "Out in the West I've seen 'em grow as big as fox-terriers. Some sort of mineral in the water develops 'em."

"Go 'way!", I said disgustedly. "A lobster wouldn't grow that big."

Uncle Harry revealed one of his two remaining teeth in a knowing grin and began.

"Me and Stevo were on a fencin' job out West at a place called Uppaquei. There was a big dam near the camp, where we used to get our water. About the third night we were there, a hawker come along and sold us two bottles of wine. We had tea, and then knocks down the plonk. We falls into a deep sleep, and just about daylight I gets woke up by a scratchin' sound."

"It was just light enough to see, and what I saw nearly scared me to death. Here's a great big yabbie the size of a dog, rootin' round in the tucker-box! I hears a yell from Stevo, and looks round to see him stonker another big cray that's tryin' to lift the wallet out of his moleskins! Then a terrible burst of snarls erupt from under the waggon, and it's Tiger crushin' a yabby to death, while another monster is hangin' onto his tail! Two more are carryin' the meat bag away between 'em, and what got me really wild was the fact that one old whiskery brute was sittin' on the pole of the waggon, smokin' me pipe! And there's more of 'em comin' from the dam!"

"We leaps out of bed in our underpants and grabs the whips, and with Tiger doin' deadly work at close quarters we drove 'em back into the dam, except for a lot of dead

233

ones that fell in the conflict."

"There was about half a bottle of wine left, so we downs it and starts gettin' breakfast. We just had the tea poured out when Tiger starts barkin', and we sees down on the bank of the dam a whole horde of yabbies. Must have been a couple of hundred. And there's one big feller, big as a St. Bernard dog, and he keeps pointin' his claw towards the camp. It's easy to see that he's orderin' a frontal attack, but his troops ain't keen to take it on. All of a sudden he comes hoppin' towards us, and Tiger goes straight at him.

"It was a close go for a while, but the old dog finally got that cray by the tail and dragged him right up to the waggon, where Stevo belted him to death with a tug-chain. We threw the body on the fire, and looks up to find that all the other yabbies are goin' like hell across the plain. It was easy to see that the death of their leader had completely demoralised 'em.

"Stevo and me were so unnerved by the battle that we went to bed and had a long sleep. We woke up durin' the afternoon, and there ain't the sign of a yabbie anywhere".

"What became of all the dead ones that you killed", I asked, thinking I had caught Harry off guard, but he was ready.

"There was a mob of crows sittin' up in the trees lookin' very full bellied", he replied. "They had evidently cleaned up the bodies of the casualties. Now this story should give you an idea of how potent the water is in Western bore-drains".

"Wine sold by Indian hawkers must be pretty potent too," I replied. "Come on, let's look for a few normal yabbies".

The Illuminated Sheep

"It's a terrible thing to see stock starving in a drought", I said to Uncle Harry. "You'd reckon the Governments would do something to combat the bad seasons."

"The Governments haven't got time", the old warrior replied. "They're too busy makin' Canberra drought and hardship proof. A famine in the Government departments would be far worse than a drought in the outback, I reckon. But there's always ways and means of givin' the stock a bit of help to boost their morale. I recall a squatter who bought a truckload of green sunglasses, and put a pair on every one of his sheep. The psycological effect was amazin'. They even ate up the waste paper at the rubbish-tip, thinkin' it was green grass!"

"But the most startlin' thing I ever saw concernin' hungry sheep was out in the west at Lightnin' Ridge. It was a terrible dry time, so bad that the sheep were eatin' anything. They even ate the potch that had been discarded around the prospect holes. And they were so poor that on a moonlight night you could see the opal chips shinin' through their ribs. You'd of swore that it was the Neon lights in Darlinghurst Road when a mob of 'em was walkin' past".

"A few would commit suicide by jumpin' down the prospect holes. One landed on a miner and gave him concussion, and a lot of 'em died from mineral poisonin'. But their potch eatin' was the cause of one old gouger gettin' rich."

"He was a tough old Scot named Wally, and he was so hard up that he decided to knock off a sheep for meat, despite the fact that they were dog poor".

"Wally waits until a mob of these illuminated sheep come along, then he captures one and cuts it's throat. On skinnin' it he finds there's a particularly bright light shinin' out of it, so he opens the hogget's guts, and what do you think he finds? A monster black opal worth a quarter of a million!"

"Whether the sheep had swallowed it whole, or whether the opal chips had solidified in the hogget's gastric juices we will never know. But Wally went home to Glasgow and retired. Bought a high-class pub and called it the Hungry Hogget Hotel."

"It wasn't safe to run sheep around the ridge for a long time after that. All the miners used to kill 'em in hopes of findin' another big opal. But when the rains came and the grass grew, the sheep gave up potch eatin', and things went back to normal again."

Uncle Harry began to scrape out the bowl of his pipe.

"This story should prove to you", he said, "that droughts can be beneficial to some members of the community".

"Which doesn't include us", I replied, as I picked up the axe and returned to the unenviable task of scrub-cutting for a starvation wage, while Harry concentrated on the construction of another unmitigated lie.

The Passing of Terry

"Women can be an awful menace at times", said Uncle Harry. "In fact never take a risk on a female of any sort".

"What regretful memories cause you to talk like this?" I asked. "What females have ever brought trouble to you?"

"I was thinkin' of something that happened many years ago", the old boy said as he packed black plug into his pipe.

"Me and Stevo were sinkin' a tank up near Graman, back in the days of the teams. There was a bloke workin' at the pub, a dirty cow that we called Hygiene, on account of he never washed, and he had a fightin' bulldog that would fight anything yer could trot out for a wager of ten quid. A lot of blokes produced fighters, but the bulldog, whose name was Destruction, was too good, and soon he couldn't get a challenger."

"At the camp early one mornin' we hears the dogs barkin', and on investigation we finds they've got the biggest tiger-cat bailed up that you ever saw. There were four dogs, but he went through 'em like a dose of mercury through a gastric emu."

"When he's done cleanin' 'em up, he doesn't clear out. Came straight to the door of the hut and starts eatin' the scraps. We fed him every day after that, and he got real tame. Then I realised that here was the cove to beat Destruction."

"We issued a challenge to Hygiene to fight in a fortnight's time, and we started trainin' Terry, as we called the tiger-cat. We give him plenty of massage and exercise, and soon he was as fit as a fiddle. Then the unexpected happens.

"The night before the fight I gets up at midnight to get a drink of water, and Terry's missin'. The little box he slept in near the stove was empty. I waited up worryin', and just before daylight he comes in and hops into his camp, and I goes to sleep wonderin' where he'd been.

"The fight was a ding-dong go. It was all Terry for the first four rounds. His footwork was amazin', and his straight left brought the hide off Destruction in strips, but in the fifth round he went clean to pieces. Ran out of gas completely. Destruction gets him by the throat and starts to shake him, so Stevo threw in the towel. We took our champeen home and patched him up, but you could see that losin' the bout had a psycological effect on him, and he died of a broken heart a week later.

"We wondered where he left his fightin' strength, but we didn't find an answer until a few weeks later. We were just sittin' down to tea when in walks an elegant little mummy tiger-cat with a baby in her pouch. She goes straight to Terry's old bed and curls up in it with a big tear in her eye. We knew then that our pug had been seduced the night before the fight, and his strenuous love-affair had effected him both mentally and physically.

"So you see, boy", Uncle Harry concluded, "as Jack London stated, the female of the species is deadlier than the male".

"It wasn't Jack London", I contradicted. "it was Rudyard Kipling".

"What matter", Harry said. "In the case of Terry it was true. God rest his little tiger-cat soul."

Snakes and Adders

When I was a small boy, my family lived in the bush. And it really was bush, still the frontier in the lare nineteen twenties. The prickly pear and scrub was impenetrable, and it contained all manner of native birds, beasts and reptiles. Particularly reptiles, and the most feared of these was the death-adder.

The myths about this reptile are legion. It is claimed that the yellow sting-like spur on its tail is more venomous than its fangs. Rubbish. It is supposed to be able to spring up to twenty feet. More rubbish. The adder is a very sluggish reptile, and relies on camouflage and concealment to catch its prey. It is also said that it makes a loud moaning noise at night. Still more rubbish. I do not know how these fables began, but they are without doubt produced by vivid imagination. One thing I agree with, however, is the belief that the adder's bite is as venemous and fatal as that of any reptile in existance.

My mother held a deadly fear of adders. I remember when one crawled into the old slab kitchen to enjoy the heat from the fire in the open galley. Mum feared to take up arms against the usurper. Showing great initiative, she hurled the contents of a pot of boiling water over him. The evil serpent was almost skinned alive.

The Stevens boys, who lived nearby, were experts at killing adders, as was another local lad named Barney Quinn. They always carried a long piece of number eight wire with a hook on the end of it, and when an adder was located under a clump of pear, he was uncerimoniously dragged out and beaten to pulp with any weapon that lay to hand. Old Stevo was the real nemisis of the adders, especially if he was in possession of the bullock-whip. One blow was enough, result decapitated adder. But I think the most daring adder killer I have seen was a bushman named Mick Macey, who married one of Stevo's daughters. Mick, on locating the

243

adder would pick up a small stick about a foot long, then squat down over the reptile and kill it with a couple of love-taps on the head, proving beyond doubt that adders cannot spring at all. How Mick was not bitten I will never know, and I often wonder how the barefoot kids of the era were not victims of this deadly creature.

Uncle Harry owned a cattle-dog named Rattler, and he had a habit of closely investigating recumbent adders. One day he became too enthusiastic and was bitten on the nose. He lived less than a half hour, his death a swift announcement of the reptile's venomous propensities.

Death-adders are rare in the bush these days. The prickly pear was their harbour, and when it was eradicated, the adder along with many other bush denizens, disappeared before the relentless march of civilization and so-called progress. And though I deplore man's ruthless destruction perpetrated on our natural fauna in pursuit of Mammon, I can muster no maudlin regret for that treacherous, unlovely and unlovable reptile, the Australian Death Adder.

The Financial Wombat

"The wombat", said Uncle Harry, "is a very docile marsupial, but his eyesight is a bit dim. Like our politicians he can never see far ahead".

"Like our politicians, he is very wasteful and has no respect for anyone's rights", I remarked.

"There was a whole heap of 'em lived in the hills near Wollombi when I was a boy", Harry began as he produced his painfully pungent pipe. "Me and me brother Herbie made a cage one day, with a trap-door. We put it in the bushes at the back of an old cow-cocy's place. His right name I've forgot, but we always called him Grizzler".

"Next mornin' we goes down and finds a big wombat in the trap. He's a real quiet feller, very docile. He lets us rub him down and pet him. In fact he was so quiet that we decides to let him go. Then we gets a bright idea. Just down the hill a bit, old Grizzler is diggin' postholes, and he's left his coat and waistcoat hangin' on the door of the cowshed. Herbie sneaks down, usin' the shed for a cover, and hooks the weskit. He comes back grinnin' and between us we get the garment buckled up tight on the wombat. We lets him out and gives him a kick in the arse, and then the fun begins."

"It seems that the marsupial is a bit flabbergasted, because instead of divin' into the scrub, he takes off across the flat, and Grizzler spots him."

"The cocky is kind of paralised for a few seconds, then with a roar of rage he takes off after the wombat, who disappeared into the bush. Grizzler went clean off his head. The roars of him were awful to hear, but he doesn't notice me and Herbie, and we make for home."

"That night at the pub Grizzler got on everybody's nerves, tellin' 'em how a wombat stole his weskit. The copper was goin' to pinch him and take him to a brain specialist, as everyone reckoned that the old boy had gone

round the bend for sure. He spent all next day prowlin' the bush with a rifle, and be good fortune he comes on the well-dressed wombat and shoots it. Then we discovers that there was a five-pound note in the fob pocket of the weskit, so the reason he wanted it back became evident".

"Didn't you and your brother regret playing such a crude practical joke?" I asked.

Uncle Harry was unrelentant.

"Not a bloody bit", he said callously. "What we did regret was the fact that we didn't find the fiver before we put the garment on the marsupial".

"You had a very dishonest outlook", I remarked sadly.

"So did a lot of famous men who made millions", the old boy concluded. "Most honest men die broke, despite what the bloated capitalists tell yer".

The Sinister Spiders

Uncle Harry was an authority on spiders, or at least he thought he was. He also disliked them greatly, and any unfortunate member of the species that crossed his path was speedily reduced to pulp by his size 10 blucher. He had a particularly bitter aversion to the trapdoor type, and on finding one of their tunnels he always destroyed it with furious trampling. I once asked him the reason for this destruction, and he related the following story.

"Trapdoor spiders are deadly and can grow to a great size, boy. And if there was enough of 'em they could be a real danger to man. In fact, out on the Narran Lakes, they attain a growth that's frightenin'."

"Just how big?" I queried.

Harry sucked on his pipe. "I don't know how big. I never saw one. But I heard 'em."

"Me and Stevo pulled into the Narran Lakes late one afternoon to do a bit of fishin'. It was a real wild place where we threw in the lines, and we noticed that there wasn't much bird or animal life about. We had a few rums, and got pretty bored when the fish wouldn't bite. After a while a big storm builds up, so we rolls up the lines and heads for the old Chev car, about a mile away. It was pitch dark, and next thing we know, we runs into a thing that seemed to be a huge disc about ten feet high. It fell with a hell of a slammin' noise, and there's nothin' where it had been standin' only level ground.

"Just then the lightnin' flickered, and in the flash we sees that these big circular slabs are all around us, fallin' shut and makin' a noise like giant doors bangin'."

Harry began to fill his pipe, and after a long pause, I asked; "What the hell were these things?"

The old boy's face assumed a terrified expression. "The lids on the homes of the trapdoor spiders", he said. ' It's a

248

wonder Stevo and me didn't fall down one of the holes and get eaten alive. There must be somethin' in the atmosphere around the Narran Lakes that makes 'em grow to a tremendous size. Or it might be in the ground".

"Or it might be in a rum bottle", I suggested slyly.

Harry refused to bite. "Could be anything. As these know-it-all geologists say, there's all kinds of chemicals and minerals under the earth of Australia. And the wealthy foreigners are just wakin' up, and they'll soon be tunnellin' worse than the spiders."

The Terrified Tree

"Do you think plants and trees have feeling?" I asked Uncle Harry, who was busily employed cutting Bathurst burrs.

"What made you ask a question like that?", he demanded, pausing to lean on the hoe and light his pipe.

"The burrs", I replied. "They shrivel and go sort of pale as soon as they get cut".

Harry debated silently as he puffed.

"It's a very moot point", he announced at last. "And I can recall a happening that proves to some extent that certain species of our natural flora have some form of feeling".

"Such as what?" I asked.

"Gum trees", Harry replied. "I'll tell you about it".

"Many years ago, me and Stevo were pushin' the teams along a lonely road out in the west near Cobar. The vegetation was scarce, but beside the road there's a young gum saplin' about six feet tall. Just for somethin' to do, Stevo uncoils his whip and gives that saplin' a terrible belt. You could see it quiver and bend. Stevo was usin' a short fall, and it cut clean through the bark into the wood".

"That was a hell of a clout mate", Stevo says, and on we go thinkin' no more about it.

"It was about fifteen years later that we're back in the same area, and I sees up ahead of me team a giant gumtree, right where the little saplin' was that Stevo walloped.

"As I draw closer I perceives a hard ridge on the bark, high up on the trunk, and I reckernize Stevo's trademark. I stops the team and sings out."

"Bring yer whip up here, mate".

Stevo comes saunterin' up, and a strange thing happens. As soon as he got close the tree begins shakin' and tremblin'.

251

"Stand back and crack the whip", I said.

"Stevo fired a volley and the tree shook like mad. Leaves fell off it and the ground round the roots cracked and broke away. It was plain to see that this unfortunate piece of flora had never forgotten the colossal clout that Stevo had given it fifteen years ago, and it thought there was another wallop comin'. Which proves that certain vegetables have feeling."

"Get out", I said, "You make it sound as if trees have longer memories than elephants".

"Who's to say they haven't", Harry replied soberly. "And let me inform you that a man's creditors have longer memories than trees, elephants or anything else. Come on, lets cut a few more burrs, so we can pay our bills".

Morgan and Noah's Ark

I stood beside my wild Queensland mate Morgan, watching the flood-water as it rose steadily higher.

"If she keeps on long enough", I suggested, "the place is going to need another Noah's Ark".

"Don't think so, mate", Morgan returned. "Never been as big a flood as the scriptures reckon. And the Noah's Ark yarn has been exaggerated a bit, too".

"How do you explain it?", I asked.

Morgan removed a spur, and began to pick his teeth with a rowel. "You've often noticed", he began, "how any excitin' story in the bush grows as it travels. Well, them old bearded blokes in the Bible were no different to the bush storytellers to-day. Now the way I reckon it was, all the weather prophets in the Holy Land forecast a real big flood, but it didn't come when they reckoned. All the cockies got careless. All that is, except Noah. I reckon he had a farm just up the river from Mount Arrowroot, and he was scared of the flood takin' his stock, as he'd put in a lot of work breedin' 'em up to a high standard."

"So Noah gets busy and starts buildin' a big boat. It took him and his sons a long time, and all the other cockies used to come round chiackin' him, but he kept his big family of useless boys workin' at it. Just as he finished her, down came the flood, but Noah had enough room on the Ark, as he called it, to load all his stock. Camels, fowls, ducks, donkeys, the lot. She floated up on the slopes of Mount Arrowroot, and Noah never lost a single head. All the cockies who chiacked him got their stock drowned, and it wasn't long before the wool-firms foreclosed on 'em and Noah bought 'em out".

"It wasn't as easy as that according to the scriptures", I said.

'Course it wasn't, mate", Morg replied. "You ever

notice how when a bloke makes good on the land, his ability gets exaggerated? All them old Hebrew farmers kept on exaggeratin' Noah's feat until they had everyone believin' that he saved every animal in the world. And the tale's been growin' ever since".

"Don't you think Noah could have been inspired by God?" I suggested.

Morgan snorted. "Not a bloody hope, mate. Noah was inspired by greed and lust for money. And of course when he got it, he gained big status among his neighbours. Like the blokes to-day who've got the biggest car or T.V. For all we know, Noah might have been the biggest take-down in the world. Nothing succeeds like success, mate. Yer don't need God if yer got money".

I have since often given thought to the wild ringer's philosophy, and when I look at some of the citizens in our midst who have risen to wealth and power, and gained the respect of a gullible community, I cannot help thinking that there is a lot of truth in Morgan's outlook.

Compassionate Creatures

"Animals", said Uncle Harry, "are different to humans. They help one another, and show compassion".

"That's because animals live without the need for a monetary system", I replied. "If animals required money to survive, they would all be trying to do each other for gain, just like people".

"You could be right", the old boy replied grudgingly. He never liked to agree with anybody. Filling his pipe he looked thoughtfully at the sky.

"Take bower birds", he began. "They all share anything they can find by taking it to the playhouse, which is a commune. Bower-birds are the only socialists that are not capitalists at heart."

"Then there are carrion-hawks. When one finds a dead sheep, he makes a whistlin' noise to call his mates to the feast. You don't see humans callin' their mates when they're on to anything good".

"And what about the cockatoo? One of 'em always sits up in a tree, and he screeches out if he sees a bloke comin' with a gun. Now I ask yer, how many of your mates would let on if somebody was goin' to do yer in? I'll tell yer. Bloody none!"

"Very interesting", I replied. "Could you tell me of any instance when a bush animal showed real compassion?"

Harry drew on his pipe, and I could see his mind was racing. At last he began.

"It was out near Broken Hill, and I was comin' along in the old Chev. Hell of a drought on the land. The stock were dog poor, and so were the kangaroos."

"Up ahead I sees a mob of 'roos hoppin' across the road, and when they heard the car comin', they took off. There was one old buck that was just a skeleton. He was laggin' at the rear of the mob, and he was so weak that the

effort of hoppin' up out of the water table was too much for him, and he fell down in the middle of the road. I slowed down, and it was then that I witnessed a very heroic act."

"Two young bucks looked back and saw the old feller down to it. Quick as lightnin' they turns and hops back, and lifts him up. He was pretty shaky, but they got one on each side of him and supported him, keepin' their hops in step with his. They manouvered him into the shade of a tree and put him down, and the last I seen of 'em, they was lookin' down at him real concerned like. I reckon they was wonderin' how they could get some water to give him a drink".

"Are you sure you didn't give yourself a drink before you left Broken Hill?", I asked.

"I can see you doubt my story", Harry replied. "it's quite authentic. As I said before, animals help one another, and like me, they never resort to deception or untrue tales".

Heelers and Holders

Every time I see a pampered and useless dog (and they are in no short supply these days), I recall the very efficient and well-disciplined cattle-dogs that belonged to the old teamsters. Believe me, they received a hard education.

Uncle Harry didn't like his dogs to get under the waggon, as far too many were run over and crushed. Harry would tie a young dog to the front axle on a short chain when travelling in scurbby country. After a couple of miles the dog would have received such a hiding from the sticks that flew up under the big wheels that he would yell for mercy, and Harry would release him. Result, he would never get under the waggon when it was in motion, but would keep well out on the side of the road. One course of the rather drastic treatment was mostly enough.

Stevo's dogs came in two types; "Heelers and holders, mate". A heeler was a small red or blue cattle dog, used for biting the heels of the bullocks when they were slothful or disobedient. They were all heart, and would endure severe kicks without yelping, and come back for more.

Holders were large powerful canines resulting from a cattle dog —— bull terrier cross, mostly white, with brown spots or a blue tinge. I have seen two of them latched onto a yearling steer, one hanging to the nose, the other swinging on the dewlap, while Stevo and his boys ran up to throw the steer. Once they tackled on, nothing short of death or a word from their master would get them to let go. Hence the term "holders".

I recall a very intelligent bitch Uncle Harry had called Misty. When the team was brought to the camp and Harry had yoked what bullocks he required, Misty would drive the spares along behind the waggon, and they knew better than to try and break away. Harry would never look behind. He knew his spare bullocks would be coming.

The bullockies had no use for a wayward or lazy dog.

Stevo was particulariy ruthless with this type of canine, which he always referred to as "useless bloody sooners, mate". If the offending animal could not be foisted onto an unsuspecting mark, it was despatched swiftly and expertly with a bullet. Most cattle dogs were snakey, savage and silent, and very suspicious of strangers. One I remember well was a bitch of Stevo's called Dot, and she was as savage as any wolf. She became dangerous to women and children, and the old bullocky was forced to destroy her, despite her value with the team.

The bullockies were stern and ruthless men with their dogs, and demanded discipline as hard as any conceived by a Nazi general. But their dogs were always well fed, fat and free from vermin. They always did their work well, with courage and dignity, and this causes me to ask myself a very moot question as I look at the careless and apathetic world of to-day. Would a bit of harsh discipline be a benefit to a certain other animal that is not canine?

The Gigantic Reptile

"Some of the snakes in South America grow awful big", I remarked to Uncle Harry. "There's a species called the anaconda that grows to forty feet in length."

"It's quite possible", said the old boy, "I knew a sheila once named Anna Conder. She was pretty long and snakey lookin'. But there's snakes in Australia just as big as the ones in foreign places."

"I remember years ago when I was a young feller, I was swaggin' it across the Macquuarie Marshes. It was just after a lot of rain, and there was water everywhere. It was a bright moonlight night, so I walked on after tea for a few miles, lookin' for a dry place to throw down me blankets. Suddenly I come onto a big log layin' in the grass."

"It was about three feet high, and four feet wide, and the bark was a queer mottled colour, but it was just right to spread me bed on. I stretches out, and I'm asleep in a few minutes."

"I dunno what time it was when I woke up, but the moon was high in the sky and I discovers I'm movin' along at a great rate and me blankets are wet with the fine spray of water that was flyin' up all around me. I looks ahead, and sees with a hell of a shock the head of a giant reptile movin' forward. I realised straight away that I'd made me bed on the back of a huge snake, and now he's swimmin' along the main channel of the marsh."

"I'm wonderin' how I'm goin' to escape, when up ahead of me I sees a big limb hangin' out across the channel. I gets on me toes, and as the serpent swims under it I leaps up and swings meself onto it, hangin' on for dear life. The reptile was travellin' at full speed, and I was nearly washed off be the wake of his passin', but after a while I scrambled to safety, and heads off in the direction of civilization. Due to campin' in such a bad spot I lost me swag and all me tucker,

and after that I never disbelieved any yarn I heard about big snakes".

"What species of reptile do you think it was?" I queried.

"Dunno", Uncle Harry replied. "The markin' on it's hide suggests it was a great big carpet, but more likely it was a plesso-sorearse or some other prehistoric reptile, even a sea-serpent or a son of the Loch Ness monster. It's quite possible".

I didn't venture any further opinions. In Uncle Harry's mind anything was quite possible.

Tall Timbers

"The trees down in Gippsland grow mighty tall", I said to Uncle Harry. "They would be without doubt the biggest in Australia."

"It's a debatable point", replied the old boy, ' very debatable. I would argue that there are trees on the North Coast that would equal them".

"I remember a time when I was up there at a place called **Kikkajikalong** haulin' timber with the bullock-team. There had been a big storm, and I was caught with a load of logs on the waggon. The river was runnin' a banker, fifty yards wide, and I had no chance of gettin' over the crossin'."

"I was just about to turn back when up the river I notices a tree, one of the smaller ones on the bank, has fallen across the stream. I goes up and examines it, and after takin' a careful measurement, I finds it's plenty wide enough for the waggon. I trims off a few roots with the axe, and calls me leaders up on to it."

"I'm well on the way across when what do I see? A team of bullocks comin' the other way. Me and the driver meets right in the middle, and I finds it's Hidebound Harris, a tough costal bullocky."

"One of us has got to get off", he says. "There ain't quite room for us to pass. What can we do?"

"There's an easy way out", I tells him. "Watch this".

"I had my eye on a limb that was runnin' out off the tree-trunk, and it had given me a bright idea. I alls me leaders in, and they starts walkin' out on the limb. I had Brains and Brawn leadin', and they were two pretty intelligent bullocks. Very carefully they moves out on the limb, and the body bullocks foller, then the pin bullocks and the polers, pullin' the waggon after 'em, thus leavin' the main trunk clear for Hidebound to go straight across. When he got safely over, he comes back after unhookin' his team, and

latches onter the rear of my waggon, and pulls her back to the main trunk, all my bullocks, who were pretty brainy, walkin' backwards. We shakes hands and heads off without any more trouble So this story should give you an idea how big the trees are on the North Coast".

"I'm a bit disappointed", I said. "I thought you were going to tell me that your team backed the waggon onto the tree-trunk".

Uncle Harry looked pained.

"Now what would I want to tell you an impossible lie for", he said. "Any new-chum knows you can't reverse a bullock-waggon. I was only trying to convince you how tall the trees grow on the North Coast".

I gave Harry best for the time being. I didn't want to hurt his feelings by insinuating that he might be prone to exaggeration.

A Really Bad Horse

"Yer don't see many really bad buckjumpers these days", said Uncle Harry. "The modern mechanisation has done away with 'em. Instead of breakin' yer neck ridin' a bucker, yer break it drivin' a fast car".

"The day of the horse is done", I agreed. "But I think horse-power was safer when the horses had it".

"Not necessarily", replied the old boy. "I remember the days when there were some really bad buckers around the bush. A horse called Funeral Service comes to my mind. He was only ever ridden once".

"Who was the successful rider?" I asked.

"As a matter of fact it was me", Harry replied as he fired up his pipe. "A terrifying ride, but I mastered this dangerous animal".

"It was at a station on the Flinders river, and Funeral Service had thrown all the big-gun riders for miles around. I decided to tackle him, and when I gets there with me gear, he was tied to a post in the middle of the yard. A big lanky grey with fire flyin' out of his eyes. I climbed through rails that were sticky with the blood of a ringer he'd killed that very morning, and throws on me saddle. He snorted and shook, and stamped hoofs that were smeared with the decayin' brain-tissue of blokes he'd trampled to death, but I managed to get me gear fastened."

"There was a big tall gum-tree just outside the yard, and a couple of cockatoos were nestin' in it. Their squawkin' didn't help me nerves much, but I reins him up short and on I jumps."

"Yer never seen a horse buck like it. High and twisty and full of jar when he hit the ground, but I'm sittin' like a politician at a banquet, nice and easy and in complete control. He put in an extra high one, just as I'm flexin' me fingers to keep balanced. I feels me hand close on somethin', but I was too occupied to see what it was. After a few extra

savage bucks, the horse give up and starts to gallop. I pulls him up and dismounts amid cheers from the onlookers. I noticed that me saddle was bent out of shape a bit from the twisty bucks, but there was no doubt that Funeral Service was mastered."

Harry drew hard on his pipe and gazed down the plain with a sly, cunning expression.

"You haven't told me what it was you grabbed when you flexed your fingers", I remarked.

"Well, as a matter of fact", the old boy replied, "it was a big handful of **Cockatoo** feathers. That will give yer some idea how high that horse was buckin'. He got right up where the birds were nestin'. Now perhaps you will agree with me when I tell you that horse-power wasn't any safer when the horses had it."

The Intellectual Kangaroo

"Hard times bring out the best qualities in a man", I remarked to Uncle Harry.

"That's right", the old boy agreed" It brings out the best in animals, too".

"Dogs and horses?", I queried.

"And also wild animals", Harry announced. "You would be surprised just how high their intelligence can go if it's a matter of survival".

"I was caretaker once on a place in Western Queensland, and there was a hell of a drought on. Even the bush creatures were starvin'. One night I leaves a plate of tinned asparagus on the kitchen table, and next mornin' it's gone, which causes me to wonder what kind of thief removed it".

"The next night I hears a thumpin' noise, and on gettin' up to investigate I find that six tins of asparagus are missin', also a can opener. I finds the empty tins next day near the stable, and all around the tracks of a big kangaroo".

"All was quiet that night, but right on daylight I hears the dogs barkin'. I gets up in time to see a big red 'roo makin' off from the fodder room with a bag of oats on his shoulder. He dropped it and made for the scrub when I sung out, and I realised I was dealin' with a marsupial of more than average intelligence. I locked the door of the feed room, and just for an experiement I leaves the keys hangin' on a nail near the door. Next mornin' the door is still locked up tight, but when I opened it, I finds a bale of hay missin'. That old 'roo sure knew his stuff. Even had enough sense to lock up when he left".

"I locked up everything secure, and I reckoned I was right, but on arisin' next day I hears a hubbub out in front of the house, and here's the 'roo in the garden, throwin' the pot-plants over to a few of his relatives, who are eatin' up all

the greenery in the pots. I soon put 'em to rout, and wondered what the next move would be. I thought about shootin' the roo, but he was so clever I hadn't the heart to do it. Then I got a bright idea."

"I opened a bottle of rum and put it outside on a table, in hopes of gettin' the roo drunk so I can capture him. Very few intellectuals can resist a drop of grog. But next mornin' when I go to look, the rum is untouched, and beside it is a volume of Shakespeare that I'd noticed in the lounge room. There was a stone holdin' it open, and the follerin' passage had been underlined with charcoal."

Foolish is he who places an enemy in his mouth to steal away his brain

"I decided then that if the 'roo came back I'd go out with a flag of truce and try and converse with him by signs. But that afternoon the rain clouds rolled in and the drought broke. I never saw the marsupial master-mind again".

"What do you think happened to him?" I asked.

"Dunno", Harry replied. "Perhaps some creature with an inferior mentality shot him. You should be aware, boy, that there's a bloody lot of humans with less sense than animals. And a bloody lot less survival value."

The Giant Cod

"The river is a bloody gloomy place at night", I remarked to Uncle Harry. "Sometimes it scares me a bit."

"The only thing that scares me", the old boy replied, "is somethin' I don't understand. Fear of the unknown is the worst fear of all".

"I remember a night in July when there was a hell of a dense fog, and I was fishin' in the Culgoa, in a terrible dark and lonely bend. I throws out me line and waits for results."

"About midnight I hears a big splash, but it's too pitch dark to see anything. Like the inside of an Angus cow in an eclipse. The splash gets repeated, then it gets continuous. It's freezin' cold, and there's no wood to light a fire."

"After a while the splashin' was accompanied by great pantin' grunts, as if some huge creature was exhausted, and at the point of death. I sits there shiverin', too frightened to move, prayin' for daylight to come. Slowly the fog lifts, and as it grew lighter and the sun rose, I gets the shock of me life".

"When I threw out me line in the dark, it got caught on a submerged log that was stickin' out of the water. The hook was danglin' about five feet above the surface, and here's this enormous codfish leapin' up and tryin' to grab the bait. He couldn't quite reach it. His jaws used to snap together just short of the target, and the pantin' noise I'd heard was his awful grunts of frustration".

Uncle Harry lit his pipe, and sucked at it until it glowed red and smelled foul, then he continued.

"I will be conservative in my estimate of that fish's weight. I would guess it would be in the vicinity of seven and a half hundred weight. And let me tell you boy, that fish was completely exhausted."

"How do you know it was exhausted?" I asked. "There was no way you could tell!"

"If you have listened carefully to my tale", the old boy said, "You will recall it was a freezing cold night in July. But that big fish was so knocked up that the sweat was pourin' off him, and his tongue was hangin' out with exhaustion".

I didn't have any more to say. When Harry was in top form he was unbeatable, and on this occasion he was at his best.

The Amorous Policeman

"The new copper looks like a tough nut", I said to Uncle Harry. "He pinched a couple of the boys last night for being drunk at the pub".

"As long as he isn't crooked he'll be all right," the old boy replied. "I don't mind 'em tough, but when yer get 'em tough and crooked, it's time to look out".

"I remember a copper down country when I was a boy. Horrible low coot called Snake-eyes Hennessey. Real hard bugger, and crooked as a snake track, also a big hand with the women. Always sniffin' round after some other bloke's wife. A real ram".

"One day a dairy farmer named Milkimm pulls me and brother Herbie up as we're comin' home from school. He knew we were game for any form of devilment."

"There's a bloke hangin' round after me daughter", he tells us. "He sneaks out at night on horseback. I'll give you boys two bob each if you wait along the track on the limb of a box-tree with a woolbale. When he rides under the tree, drop the bale over him. I'll be waitin' close by to give him a hidin'. I don't know who he is, but I'll find out when I get hold of him".

"That night Herbie and me climbs out on the limb of a low box-tree about nine feet above the track, and gets the wool-bale in position. It was a pitch black night, and we waited for a long time amongst the mopokes and possums."

"We were just about to give up when we hears a horse walkin', and a shadowy shape appears underneath us. More be good luck than good management we made a perfect drop with the bale. There's a snort and a wild yell, and next thing the horse is gallopin' back towards town, while there's oaths, kicks and blows goin' on underneath us. Milkimm had been waitin' in the scrub nearby, and he was dealin' it out to the bloke in the bale."

278

"We climbs down and makes for home like greyhounds, where we sneaks into bed, thinkin' what a joke it is. But we gets a big surprise next day, when we finds out the bloke in the bale was old snake-eyes Hennessey himself. He's got Milkimm in the slammer, charged with assault, but that wasn't the worst part of it."

Uncle Harry paused in his narrative to light his unlovely pipe.

"Some of the boys at the pub caught Hennessey's horse after it galloped back to town, and it give them a bright idea. They painted the seat of the saddle, the unguent used bein' obtained from the dunnikin at the back of the pub. Then they ties the horse close by. When Snake-eyes found it he jumps straight on to ride it home. You can guess the kind of mood he was in after he sits on the annointed saddle."

"What happened to Milkimm", I asked.

"He got fined a few quid for assault", Harry replied.

"I'll bet he took it hard", I said.

"Not as hard as me and Herbie took it when he wouldn't pay us our four bob", Harry said sadly. "At least he didn't let on that we were mixed up in the mess. Always remember, boy, when you take on a job that looks a bit doubtful and dangerous, make sure you collect your wages in advance."

The Terrible Tree

"It's easy to fool a real new-chum", said Uncle Harry. "In the old days they'd believe anything".

"We today are not much better", I replied. "We believe what the politicians tell us". "Too true", the old boy said as he lit up. "To succeed in politics you have to be a first-class con. But even the average bushman could fool a new-chum".

"I remember a Scot named McIntosh who was workin' on a scoopin' job with me and Stevo near Wallangra. He knew nothin' about the outback. We had our camp in a clump of wilgas right near the job, and Mac spreads his swag under a little saplin' about six feet tall and as thick as a billiard cue. Not much bigger than a bloody toothpick. Stevo notices it and gives a big grin."

"That night after tea we were sittin' near the fire, and me old mate starts tellin' stories about blokes gettin' killed by fallin' trees. He made their deaths sound pretty grisly, and I notices Mac takin' it all in. Stevo had thought up some terrible yarns about it, and he soon had Mac's eyes bulgin', as he raved on about all sorts of trees fallin' on fellers and crushin' em."

"It don't take a very big tree to kill yer, mate," Stevo says in a real serious voice. "Even a little one falls with terrific force. Never pays to camp near a tree when yer in the bush."

"We has a drink of tea and goes to bed, and I could see a real worried look on Mac's face. Yer could see that Stevo's tales had taken a big effect on him."

"It must have been about midnight I woke up, and what should I see but McIntosh climbin' out of bed and makin' for the waggon. He rummages in the tool box and finds an axe, then he starts back. I wondered what the hell he was up to, was he thinkin' of murderin' me and me mate?"

"He goes up to the little saplin' near his bunk, and in

281

about two swipes he cuts it down, then grabs it and throws it aside."

"What's up Mac?" I call out, and he turns to see me awake.

"Ahm gettin' reed o' yon dangerous tree, mon", he answers. "I wilna take the reesk a' bein' crushed if it falls".

"A few feet away I can hear Stevo chucklin'. He really had Mac thinkin' it was big enough to kill him if it fell on him".

"Wasn't you ashamed of deceiving the poor unenlightened immigrant?", I asked.

"Not a bit", Uncle Harry replied. "Smarter men than Mac have been conned when they came to Australia, and it's goin' to keep on happenin'."

A Discourse On Nature

"You hear a lot of wild tales about the habits of bush creatures", said Uncle Harry. "People tell the most impossible tales about them".

"About other things that happen in the bush, too", I remarked slyly, but Harry ignored the inference of my remark, and waving his pipe enthusiastically he began his address.

"Take the ring-snake or bandy-bandy. For every ring on his body, you're supposed to throw a fit if he bites you. A lot of rot".

"Then there's the story of the death-adder's tail. The yellow sting on it is supposed to contain venom. Impossible. It's only a decoy to draw his prey. Also he's supposed to make a loud groaning noise at night. Rot. There's nothing dumber than a death-adder, unless it's a newspaper reporter."

"People will tell you that a wild pig will cut his throat with his dewclaws if he tries to swim. Let me tell you boy, a pig's dewclaws are as dull as the mind of the average university student, and the hide on his neck is as tough as that of any politician."

"I'm a bit doubtful about the kookaburra, too. Bushmen claim he kills snakes, but I can't see how a little bird like a kookaburra could kill a snake of any great size. Also he's too smart to take on a job he can't handle. Did you ever notice how kookaburras in the early morning sit on a limb and laugh. It's my belief they're laughing at the poor human mugs who have to go to work for a living."

"Then there's the legend of the whip-snake, that can crack his tail just like a stockwhip. The bloody thing doesn't exist, and neither does the hoop-snake. He's supposed to grab his tail in his mouth and bowl himself along like a hoop. A dreadful exaggeration."

"And another tall yarn is the one about the brown

snake, that when in danger it swallows its young, and spits them out again as soon as it reaches safety. A shocking untruth".

"There is also a theory", I broke in, "that the kangaroo is born in the Mother's pouch, through the teet. This is another impossible assumption".

Harry suddenly stood stock still, a look of amazement on his face. He pointed accusingly at me with the stem of his pipe.

"It's easy to see you know bloody nuthin' about the bush", he said in disgust. "Everybody knows that the kangaroo is born in the pouch. I didn't think you would doubt a true fact of nature. It's looks as if you'd sooner believe the unfounded rumours".

I gave up then. Uncle Harry was a long way too inconsistent for me in his opinions of bush creatures and their history and natural functions.

Wild Cats

In the bushland of my boyhood an amazing number of domestic cats went wild. They fell upon birds, rabbits, bush mice and rats for sustenance, and in some cases snakes and lizards, not forgetting farmyard chickens and eggs. They were expert thieves, and operated mostly at night, for their dark deeds would seldom suffer the light of day. Cats of all colours resided in the prickly pear, and at mating time made the night hideous with their yowling. No woman in the pangs of childbirth, no martyr twisting in agony on the rack, ever produced the terrible moans and screams that issued from two old Toms fighting for the favours of some lean, famished female feline.

They lived a desperate, hunted existence, for if skinned the hide was worth three shillings and sixpence at the local skinbuyers, a fortune to the grubby and merciless school-boys of the time, and rabbit traps were set around every fowl yard in hopes of catching any luckless cat. Sometimes a sleek house-cat would wander away from home and comfort, and if caught would be speedily knocked on the head like any of it's wild fellows. All cat-skins looked alike when presented to the buyer, and many cat lovers mourned the disappearance of their pets.

I remember an occasion when Uncle Harry made great efforts to capture a large black Tom that was playing havoc with his fowls, but was too devilishly cunning to be caught. Harry confidently set several snares, but the only result was his half grown cattle-dog Nip, who foolishly hanged himself, and the setting of rabbit-traps produced several fowls with broken legs. Harry took to carrying a shot-gun, but Tom must have had a Radar installed, for he failed to show him-self whenever the weapon was in evidence. At last Tom fell to a strategically placed poison bait. In his mad convulsions he dashed howling into the kitchen and died on the table, breaking an antique tea-pot and several cups and saucers in the process. It was a Pyhrric victory for Uncle Harry.

287

One respected lady who lived near the village would never dispose of wild cats, but encouraged them by leaving food out. Result, a large number of diseased, runny-nosed, sore-eyed cats became permanent boarders, to the chargrin of her hard-working husband, who silently cursed when the bill for cat-food arrived.

Many old isolated bushmen and their illiterate wives would not kill a cat, as such an act was believed to promote seven years ill fortune. Their places of abode became feline menageries until famine reduced the cat population. It was a popular fallacy that cats kept snakes away, and though some cats would tackle a serpent, it was a common sight to see snakes and cats living in the same burrow.

The wild cats were also the bane of the rabbiter, as many trapped bunnies were devoured by the starved felines. A trail of baits laid for foxes always caused a high mortality rate among the cats, and their bloated carcases could be found along the track at regular intervals, smelling to high Heaven.

I knew one old bushman who castrated all male cats, claiming the she-cats would go away if there were no Toms round the place. He was an expert at dropping the front end of a tom-cat into a rubber boot, to hold it while he operated. The bush around his home was heavily populated with sleek desexed felines, as well as countless entires and females.

Wild cats are pretty rare these days. When ten-eighty poison wiped out the bush birds, and myxomatosis eradicated the rabbits, the wild cat's natural food was gone, and those that did not return to domestication died in the bush. But sometimes I am reminded of earlier days by the sight of a ragged survivor streaking for cover in the trees along a bush track, and I feel that the survivors of the Western world will be doing the same before many more decades have passed.

The Aviating Bull

"The drought is pretty bad", I said, looking at Uncle Harry for conformation as he filled his foul pipe. "This is the worst one I have ever seen".

"It ain't as bad as Nineteen-two", the old boy replied argumentively, "why, the emus were so poor that you could run 'em down on foot. Only had to stick to 'em for the first hundred yards, and they'd fall over from malnutrition. And the cattle and sheep were so poor that a gust of wind would knock 'em down."

Harry's eyes lit up in concert with his pipe, and I knew that a monumental lie was on the way as he began.

"I was workin' on a station in the west durin' that drought, and there was an old bull in the homestead paddock, so poor that even on a summer day he couldn't cast a shadow. One afternoon a really fierce whirlwind came along and picked him up like a scrap of paper! Away races the willy willy across the plain carryin' bullo a hundred feet up in the air! I takes off on foot chasin' it, and it's almost out of sight when I sees it deposit bullo in the fork of a kurrajong tree, about fifty feet up."

"I goes and reports to the boss, but he was so busy dodgin' the bank manager to care. Said the bank was about to foreclose on him, so one old bull didn't matter much."

"About a week later I goes out to have a look around, and here's bullo sittin' in the fork of the tree, and believe it or not, he's mud fat! He'd eaten all the kurrajong leaves, and that was the only sustainin' tucker he'd had for months. Gave him a new lease on life."

"We got him down with the aid of blocks and tackle, but it wasn't long before he was dog poor again. Ran himself ragged chasin' after every whirlwind that came along, in hopes of it liftin' him into a tree again where there was some good fodder. At last he passed away, with his eyes trained hopefully on the foliage of a big kurrajong."

290

"Why didn't you lop the trees to keep him alive?" I queried.

Uncle Harry assumed a knowing and practical expression. "What was the use? As I already told yer, the bank was about to foreclose. When yer in the clutches of the money-lenders and about to lose all yer got, why worry over one old bull full of kurrajong leaves. Where's the value in him?"

I fell silent, wondering where the value was in one old sinner full of bull.

Fox for Breakfast

In the small town where I spent my boyhood days, there was a butcher's shop that was never a very profitable business. Far too many self-appointed butchers prowled the night with knife, bag and silent working dog, and acquired their mutton at the risk of capture and court appearance. The butcher's shop changed hands with monotonous regularity, and at last it fell into the hands of a cove I will call Sid.

Sid was a good drinker and a dedicated practical joker, and the meat he killed was excellent, often acquired without the owner's consent. One night the town larrikins decided to have a joke with our butcher.

Several of the lads had been hunting during the afternoon, and had shot a large fox. After darkness spread it's cloak to cover any unlawful deeds, we headed for the silent butchery. Sid never locked the back door, and we entered with the body of the fox, all it's skin removed except the face and paws. With great ceremony we hung the carcass, labelled "today's special", beside a large fat sheep, then departed as stealthily as we came.

Sid was over-indulgent at the bar that night, and on arriving late next morning to open the shop, he was greeted by a group of irate customers who gave him a torrid time until he made explanation to the effect fox was not part of the saleable goods. We expected him to complain to the local constable, but he had other plans.

On the following Saturday night a dance was being held for the youth of the community, and on going to the hall to open it for the event, the organisers were greeted by a foul and unpleasant odour eminating from the supper-room. There was great consternation, all hands believing that some transient had entered the hall for shelter, and died there.

The constable was hastily summoned, and on entering was greeted by a unique dance decoration. Hanging from the central lamp-bracket was the decomposing corpse of the fox, and the heat from the light was causing his bodily juices to

drip unpleasantly on the floor, adding a distinct flavour to the original effluvia of decay. It was some time before the flabbergasted audience found speech.

A few blokes with brave hearts and strong noses removed the offending animal, and various unguents were burned to clear the air after the floor was washed with disinfectant. Despite the late start the dance was well patronised, and foremost among the revellers was Sid, remarking that the joke with the fox was "a bit over the fence", and that the jokers "ought to be sent along".

Time has passed, and so has our humorous butcher, for I grieve to state he died in the service of his country during the Pacific war. Whenever I see his name on the local memorial, I remember the hard old days, and the occasion of the offensive fox.

Brains

"You don't see many sheep-dogs with sense these days",
I said to Uncle Harry. "They don't get enough work to make
them good".

"That's true", Harry agreed, "and your remark reminds
me of old Brains".

"Who was Brains?" I requested.

Harry produced his pipe and lit up before commencing.

"Brains was a long skinny red kelpie I owned years ago.
Smartest dog you ever seen, but like a lot of intellectuals he
suffered from weak eyesight. However I overcame it be
gettin' him a special pair of glasses from an optometrist. He
soon learned to wear 'em, and became an object of envy to
all the dogs about."

"There was a terrible drought on the land, and I had to
shift a mob of two thousand wethers from Bollon to St.
George on the Queensland side. They were dog poor and mad
for a bit of green feed. I pushed 'em to within three miles
of their destination, and they wouldn't go a yard further.
Threw the towel right in".

"I'm wonderin' what the hell to do, when I noticed
Brains go streakin' over to a new haystack in a paddock
nearby beside the road. Back he comes with a big mouthful
of green hay. He puts it carefully on the ground then rummages round in the tucker-box til he finds a piece of twine.
Next he holds out the twine to me, and when I take it he
runs over and puts his tail on the hay. I woke up what he
wanted. So I tied the hay securely to his tail. Straight away
he give a bark of joy and trots over to the lead of the sheep,
wavin' his hay-loaded tail".

"You never saw a mob of sheep come to life like it!
When they saw the green hay they took after it at top
speed, with Brains streakin' along just ahead of 'em. In a
couple of minutes they were out of sight, and when me and
me cart got to St. George they're all safe in the truckin'

yards, with the dog lyin' in the gateway waitin' for me to wipe dust off his spectacles. But more was to happen".

"After we got paid by the agent, we went through to Dirranbandi, and on arrivin' we find Brains ain't with us. We goes for a beer wonderin' what to do, and a ring comes for me. It's the agent at St. George, to tell me old Brains is with him, and he wants to know what to do."

"Hold the telephone to his ear", I says, and as soon as the bloke complied I let a loud whistle into the instrument. Next minute the agent's voice comes across again.

"Cripes", he says, "that dog just took off like a rocket towards Dirranbandi. He really knows his stuff".

"Sure enough when we walks up next mornin' Brains is lyin' beside the telephone in the bar. He was a dog you could call extremely reliable".

"What was his final end?" I asked.

"Dunno", Harry replied. "When he got too old to work I gave him to the C.S.I.R.O. Last I heard he was givin' lectures to young kelpies on the finer points of handlin' sheep. And I don't reckon you'd say I was exaggeratin' if I said that he's most likely there yet".

"Thanks for a very sincere story", I said. ' i would never dare to suggest that you exaggerate, old Uncle."

The Germ Destroyer

"Fire", said Uncle Harry as he watched the pile of burning rubbish, "is the complete destroyer. Kills all vermin."

"I've heard there are certain germs resistant to it", I replied.

"Not if they get really drunk and fall in it", Harry said. "And any tucker cooked on a hot fire is safe to eat. No microbes on it after the heat goes through it".

"I recall a time when I was wood-and-water joey at a pub along the Cobar road. I had a big useless cattle-dog called Pincher, and it was a bloody suitable name. The bludger would pinch anything that would fit in his jaws."

"The cook at the pub was a big genial German called Fritzy, and he could cook meat pies like no bugger on earth. He had to be real clean, as the publican's wife was a real crank on hygiene. She was a great social-climber too, and used to invite the squatter's wives to a pie dinner every Sunday."

"One Sunday morning about ten o'clock I'm cuttin' wood near the kitchen, and out flies Fritzy". "Vill you blease guard bie, Harry?", he asks me. "I coom back in minute and but on for dinner".

"I looks in the door, and here's a big pie sittin' on the table ready for the oven. I nods to Fritzy, off he goes to the dunny, and a minute later I looks round to find Pincher on the doorstep with the pie, lickin' and chewin' at it. I nearly passed out, but pullin' meself together, I heaves a stick of wood at the hound. He dropped the pie and bolted."

"I rescued the pie, got it back on the table with all speed, and wiped the dog-slobber off it with a tea-towel. The tooth and claw marks I pressed out with the bowl of me pipe, and be the time Fritzy returned nobody would have suspected a mishap. The pie was a great big dinner success, and the guests were none the wiser. They complimented Fritzy on his cookin' effort."

"Wasn't you ashamed of giving them the dog-befouled pie?", I asked. "It could have been contaminated".

"Not at all", Harry replied with certainty. "Hot fire kills all germs. And the yarran logs Fritzy was burnin' in the stove were really hot. But right now, all over the world, there are power-mad germs workin' on a thing that will kick off the biggest fire ever. And they don't seem to realise that it's goin' to kill them like everything else. Do you get me, boy".